EMMA'S SECRET DIARIES

Readers of *Emma's Secret World* and *Emma Enslaved* will remember just how emotionally and physically exhausting my relationship with Ursula was. Now, encouraged by my long-term lover, Henry, I have broken with her and started looking for a new relationship.

I have always wanted to keep a diary and thought this would be a good time to start one. So here goes.

Hilary James is a pseudonym of Allan Aldiss.

By the same author:

EMMA'S SECRET WORLD
EMMA ENSLAVED
EMMA'S SECRET DIARIES
EMMA'S SUBMISSION
EMMA'S HUMILIATION
EMMA'S SECRET DOMINATION

A NEXUS CLASSIC

EMMA'S SECRET DIARIES

Hilary James

This book is a work of fiction.
In real life, make sure you practise safe, sane and consensual sex.

First published in 1995 by
Nexus
Thames Wharf Studios
Rainville Road
London W6 9HA

This Nexus Classic edition 2004

Typeset by TW Typesetting, Plymouth, Devon

Printed and bound by Clays Ltd, St Ives PLC

ISBN 0 352 33888 1

Contents

Part I
ISABELLA

1

The first weekend

The weekend is approaching and I'm moist with excitement and apprehension.

I've been having the most awful time with Henry, who has been constantly chasing after other women in his hunt for a suitable wife now that he is widowed. I half feel that he is doing this deliberately to annoy me. However I have taken his advice and broken with Ursula for once and for all.

But with Henry being otherwise occupied, and with Ursula being out of bounds, my body aches for physical excitement. I feel so empty without all the thrills of my extraordinary relationship with Ursula – despite all the humiliations that she imposed on me. I know that I loved it all and I crave to be degraded – it somehow heightens my sexuality.

I just wonder whether other women know to what depth of excitement you can be driven to by being made to feel like a slave or a dog ... to be chained or to be kept caged in a kennel ... to be kept frustrated, just waiting for the summons to please ... oh, how I miss it all!

Certainly I have never found it at home with my charming, quiet and devoted husband, John. But then marriage is something quite different. Marriage provides a firm base to life – day in, day out. John is well connected and through him I have an amusing circle of friends and relations. We get on very well. He is utterly dependent on me. He never asks too many questions when I go off for a few days. I would never, I know, leave him – not even for Henry.

But now what will this unexpected weekend bring?

I met the rather older, but well known and wealthy,

Mark at a party some months back, and he left telephone messages for me several times. But I did not bother to return his calls as I had then been so involved, quite separately of course, with both Ursula and Henry. But then at the end of February, when he sent me another invitation, I accepted.

It was merely for dinner with some friends at *Le Caprice* in Arlington Street, he had explained. There was no question at that stage of anything unusual.

The evening went well and it was assumed that I would be staying with friends. So Mark just kissed me briefly and said, 'My driver will take you home.' So that was fine. Next day I received a present of a rather lovely evening blouse and I felt quite flattered.

This was followed by a few similar evenings – always at very pleasant eating places: the River Cafe at Thames Wharf or Bibendum on the Fulham Road, which I adored. Ursula used to go there a lot, and I secretly rather hoped to see her, but I never did.

Then one evening, at the Mirabelle in Curzon Street, Mark kept on talking about how someone called Isabella adored French cooking and that he always took her there. She would apparently be flying in from Paris the following week.

At first I did not pay much attention, but Mark talked a great deal about Isabella: about how she was married; about how she was a former French model for the House of Dior; about how she was the centre of the Parisian social scene; and about how she would occasionally fly over from Paris. Evidently they were old friends.

He then told me that his wife would be away for the weekend of the 28th, and asked whether I would like to join him at their country house near Marlborough. He casually told me that Isabella might be there as well – but instead of feeling jealous, I felt that this could only make it all the more exciting.

However, he continued, as he is a well known man, I must observe some simple, but strict, rules. I was to drive to Marlborough and park at a certain hotel and ring him. I was to leave my car at the hotel and he would then have me driven to the house. All this made it sound even more exciting!

The weekend has at last arrived and I'm at Mark's house.

It is a lovely Palladium style building surrounded by a beautiful park where fallow deer graze under large oak trees. Mark has been attentive, but slightly cold – as if he wants to keep a certain distance between us. Greeting me, he simply said: 'Well, Emma, you must look after yourself until dinner as I've things to do.'

I found that I had my own bedroom and bathroom at the top of the staircase of the galleried hall, and had no difficulty amusing myself. In fact I rather enjoyed being on my own. I even took the chance to write up this diary!

It's now eight o'clock sharp and there's just been a knock on the door. The butler said, 'Dinner will be at eight thirty, Madam.'

I wonder what will happen this evening? I'm on tenterhooks!

Well, down I went feeling a million dollars, wearing the pale blue, off the shoulder, wild silk dress that Henry gave me.

We had drinks before dinner and I was introduced. It was all very polite and sophisticated. Nobody asked if I was married or how I knew Mark. He himself was very polite and, although I did not sit next to him at dinner, I felt no jealousy and found it all fun.

I adored the intellectual and amusing conversation and after dinner we played a brilliant variety of charades. I was given 'Marie Antoinette' to act and it was quickly guessed – which bucked up my self confidence.

Then shortly after midnight everyone except Isabella began to leave. She was, I thought, just divine: very French and about 40 – though it's difficult to tell for she still has her model's figure and good looks. She walks beautifully and looks exquisite. She told me that she had known Mark for some years and although she was married in France, she came to London frequently and stayed with him.

5

Then when the other guests had left, Mark also suddenly went out saying that he would join us again in a few minutes.

Soon Isabella and I were sitting very close to each other on the sofa. Isabella had complained of the heating being too much and asked me to help her take off her dress. Underneath all she was wearing was a lovely La Perla teddy. This was the underwear that I had always longed for. I had often asked Ursula to buy me some, but somehow Ursula had always forgotten. In retrospect I suspect that Ursula just bought for me what she liked to see me in, and not what I wanted.

Seeing Isabella looking so exquisitely seductive, I could feel myself getting wet. I began to long for Isabella to put her hands up my dress. I spread my legs. Luckily I had no pants on – just stockings.

But Isabella did nothing. I was desperate. How awful if she did not fancy me! I was already mesmerised by her, but she just sat smoking a cigarette, seeming rather indifferent to me.

What should I do? What could I do? This was something you did not learn in books. I was used to Ursula and Henry setting the pace. As I was their little slave, the question of me taking the initiative had never arisen. Dare I make the first move? Isabella seemed so haughty that I feared she might reject me.

Isabella now put on some music and began to dance with herself around the room. She undid her hair and let it flow down her back. I was amazed at her delicate little dancing – pretty little steps and so well co-ordinated.

'Can you dance?' she called to me.

'Just a little,' I replied, knowing full well I did not have the lightness of step of Isabella nor her wonderful movements – the swing of her hips. Nor did I have her long legs, her flat tummy, or her gorgeous La Perla.

'Change into something exciting,' whispered Isabella. I thought that in my long dress I was already looking quite exciting. What could Isabella want?

I went to my room and looked at my clothes hanging in the cupboard. Everything suddenly looked rather tacky.

My negligées were not nearly fine enough. Then I wondered about the basque that Ursula had given me. It really was one of Ursula's own ones, so it was slightly too big for me. Ursula used to say mockingly, 'Those little tits will fill it one day – you just wait – I'm going to have you specially treated.' Oh, how I hate Ursula now!

I put the basque on together with my stockings and some high heel shoes. How I wished I had kept the present of the hugely high heel shoes that Ursula had sent me recently. But I had angrily sent them back. What a fool I had been. Oh, how I longed for them now!

Isabella called up through the door, 'Put long gloves on. I like gloves.' I smiled. Isabella was obviously a glove fetishist. Luckily I never went anywhere without gloves.

Feeling slightly gauche, I returned to the still dancing Isabella.

'Ah,' cried Isabella, 'that's a bit better . . . Let your hair down . . . Darling Mark likes flowing hair.'

This was the first mention of Mark, who still had not returned. In fact I had almost forgotten about him.

'Oh, I, your shoes! Don't you have any higher ones? Mark will be cross.'

I was embarrassed. I felt so inadequate by comparison with this divine waltzing creature.

Isabella held her hands out to me. 'Relax, little girl, relax.'

Her hands were like little pearls as they touched my flesh. Obviously they were hands which never worked, never washed up, never gardened . . . They were hands made to play with a body. I could feel Isabella's soft little touches.

'Come and dance, darling.'

At first we danced apart, joking and laughing – just little steps, and Isabella was so encouraging. Then she said, 'Let's have something softer – slower – a waltz perhaps.' She lowered the lights. The room was quite dim now . . . soft music . . . the delicious, intoxicating, smell of Isabella's sex. I could see that Isabella was aroused, but I did not think it was due to my presence. What was Isabella thinking about? Some private fantasy?

7

'Now you look more attractive,' Isabella purred. We started to dance close together.

I was throbbing. I adored the femininity of the other woman. I knew I could be Isabella's little slave, but there seemed no question of this – the subject simply didn't arise as we danced cheek to cheek, our soft hot flesh touching.

'Use your hands, Emma!' whispered Isabella. I started to do so, and had just put my hands on her breasts, when Isabella rang a little bell and, to my astonishment, in walked Mark – just wearing some tiny leather briefs! They were extremely tight and his manhood looked gigantic inside them.

Isabella waltzed over to him. 'Darling, you must see Emma dance . . .'

We started to dance again. 'Use your fingers quickly!' cried an agitated Isabella. I undid the La Perla and gradually took it off, to reveal a naked Isabella. Her body was unbelievably taut, and she had a very small little mound of hair around her body lips – almost as if it were sculptured.

My own hair had been removed – something that both Ursula and Henry had insisted on. It was still smooth with not a trace of stubble. Both Mark and Isabella were frightfully excited by glimpses of this below the basque.

'Isabella!' cried Mark. 'Do let me see more of Emma's little belly and beauty lips.'

We danced around Mark and Isabella gently lifted the basque. I could feel Isabella's wet beauty lips when she pressed against mine. Soon Mark was standing between the two of us. His leather briefs were obviously bursting.

'Come!' said Isabella taking my hand . . .

2

A tantalising threesome

Leaving Mark downstairs Isabella led me up to her bedroom. She put on a lovely satin peignoir, but left me in just my basque.

'Would you like to play a little game, darling?' she asked, in her fascinating French accent. I, of course, love games, but not knowing Isabella well I was too embarrassed to say a word. I just nodded eagerly.

'Very well! We're going to pretend that I'm the Sultan's favourite wife and you're my slave girl. The Sultan is going to visit me and it's your job to get me ready for him and, when he arrives, to get him ready for me! And to give him so much extra pleasure that he comes back to me more often! But remember your task is just to give pleasure – not to receive it, unless I give you permission. Understand, my little slave?'

Again all I could do was nod eagerly.

'Very well! Now kneel down in front of me whilst I sit at my dressing table and titivate myself. That's right, crawl down!'

Moments later I was kneeling at her feet under the dressing table. Her lovely long legs were either side of me. She untied the sash of her negligée. She started to freshen up her lipstick.

'Now slave, I want to feel your tongue all the way up the inside of my right leg.'

This was something I knew how to do – and do well! Soon I heard her gasping with pleasure. But, then, just when my tongue approached her holy of holies, she pushed away my head murmuring, 'No, slave, the other leg first!'

Again my tongue slowly and tantalisingly climbed up her leg. This time she opened her legs and sat back.

'Now slave, excite your mistress. Get her ready for the Sultan!'

I ran my tongue gently up and down her beauty lips. I could feel them getting more and more moist. I thrust my tongue down between them.

'Yes, that's very good, slave. Now come up a little higher.'

Moments later my tongue was gently caressing her beauty bud. I could hear her gasping. 'Wonderful, wonderful,' she murmured.

Then she stopped me.

'I think I'm now more than ready for the Sultan!' she laughed. 'I can see that you're very good!'

I blushed with pleasure.

'Now come up and brush my hair! When the Sultan arrives, I want him to see me sitting, looking gorgeous in my peignoir, whilst a half naked slave girl brushes my hair . . . Now start brushing!'

She handed me the silver hairbrush. Looking in the mirror I noticed that she looked very beautiful and was clearly very excited. How I wished I was the Sultan and not a mere slave girl!

'Now listen carefully, slave,' she said. 'When the Sultan enters you're to fall to your knees with your head to the floor – and stay like that until I click my fingers. And keep silent – slave girls don't dare to speak in the presence of the Sultan! Then when I click my fingers, your task will be to kneel down and lick his bottom and tickle him behind his manhood – that's what he really likes, and that will make him really virile for your Mistress. So, slave, if you want to please me make sure you lick and tickle well!'

I was rather shocked. It was what Henry liked me to do too, but I hardly knew Mark and it was such a personal thing to do. But I knew I'd do anything to please Isabella!

Before she could explain any more, there was a knock at the door.

'Come in, Sire!' called Isabella, evidently giving Mark the code word that would confirm that his role was to be that of Sultan. Obviously it was a game that they had played before.

Mark came into the room. He was dressed in a long silk dressing gown. In his hand was a short dog whip.

Isabella gave me a nudge. Quickly I fell to my knees and lowered my head to the carpet, like a respectful slave. I could feel my juices running, I was so excited. Out of the corner of my eye I saw Isabella walk across to him, take the whip out of his hand and kiss him on the lips.

Moments later I heard Isabella snap her fingers. It was the signal! Hastily I rose to my feet, trying hard to be graceful in just my little basque, and minced across the room. I could see that Mark was eyeing me, even though it was Isabella that was kissing him. I went behind him, and fell to my knees. I hesitated for a moment. Could I really do it? There wasn't much chemistry between Mark and me, not on my side anyway. But he was a rich and powerful man. And there was all the chemistry in the world between Isabella and me!

I put my head under the back of Mark's dressing gown. He was naked under it. It was dark, but I could smell his aroused masculinity. Again I hesitated. Could I really go on? Was I just being used as a tart?

My hesitation ended abruptly when Isabella reaching behind Mark, and, guessing my doubts, gave me a sharp cut across my bottom with the dog whip. My God, I thought, I must remember that I'm just her slave girl. I must do whatever she says.

I raised my head and parted Mark's buttocks with my hands. I reached forward with my tongue. I felt Mark give a little jump. I heard a little sigh of pleasure from Isabella. He would, I knew, still be kissing Isabella passionately. His passion would now have been heightened by my tongue and his passion would fuel Isabella's. My role was really, I knew, just a secondary and humiliating one, but somehow I felt proud – proud to be used to increase my Mistress's pleasure. I felt deeply satisfied and excited as I thrust my tongue in and out more deeply.

I remembered what Isabella had said about my fingers. I reached forward slightly and with my finger tips began to tickle Mark behind the sack of his manhood. Again I felt him give a little jump. Again I heard Isabella give a little sigh of pleasure. Again I knew that my Mistress's pleasure would be increased – and I was responsible for it!

Greatly daring, I reached forward with one hand. I brushed his aroused manhood. I had never seen it. I longed to hold it, and to cup his spheres, but I dare not even touch either without my Mistress's consent. I felt her hand then reach down and angrily push mine away. I took my hand back. I must not trespass on her ground!

As I licked and tickled from behind, I could feel her massaging his manhood. She was giving him his principal pleasure. My role was only secondary – as befitted a mere slave girl.

Then I realised that Isabella was now rubbing Mark's manhood against her beauty bud. Another sharp tap on my bottom from Isabella's whip made me realise that my role was just to ensure that his manhood remained aroused – after all he was not a young man. I applied myself diligently!

'Darling,' I heard Isabella whisper after a couple of minutes, 'come to bed!'

They moved to the large high four poster bed. I did not know what do.

'Emma, kneel down – head to the floor, and keep your eyes closed,' ordered Isabella.

Kneeling down by the side of the bed, and yet unable to see what was happening through the curtains that surrounded it, I could hear everything. It was so frustrating – and yet terribly exciting. Soon Isabella was crying out with excitement.

Then there was a pause and I heard Isabella whisper, 'Darling, let's make more use of Emma!'

Moments later she called out: 'Emma, stand up!'

I was now standing by the curtains, with the top of the bed level with my moist beauty lips.

'Now don't pull back the curtain – just slip your hands between them.'

I could not see my hands now, but I felt them being gripped by Isabella. She guided down, and made me hold something hard and warm – and yet slippery and velvety. It was Mark's manhood. Hastily I let go – I had never before held it. But Isabella's hands caught mine again and took them back to where they had been.

'Work, Emma! Work!'

Nervously I started to massage him. I heard a chuckle from Isabella and a grunt of satisfaction from Mark. It was so embarrassing not being allowed to look through the curtains!

'I think, Mark, you deserve an exciting little sight!' I heard Isabella say. Then she called out. 'Now keep your right hand doing what it's doing now, but hold your left breast in your left hand.'

Mesmerised, I did what I was told.

'Now with your left hand, put your left breast through the curtains so that we can see it properly – and keep the curtains closed! All we want to see of you is your breast.'

I felt utterly humiliated as I obeyed the very explicit orders. All I could see in front of my eyes were the drawn curtains, but I soon felt fingers on my breast, kneading my nipple. Was it Isabella or Mark? I could hear more gasps of pleasure from Mark. I felt that I had lost control of my body – the mere sight of my breast was apparently stimulating and arousing Mark. I was not really involved at all. I might just as well as have been a picture or a photo – but I could not help feeling that it was terribly exciting.

Suddenly I heard Isabella's voice again.

'Emma! Go to the foot of the bed and start crawling up under the bed clothes.'

Breathless with excitement I obeyed. My hair was suddenly gripped and pulled up between outstretched legs. But they were not, as I had expected, Mark's hairy rough skinned ones, but the long soft legs of Isabella. I felt the bedclothes being flung back to bare my naked bottom. I felt a stroke of the whip.

'Now excite me, for a change,' Isabella ordered.

In the darkness, under the bedclothes, I groped with my tongue for her beauty lips. I ran my tongue up and down them several times. I was rewarded with little cries of pleasure. Then I gently parted the lips with my fingers and once again lowered my tongue to her beauty bud. The response was immediate and violent.

'Go on!' I heard her cry. She gripped my head with her hands, pressing me tightly to her sex. 'Oh . . . Oh . . . Don't stop!'

I looked up from my task, and saw that Mark was lying by her side. He was now kissing her on the mouth. With one hand he was playing with her nipples. With the other he now reached down and with his middle finger pushed aside my tongue and began tickling Isabella's already high-ly aroused beauty bud. I was relegated to the subsidiary task of tickling her beauty lips with my tongue.

Isabella now became highly aroused. Her breaths came in short gasps, interspersed with little cries of delight. I could not help feeling jealous of Mark and more than a little put out – surely I, as a woman, could have aroused the lovely Isabella's beauty bud far better than any man?

Then I saw that Isabella had partly turned towards Mark. They were kissing passionately and playing with each other's nipples. Yet I was sure that most of her pleas-ure was coming from me – even if it wasn't being acknowledged and even if I, myself, was not being given any pleasure. I was just there to serve.

Then Isabella pushed both my face and Mark's hands away.

'Suck him, Emma,' she cried, gripping me by the scruff of my neck and thrusting me forward. 'Do it!' she ordered when she saw my hesitation. I lowered my head and took his manhood into my mouth. Thanks to Henry it was a task that I knew I could do well, very well.

Moments later, and with Mark clearly approaching a climax, Isabella thrust me aside and took my place.

'Get down between his legs and lick!' she muttered.

I lay down between his outstretched legs. In front of my eyes I could see his erect manhood now held in Isabella's hand – and Isabella's mouth moving up and down. She flashed me an angry look and I reached out with my tongue. Clearly I was not deemed worthy to receive his seed in my mouth. Once again my role was merely second-ary.

Moments later I felt Mark's spheres twitch. He gave a deep groan and ejaculated into Isabella's mouth. She flashed me a look of triumph.

'Oh, darling,' he cried to Isabella, 'that was wonderful . . . wonderful.'

Then whilst Mark watched, Isabella and I kissed and excited each other. We were both highly aroused. It was unbelievably exciting. In no time, our mouths glued to-gether, our breasts pressed against each other, and our hands gently tickling our beauty buds, we reached our cli-maxes and relaxed into each other's arms.

It was something that we repeated later during the night whilst the exhausted Mark slept . . .

That night was unbelievably exciting for me. I knew now that, regardless of what Henry might say, I really do enjoy making love with women to the orders of a strict Mistress.

As I lay in Isabella's arms, satiated, I thought what fun it would be if me and Henry could have another girl . . . Dazed, I started to fall asleep, wondering why Henry thought I was jealous. In fact it was all Henry's fault, I decided. Henry makes me feel inferior. If a threesome is going to work then you've all got to be physically attracted to one another. You can play games, but when the games are over no one must feel left out of it, or one not as good sexually as the other. The understanding must be that you each bring something different. But Henry would never learn this – anyway, he'd been such a bastard recently, did it really matter?

The three of us spent a blissful night together, but early next morning Isabella had to fly back to Paris. So Mark took her to the airport and I stayed on sleeping, exhausted.

How Henry would love to hear all the details, I thought. But then I stopped myself thinking of that, and instead only thought of how he had wounded me – the bastard!

Mark came back and got into bed again with me. We both missed Isabella, and although we had a happy relax-ing time, we were too exhausted for more fun and games.

He was interesting and clever, and I enjoyed being with him.

Oh, how complicated life is getting!

3

The plot

I have now developed a craving for Isabella.

It is a craving that has increased the more I find myself staying with Mark. It was in his house that I met her. It is in his house that I hope to meet her again.

It is an unnatural craving – like being desperate for a drink, a drug or just sweets. It was more than a crush – crushes come and go but this craving stays. Isabella is in my thoughts first thing in the morning, last thing at night, during the day, all the time . . .

I even wildly imagine that I see Isabella in the street . . . at the hairdresser . . . in Harrods . . . at a fashion show – then, when I rush up and find it isn't her but just another model, I feel crushed, and so unhappy.

I can feel the craving getting worse. At times I wake up hoping to feel a delicate finger on my moist, wet little beauty bud – but of course it is only wish fulfilment, and then I feel madly frustrated. I had thought of keeping a separate diary of my longings and sending them to Isabella, but on reflection feel that this would be foolish.

However, I obtained Isabella's telephone number from Mark's address book one afternoon when he was out shooting and I now plan to ring her. I have rehearsed several times what I am going to say – 'Hello Isabella, how are you? When are you coming over to England?' or 'By the way, I'm planning to come over to Paris quite soon . . .'

But I have thought that this all sounded rather feeble. Perhaps I could get Mark to telephone? But now every time I mention Isabella's name to him, he just gets all furious and shouts that I'm not to mention her name in his house. However I know that when I make love to Mark he becomes soft and yields to my every wish. Of course, it isn't real love making, but I know how to amuse him and that is all he wants.

So I've hatched this little plot to get Mark to phone Isabella – and then some weekend when I know that Mark will be away, I will try and arrange for Isabella to come over. But will Mark agree to all of this? I know that relations between the two of them are now difficult. Isabella has obviously become bored by Mark and he is very hurt. I will need to be unusually subtle. I also know that I will have to please Mark a great deal – even though I am not really interested in him and, quite honestly, regard making love to him as a bit of a bore.

Mark has been ringing and writing, and is constantly on my back trying to persuade me to come and stay. But I'm just too busy. My relationship with Henry has improved and has now returned to the excitement of earlier years – so really Mark has been put on the back burner. I had, I admit, been initially very excited when we first met, but that was because I had fallen in love with Isabella.

Indeed, I am now hopelessly infatuated. It has happened so quickly. It is the most exciting thing that has ever happened to me. I had never really loved Ursula. That had been more a case of fear and awe – and of being in love with Ursula's lifestyle, with the art world and with the people in it.

I have to admit that I have also loved Henry. But then we have had our separation and differences. Since then, although we've been back together and have had some marvellous moments, I know that they could only be fleeting ones, for he simply has to find somebody else: somebody who will marry him and look after him . . .

Isabella was married, of course, but that was all a mere beautiful *marriage de convenance* for her and her husband and everybody knew it.

Finally, last week, I plucked up the courage and telephoned Isabella.

Hearing her beautiful voice, I felt suddenly paralysed and just didn't know what to say. Anyway, I thought,'

Isabella was a very busy person and might even have forgotten me, and then I would feel the most terrible brush-off. So, trembling, I put down the phone.

It was therefore now even more important that I humoured Mark and got him to phone Isabella – for I just couldn't do so myself.

So I have decided to relent and agree to go and stay with Mark again.

It's never awful staying with Mark – in fact it is extraordinarily pampering. The lifestyle is wonderful and Mark is increasingly falling in love with me, whilst also being, like me, infatuated with Isabella.

So why, I wonder, had I made such a fuss about staying with him? After all, I have no difficulty in persuading my dear undemanding husband that I'm going off on business for a couple of days. No, I think, it is partly because the 'me' that Mark has fallen in love with is really just a shell. It is like falling in love with the icing on a cake and not the cake itself. The majority of men do this, but I think they are either very stupid, or naïve. But anyway why should I worry? If it's just the icing he loves so much, then so be it – and let him enjoy it. He would never reach my real self, the real cake, only Henry had ever done that. And he, alas, is away – always so busy trying to get married.

On the Saturday night there was a dinner party, so we were all rather busy. But on Sunday we took a walk around the gardens and Mark drove me round the estate pointing out where he was planning to put in new trees, and describing his plans to have a golf course.

I quietly listened to it all and he became more and more enchanted with my gentle words of encouragement and with the interest I showed in all his future plans. That evening, after dinner, Mark was indeed a mellow man – he felt so at ease with the world – and as we sank into bed he was quite happy to listen to my suggestions.

Picking my moment, I said in a straight-forward way that I had liked Isabella and whatever the differences between the two of them, would he please now ring her up and invite her over in two weeks time when he was going to be in Scotland, and let me use his house to entertain her.

To my amazement, Mark agreed, and after one or two attempts to get through to Isabella he eventually did so.

There followed a few strained sentences in French – I could here Mark say. '*Oui, c'est en Novembre. Oui, oui,* Charlie will collect you from the airport, *oui.*' Then it was, '*Au revoir!*'

Mark looked at me. It was all arranged.

Then I gave him his reward while I fantasised about Isabella – and eventually we slept.

4

Isabella returns – and bitter disappointment

The weekend is approaching fast. I am consumed with a heady mixture of agitation, longing and craving.

I have told my husband that I will be away, staying with a girl friend. Anyway he is so busy with his oceanographic reports that he scarcely notices whether I am there or not.

True to his word, Mark has arranged for Isabella to be met and driven to his house. I have decided to go there on the Friday, as Isabella will be coming just for Saturday and Sunday.

All day I've been preparing myself: first to the hairdresser, then to the beauty clinic for a wax and nail varnish, then to buy some sheer stockings – and all this just for Isabella.

Friday night alone at Mark's was a relief – I could get my beauty sleep, relax, do as I please, and think only of the pleasure I was going to give Isabella when she arrived the following morning.

I decided I would tell Isabella that I adore her and want to go back to Paris with her.

But it was not until four thirty in the afternoon, after a very prolonged delay in London that I at last heard the swish of a car's tyres on the gravel outside. I rushed to the window. There, standing as statuesque as ever, was Isabella!

Oh, the sheer joy! It was all just too exciting! But just as I was getting carried away, I gave a gasp of horror as I saw Isabella put her arm around another beautiful young model, one who had obviously come with her.

My God! I almost cried aloud. Just what does she think

she's doing? I asked her here on her own. How dare she bring another girl and arrive six hours late. No wonder Mark got fed up with her – she really is impossible.

I continued to feel bewitched, furious, jealous and, as ever, in awe of Isabella. Yes, there was Isabella, talking animatedly and holding hands with this beautiful unknown model. There they were, walking up the steps of the house – then I could see no more.

I felt sick. Should I disappear, or should I go down and act as if nothing unusual had happened? Should I look at Isabella in a disinterested way and pretend that I'd only asked her over from Paris as a joke? Yes, I decided, that's what I would do.

Hastily I put on more lipstick and with a light step I bounced down the stairs and cried, 'Oh, hello Isabella! How lovely you could come. Do introduce me to your lovely friend.'

Being French, Isabella did not recognise my false tone, and responded magnanimously. 'Oh, Emma!' she cried. 'Do meet Brigette.'

I could hardly believe my eyes, the girl was so beautiful. Girl? Close up she was more like a child. She couldn't have been more than sixteen – with the lovely innocence of a little girl. Her tiny voice just said, *'Enchantée, Madame'*. She knew little English. But what did that matter if you were so beautiful? Soft skin, fair long hair, very little make-up – just plain beautiful.

Isabella was obvioulsy infatuated with the girl, and to my chagrin barely acknowledged my presence. She certainly did not seem to realise that she was only there as my guest. She brushed past me with another casual, 'hello' – no kiss, not even a 'Darling', and the little Brigette ignored me totally.

Isabella was now lording it about the place – being over-friendly to Mrs Price, the old housekeeper, who of course loved Isabella, as she always brought her presents from Paris. She had never bothered much about me! I had even noticed Mrs Price putting flowers in Isabella's room and cooking a special vegetarian lunch ready for her. In my anger, I was now delighted that Isabella hadn't arrived in time to eat it.

Only a few minutes earlier, Mrs Price had said to me how shocking it was that Isabella hadn't telephoned and what bad manners it was. Now she was all sweetness to her – and to Brigette.

Their rooms all adjoined one another and were separated by bathrooms with inter-connecting doors. The bathrooms were almost indistinguishable from the bedrooms; they had the same thick carpets and French furniture, but a bath sat like a throne in the centre of the room. Mark always had the bathrooms well stocked with Floris soaps, gels, lotions and scent. Indeed, they were almost like an advertisement for Floris!

Isabella had now arrived in the adjoining bedroom to mine. Officially it was Mark's wife's dressing room. But as she was always away now, it made a very comfortable guest room. I had specially told Mrs Price to put Isabella in there. However, Isabella now said, 'Darling Brigette, you can have this room,' – and the stupid Mrs Price of course agreed, and told Isabella that she would make up the room on the far side for her.

I was incensed! Mark would certainly not have allowed this. I understood now why they had fallen out. Isabella was quite impossible with all her grand manners, directing everybody about as if they were children. I felt I must exert myself.

'Isabella, I had this room specially prepared for you. We were not expecting you to bring a friend.'

Isabella pretended she could not understand my slight Irish accent, which was a ruse she had always used when she wanted her own way. So, without batting an eyelid, she began to stroke Brigette and said, 'Now, *ma petite enfant*, have a wash after your long journey and I will join you in a few minutes. I am just going to discuss with Mrs Price what we are going to have for supper.'

Hearing this I was again consumed with rage and slunk off to my own room distraught with jealousy – and almost hatred for the horrible Isabella.

Minutes later I heard Isabella return and, through the connecting doors that Isabella had left open, I again saw the beautiful young girl – tall, slim and with long blonde hair. She only had a peach coloured silk dressing gown on, and there she was, literally kneeling at Isabella's feet and gazing up at her.

Isabella raised her up and slowly led her towards the bathroom. Again consumed with jealousy, I watched in amazement as Isabella inspected the girl's body and plucked at her fair skin with a large pair of tweezers.

'*Ma petite Brigette . . . Ma petite cherie . . .*' she whispered, together with a lot of other endearments which I did not understand. I could not see a single hair on the girl's body, but then she was at a slight distance. Isabella now parted the legs of the '*petite enfant*', and gently removed some stray hairs with the tweezers. Throughout all this, Brigette was just staring at Isabella as if transfixed.

I was in a turmoil inside. I had known a little bit of jealousy before – when Henry had started to have a fling with lots of different women, but this had made me more annoyed than seriously jealous – annoyed, not so much at Henry's behaviour, but with the stupid women who, for some strange reason, threw themselves at him. How could these women be so stupid? Anyway, as women, compared with Isabella, they didn't really count. Indeed, I had a strange contempt for them and their silly empty lives.

I knew from experience that women like Isabella were most fastidious. With Ursula, of course, the mere touch of an offensive bristle, and I would have been beaten. I now saw Isabella pick up a hairbrush. Was the girl going to be punished?

But then Isabella put down the tweezers and started to brush and pat the girl's body. This was obviously some sort of toning for her body. She patted Brigette's little breasts several times and then gave an order in French.

Instantly the young girl raised her arms and began some exercises. Holding herself erect, and clasping her hands behind her back, she began to push out her chest. After doing this several times, her face began to show a lovely rosy glow, and her delicious little ripe nipples began to stick out and up.

I could stand it no longer. I was now in a highly aroused state. Watching the beautiful blonde girl, who was such a willing slave of Isabella's, had been very erotic. But I wanted to be Isabella's willing slave too. After all, that was the whole purpose of the visit. I had made it clear to Isabella that I would obey her every wish – and I had also let on that I was not really sleeping with Mark – or with any man. I had promised Isabella that I just wasn't interested in men anymore, and Isabella had seemed to be excited by that conversation on the telephone.

I wondered whether to interrupt but, just as I was going to do so, I saw Isabella touch Brigette with a little cane. Instantly Brigette knelt again at Isabella's feet. Isabella's legs were well apart and Brigette put her beautiful long pink tongue into her little parting. In and out it went in a perfect rhythm.

It was as if Brigette had been specially trained – and as each lick went in, Isabella's subtle body swayed excitingly in time to the girl's tongue, her pale white cheeks gradually taking on a little pink flush. Brigette herself appeared to be obtaining no satisfaction from all this.

Suddenly Isabella stooped down slightly and began to caress Brigette's soft abdomen. Then she raised the young model from her knees and ordered her to position herself on the bed like a willing little slave. But, I heard Isabella say, before she did this, she was to have ten little strokes from her cane.

I watched. Surely Brigette would cry out. Down came the first gentle stroke – on the girl's tender breast. There was not a whimper – not even a sniff or a sob.

I now knew for certain that Brigette really had replaced me. I began to fantasise how I might oust Brigette. But how? I knew only too well how to play the perfect slave. At least Ursula had taught me that . . .

I heard another stroke. This time it was across little Brigette's belly. Still not a whimper. It was extraordinary.

Then Isabella noticed me through the open doors. She

cried out in a harsh French accent, 'So, Emma, you're admiring my new little slave, are you? Well come and watch! You may learn something.'

Then she suddenly strode into my room and seized me by the hair. She pushed me to the floor, screaming, 'Get into the corner of Brigette's room and watch from there. Yes, watch me, just watch.'

I was on fire with rage. Isabella had taunted me enough. It was too much. In a sudden rage, and forgetting all about being Isabella's obedient little slave, I suddenly let fly, grabbing Isabella by the feet and dragging the statuesque beauty to the floor.

At first, thanks to my rage, I found myself the stronger. Little Brigette cried out, '*Arrêtez! Arrêtez!*' But we didn't hear. I was clawing at Isabella, who was thumping me with her fists.

'You'll pay for this, you horrible little beast, you wretch!' she yelled.

Now Isabella was on top of me, holding me down. I was literally pinned down under her. I could hardly breathe, let alone speak.

'Brigette!' Isabella yelled. 'Get my cane from the dressing table.'

Mistress's little pet that she was, Brigette scuttled away to please her adored Mistress, whilst Isabella continued to hold me down helpless. Back she ran a few moments later.

'Now Brigette, you are going to learn to cane this wretched little beast and teach her to control her temper. Start with her breasts!'

Isabella slightly adjusted her position, still pinning me down. 'Now wait, Brigette, until I count ... one ... two ... three ... four ... five. Now, Brigette, now!'

Brigette was not trained to thrash another woman. The first stroke was very mild. I hardly felt it. But Isabella was a good teacher, and soon Brigette got more confident. The next few strokes got harder and harder. But I had known far worse – both from Henry, and especially from Ursula. I began to wonder if Brigette felt sorry for me and I found myself beginning to love this gentle and beautiful creature.

Isabella was shouting again, 'Brigette, you little fool, this won't do at all. I want to see Emma being severely punished. We'll tie her up and then I'll show you how to use a cane on a woman . . .'

The next minutes were terrible as, tied to a radiator and made to bend over, I was alternatively beaten by Isabella and then Brigette. Soon, weeping with pain, I was left tied in a corner of my own room feeling miserable. In the distance, through the doors, I could hear giggles and laughter as Isabella and Brigette frolicked with each other. I felt so jealous.

Then I heard Isabella say something in French, and she came and opened the connecting doors wide. I could now see into Isabella's room.

Brigette lay panting on the bed after all her exertions of tying me up and than practising beating me. She had also evidently felt an intense excitement at having been allowed to beat me. She now knew that she could enjoy giving pain as well as receiving it.

Isabella was obviously intoxicated with Brigette. I watched as her hand moved into the girl's wet little crevice, and Brigette responded instantly with little wriggles and cries. Then Isabella moved her long tongue between her young friend's parted legs – giving me a beautiful view of the girl's perfectly hairless cleft, and the dainty beauty lips that guarded her treasure.

The outer lips were pouting proudly – a typical young girl's, fleshy, firm and straight – a perfect foil to the inner pair which were as convoluted and luxuriant as any I had ever seen.

When Isabella pushed her tongue between them, she evidently found Brigette's little treasure closed as tightly as a child's – no one would ever have guessed that Isabella had already drunk several times from this oasis of love.

Now, as if she wanted to make up to Brigette for the awful scene that I had made, she put her lips gently to that divine opening and slid her tongue as far inside as she could manage. At the same time, she eased her own thighs apart and let her darling Brigette take similar liberties with her own more voluptuous and seasoned delicacies.

It was clearly a luxuriously sensual feeling for both of them, and over the next half hour or so time lost all meaning for them. As I writhed with frustration, unable to loosen my knots, they just wallowed in the sensual delights of each other's intimacies and relished their perfect agreement on doing what pleased them most.

But suddenly it was all getting too much for Brigette. She cried out for Isabella to stop. But Isabella was at the point of reaching a genuine orgasm and hit the silly girl with her fists.

'Work your fingers, you little slave,' she screeched.

Isabella's body was on fire. Her nipples were burning. Nothing would stop her now. It was amazing what the little slave Brigette could be made to do – when forced. Isabella's belly was tingling – she almost looked demented. Poor little Brigette was forced to continue until swooning with screams and almost inhuman yells Isabella reached the peak of a tremendous climax.

Her whole body went rigid and then jerked in spasms as if she had fallen onto a live electric wire. Then she relaxed beside her gorgeous little slave girl and they both descended into a deep sleep – until they were awoken by loud cries from me.

'Please, please, Isabella, untie me! ... You must! ... Help! ... Help!'

Isabella's mouth curved into a cruel smile. She beat out a little tune with her fingers and laughed, telling Brigette to listen and enjoy my silly little wails and cries. Indeed, they both got excited again just listening to me. And as they laughed and again made love, I was completely ignored.

5

Humiliation

'Supper's ready!' I heard Mrs Price call up – the supper that I had so carefully ordered as a little romantic occasion for just Isabella and me.

'Thank you,' Isabella called back. 'There'll just be the two of us – Emma's not feeling well. Don't you bother to wait for us. You go off and watch television! Just leave it all on the hot plate and we'll help ourselves.'

So much, I thought bitterly, for my romantic candlelit evening with Isabella!

But clearly Isabella had planned it all. For when she now untied me, she produced from her suitcase a pretty white frilly maid's pinafore and a rather ugly matching bonnet.

'Now, Emma,' she said, 'put these on, and if you're very good and obedient, I'll let you be my maid servant this evening. You can bathe Brigette and me, and then wait on us at table. Just wear these and black stockings and shoes – nothing else. And also put on these white gloves – we don't want your dirty hands and fingers touching us or our food. And scrub your face – I don't like make-up on a maid servant ... And hide your hair under the bonnet – I don't want any dirty hairs falling into my food. Now hurry up – and not one word, unless you want another thrashing!'

Mortified, I bit my tongue to keep back my protest, and washed off all my pretty make-up and lipstick. I put the pinafore over my neck and tied it round my waist. It left my back and my sore little bottom bare. Then I put on the bonnet and shoes and stockings.

I glanced in the mirror. Except for being half naked, I looked, with my ugly bonnet, just like a rather plain maid servant. I gave a sob of despair – the pretty, blonde, well groomed woman of the world had completely disappeared.

'Hurry up and run our bath, Emma!' ordered Isabella. 'And make sure its not too hot.'

I scurried off and ran their bath.

'It's ready,' I reported with a little curtsey.

'Good, now take Brigette to the loo.'

I swallowed my chagrin as I stood by the girl who had replaced me in Isabella's affections as she sat on the loo, spending a penny. I forced myself to clean and dry her. I wouldn't have minded doing this to Isabella, but to have to attend on this chit of a girl was too much. But I did not dare protest – nor stop smiling ingratiatingly.

The two of them got into the bath.

'Wash us properly, Emma.'

Again I bit my lips as I washed off the signs of their love-making – from which I had been so cruelly excluded.

'Now dry us carefully!'

Moments later, wrapped in large towels, they went back to their rooms. At least, I thought, I will be able to dress Isabella and brush her hair. But again I was to be humiliated.

'That will do now, Emma,' said Isabella. 'I like Brigette to attend on me when I get dressed and do my face. You can go downstairs and wait in the dining room. Stand with your back against the wall and hold a napkin folded over your arm. And don't move until we come down and I tell you to serve us.'

Nervously I crept down the big staircase. Supposing Mrs Price saw me! But luckily, she had gone off, leaving the candles lit, the food on the sideboard and the wine in the coasters.

Hastily I picked up a napkin, draped it over my arm, and went and stood by the wall. At least my naked bottom was hidden!

The minutes ticked silently by. I did not dare move. How differently things were turning out from what I had planned, I thought sadly.

At last I heard laughter and footsteps. Two very beautiful creatures stepped into the dining room, their arms round each other's waists. Isabella, her hair up, was dressed in a lovely long tight-fitting sheath of blue silk that showed off her wonderful figure and colouring. A diamond bracelet was on her right wrist and a matching necklace showed off her bosom. Were they presents from Mark? I wondered.

But it was Brigette who really caught my eye, for she was dressed like a little girl in a short and pretty child's party dress with a satin bow round her waist, and another in her hair; all blue to match Isabella, except for white socks and flat-heeled black shoes with a buttoned strap across the instep.

They were chattering away in French and I could scarcely understand a word. They sat down, still laughing away. They ignored me totally. The contrast between their lovely dresses and beautifully made up faces, and my own near nakedness, scrubbed face, and ugly bonnet, was overwhelming.

Suddenly, Isabella clapped her hands and called out, 'Serve the wine, please!'

I rushed forward, almost stumbling in my efforts to please, picked up the wine and poured a little into their glasses. They paid no attention to me. I put the bottle back into the coaster. How I longed for some myself.

Soon I was rushed off my feet, serving the delicious dinner that I had asked Mrs Price to prepare for what I had intended to be a romantic dinner for just Isabella and me. My mouth was watering more and more as I served each course and then stood silently back against the wall as, still laughing and chattering, they tucked into it. I didn't dare say a word, or move until both of them had finished and, hand in hand, gone up to bed together.

My whole plan for entertaining Isabella in Mark's house was completely ruined. She had treated me as humiliatingly as Ursula did. But the beauty of Isabella was so bewitching that, as I cast the bitter memories from my mind, the fantasy of another weekend with her kept creeping back . . .

6

A final snub and a new start

May 18th! It is a date underlined in red in my diary.

It is now May 6th. Twelve days to count down! Twelve days before seeing the gorgeous Isabella again. Would she be alone? Where would we go? What should I wear?

Isabella had been so blasé when she rang me.

'Emma, *ma petite* . . . Is that you? . . . I shall be in London for the Jasper Conran fashion show, and the following day, darling Jane Newsome and I will be together – it would be nice to see you . . .'

'But where?' I had gasped, taken aback. Isabella had been so cold on our last meeting and had treated me abominably. Had she forgotten? Was she trying to make it up again? All my old longings for Isabella came out again.

'Oh, don't you have a key to Mark's house?'

'No!' I had replied feeling very miffed as Mark had never even mentioned a London house to me!

'Then go to Tite Street, and we can meet at Jane's. Be there at two thirty if possible. *Au revoir!*'

I had looked at myself in the mirror. Gosh! I thought. Straight to the beauty salon for you! Isabella was almost neurotic about appearance. The slightest sight of any body hair would infuriate and disgust her.

And why was Mark being so secretive? I had always longed for a London flat. Was he keeping another woman there? My head buzzed. Perhaps, I thought, I could stay at the beauty club that Ursula had introduced me to. It was attached to a very smart hotel. I could afford to spoil myself for one night and have my hair, nails and body hair all attended to – and a pedicure. Then I would be relaxed and ready for darling Isabella.

Should I tell Mark? Perhaps not. Or Henry? No, I have decided. The brute would probably adore Isabella!

At last May 17th has arrived. One more day! I had a massage. I have gone on a two day water only diet, with lots of lemon. So, my body is rid of all impurities and I have to admit that my lovely beauty lips are as soft as those of a baby girl.

I even felt that the beauty therapist who removed all my hair slightly fancied me. She slid a moist finger onto my little wet beauty bud, and we both got quite excited. She was the dark girl, Maria, to whom I usually went. I had told her about my love for Isabella, and Maria adored being taken into my confidence. We had both laughed and excited one another at the thought of all the thrills that I was going to have when I met Isabella.

I am now highly aroused and my body is in perfect trim – ready for presentation to my Mistress. With my blonde hair cascading down over my shoulders, I feel ready for anything . . .

The 18th arrived.

Everyone, of course, knew of Jane Newsome, the fashion designer, but few knew that she was a lesbian as she had a husband. But he enjoyed her lesbian friends and sometimes even found some more for her. I only knew of this from Isabella. I had never actually met Jane – only seen her.

At two twenty, looking very elegant, I arrived at Tite Street. A tall black man opened the door and said: 'Miss Isabella said you come. But she out. She told me to show you upstairs.'

I followed the faintly sinister man upstairs into a huge bedroom. 'Miss Lucy will attend to you shortly.' Then he closed the door and left me alone.

I began to feel strange. Where was Isabella? And Jane? I thought of all the money that I had spent pampering myself to impress Isabella, and to make sure that her first impressions would be favourable. My hair was just perfect, my nails just the right colour, my little painted belly was all powdered pink, and my moist little beauty lips were shining with red lipstick.

I was just about to sit down on the bed when in walked a tall black girl, at least six foot one.

'Sit!' she yelled at me. Then she turned on a tape.

'Listen!' she bellowed.

I was stunned. It was Isabella's French accent – giving instructions.

'When little Emma arrives, take off all her clothes. Check her weight and if you see any body hair, remove it. Then, Miss Lucy, you are to give her the birch – a really good birching. And I want you to record all her cries and whimpers. I will know if you don't beat her hard enough, and then Quentin will see to you! Understand? I will be back at four and I want to find . . .'

There was a pause on the tape. Miss Lucy was glaring at me, and by now I was feeling utterly disgusted – and scared stiff. How could Isabella play such a mean trick? It was horrid!

The tape continued: '. . . and then, Miss Lucy, I want Emma to serve tea to Jane and me in the long room downstairs. She is to wear the blue gauze see-through little girl's party dress, with little girl's tiny panties – the cut away ones – and ballet shoes . . . Now start the beating and remember to record her screams.'

Before I could get my breath back, Miss Lucy was standing over me shouting: 'Take off your dress. And quick about it! Now go over to the dressing table.'

I did so quickly. I was really frightened of the big Miss Lucy and her strangely staring eyes.

'Pull your pants down!' she ordered. 'Hmm . . . Look at that fat on your belly! Miss Isabella won't like that.'

She brought the birch down across my belly. I screamed.

'Please, stop!' I cried. But Miss Lucy was looking very fierce – almost crazy. I was panting with fear.

'Stop, I beg you. Please!'

Miss Lucy just kicked me. 'Shut up, you ungrateful little slave!'

Then she began to lay into me with the birch. Finally,

she stopped and played back the tape. I heard my pathetic moans – and my pleas.

'Good! That's enough,' the black girl said. She switched off the recorder. I sighed with relief. 'But now you're going to get some secret extra strokes – just for my own amusement . . . Bend over again, white girl!'

Finally, I was dragged off to the bathroom, where Miss Lucy continued to hurt me. 'We must work on these miserable looking nipples before Miss Isabella arrives!'

She started to pull on my little nipples. I could feel that the horrible Miss Lucy was getting excited herself by punishing me. She began to taunt me: 'Look at you!' she cried.

With the tape still switched off, she began to suck hard on my nipples.

I just felt disgust – and yet no matter how awful these ghastly experiences were, I could feel myself becoming quite excited. I hated myself, but how could I stop it? Soon Miss Lucy was caressing me, putting her fingers between my beauty lips. I felt like a tap, with little drops pouring out of me.

Then suddenly Miss Lucy switched on the tape recorder again, and began to shout: 'So our dirty little slut of a slave has been exciting herself, has she? Bend over, you filthy slut!'

She proceeded to give me another thrashing.

'Please stop! Please. Stop! Stop!'

It was all recorded, together with the noise of the birch and my terrible shrieks of agonised torment.

I was almost unconscious, but soon Miss Lucy was powdering me, putting my hair into little plaits, putting a little rouge onto my cheeks and finally putting me into the little girl's blue dress.

Then she disappeared, saying: 'Wait until you hear a bell being rung twice. Then come down and serve tea to Miss Newsome and her guest. Understand?'

At four fifteen I heard the bell ring – twice.

I flounced downstairs, waited and knocked at the door.

'Come in!'

I could see, as I walked in, the tall and beautiful Isabella. She was languidly smoking a cigarette with a long holder and was stretched out gracefully on a chaise longue. On the other side of the chaise longue was the awesome but diminutive figure of Jane Newsome, looking ice-cold in a long navy frock.

The two of them were deep in conversation and ignored me. Anyway I was feeling so foolish, dressed in the stupid little girl's dress.

Isabella was cool and relaxed, smooth and soignée – utterly in command of herself. Finally she looked at me.

'Oh don't just stand there! Pour the tea,' she commanded, 'and offer the crumpets to Miss Newsome.'

I felt humiliated. But worse was to come: 'Now, Emma, go and stand in the corner whilst Miss Newsome and I talk business. That's right, run along, little girl ... Right into the corner ... Put your face to the wall.'

Then I heard Isabella say to Miss Newsome: 'While we're having our tea, darling, shall we listen to a little tape?'

I imagined that some soft music, perhaps by Mozart, might be the sort of thing these sophisticated women would listen to. But to my horror, next minute I heard myself – yes, my own pitiful cries and screams. I heard Isabella say: 'I think our Miss Lucy has done a very good job, don't you darling?'

Over the chinks of cups and saucers I could hear my own painful yells and pleas to Miss Lucy to stop. It was pathetic to hear, and yet these two women were loving it. Soon the beautiful Isabella was gushing: 'Jane, are you getting excited? Well! ... Come here, Emma! Now curtsey nicely to Miss Newsome. That's a good girl! Now smile! Well done, little girl!'

To my amazement, I found myself being almost pleased by Isabella's praises.

'That's better, Emma! Now lift up your little dress and pull down your panties ... And open your legs ... Hmm, quite nice!'

The two women's eyes were glittering. Then Isabella smiled: 'Very nice – what a good little girl!'

The graceful figure of Isabella rose from the couch. She stepped across the room. She had a superb body – shaped and smooth under a very light weight suit. She moved closer to me.

'Now bend your knees, little girl, and present yourself to your Mistress.'

I did what she told. The air was tense. I thought that Isabella was going to take me there and then in front of her friend Jane. I almost wish that she had. I knew that Isabella wanted to taste me. I almost begged her to do it. My heart was throbbing. I no longer cared that I had been humiliated. I just longed to feel Isabella's mouth on my body lips, drinking my juices. How they were flowing!

Then suddenly, Isabella smacked my face.

'Kiss my shoes, you little slut, and then crawl out of my sight. Understand? Get out! And wait for me in my bed – under the bedclothes, out of sight.'

She turned to her companion.

'Well, darling, what do you think of my new little addition to the menu? Shall we have her in with us this evening? She's obedient and well trained.'

Oh, no, I sobbed to myself, hearing how all my hopes of an evening alone with Isabella had once again been thwarted – and by my Mistress. Once again she had brutally shown her preference for another woman over me. Last time it had been that chit of a girl Brigette, and now it was Jane Newsome.

How stupid I had been to think that the cultured and intelligent Isabella would really be interested in a simple girl like me. I resolved not to see her again after this . . . never to chase after her again.

Now, a few weeks on, there has been an unexpected fallout from the break with Isabella, for not only has Isabella broken with me, but also with Mark – and he and I find ourselves spending more and more time together.

Mark has not replaced Henry in my affections, but Henry is always so busy trying to get married. Nor has Mark replaced my longing for another strict Mistress. But

37

he has provided a luxurious lifestyle into which I find myself fitting very well.

Not only does Mark use me increasingly as his hostess in his large house, but he is increasingly attracted to me as I do not object to the various good looking young men who so often also seem to be staying in the house, or who are brought there by Mark's men friends.

Indeed I was intrigued when he took me to an Indian doctor in London to have what he had described as just a little operation. When I recovered I found that my rear entrance had been enlarged – just as, I presume, had those of his young men.

Rather shocked, I consoled myself with the thought that at least it should make me even more popular with Henry, for although he did not share Mark's interest in young men, he did have what he described as his 'little proclivity' – something which I had enjoyed but had hitherto also found rather painful.

Part II

HENRY

1

The island

I thought that it all sounded unbelievably exciting.

'I'll meet you on the island,' Henry had said on the phone. 'We'll travel as strangers on the same flight. There'll probably be friends at the airport, or people who will recognise me, so keep well away as I check in and also on the flight. But I'll send you your ticket. Make sure you travel in something smart, preferably a dress that buttons down the front – and be naked underneath it!'

I felt a little thrill go through me. This sounded like vintage Henry all right – the dominant demanding Henry I so often longed for.

'When we arrive,' he went on with a laugh, 'you can come up and ask me if I am going to the island and, if so, can I give you a lift. Then we'll learn to our apparent surprise that we are both staying at the same little hotel. We'll make friends there. No one will guess that you have been my Mistress for years, or rather my slave.'

Indeed I was so excited that I arrived at the airport two hours early. I had been to the hairdresser that morning and was, I knew, looking radiant. We had not met for a couple of weeks. The build up to this meeting, this holiday together, had been thrilling. Now the feeling of anticipation was utterly overwhelming.

So it was that when I saw the tall athletic figure of Henry striding up towards the check-in queue at the airport, I felt weak at the knees. I could hardly restrain myself from rushing up into his arms, or at least from standing immediately behind him in the queue.

'Is there anywhere you'd like to sit?' asked the check-in girl, breaking my reverie.

'Yes! Next to my friend ...' I blurted out. Hastily I

corrected myself. 'No! Just put me anywhere near the back.' From there I would be able to see him.

I saw him again in the crowded departure lounge and again longed to rush up to him – and at least invite him for a drink at the bar. I saw him buy some scent in the Duty Free shop. Was it for me? My favourite scent? A feeling of almost uncontrollable jealously swept over me at the thought that he might be buying scent for another of his women. Which one? I could feel my temper rising.

I saw him in the final flight lounge, seated, his face buried in a newspaper. He still gave no sign of having seen me. Was he indifferent as to whether I was on the plane or not. Did the cad have another woman also on the plane? Also travelling to the island? No, not even he could be such a swine. I walked slowly past where he was sitting, my nose in the air. Many men were looking at me. I am, I know, a very attractive woman. But Henry just went on reading his damn paper – or had I detected a slight flicker of his eyes?

On the plane I saw that he was seated in the front by the emergency exit. Trust him to get plenty of leg room for himself! After take off, I saw him and some other rather amusing looking people stand up and greet each other in the aisle. I heard the name of the island. Goodness, no wonder he had insisted that we travel as strangers.

'Champagne, Madam!' said the air hostess, handing me a little bottle and a glass. 'With the compliments of a gentleman who said you would know who it was from.'

'But how do you know it's for me?' I gasped.

'Because he pointed you out, Madam.'

'Oh!' So he had noticed me! The feeling of utter excitment returned.

At last we arrived. At last our passports were stamped. At last I found myself waiting for my luggage. Desperately I looked around for him. Had he gone? Leaving me here alone? My heart began to beat faster. Oh, no! Dear God, no!

Suddenly I saw him, reaching forward for his suitcase from the moving luggage rack. There was no sign of mine yet. I saw him talking to the friends he had met on the flight. Might he go off to the island with them? It was now late at night. What should I do?

Suddenly I saw my suitcase. I grabbed it and put it on a trolley. Quickly I pushed it over to where he was still standing talking to his friends.

'Excuse me, Sir,' I began. I must, I knew, be very respectful in public – as well as in private. 'Are you by any chance going to the island. Is there any chance of you giving me a lift to the ferry?'

'Yes, indeed,' said Henry charmingly. My heart melted. he introduced himself and his friends. 'Where are you staying?'

I gave the name of the little hotel on the water's edge where he had booked me a small room next to his own larger one. Because of me he was going to keep away from his own villa. 'The maids would only talk,' he had said.

'What a coincidence!' he laughed. 'That's where I'm staying. Do you know the island?'

'No, it's my first visit,' I replied.

'Perhaps you would let me show you a little of it? Are you alone?'

'Yes – I suddenly felt the urge to get away for a few days and the travel agent booked me there,' I laughed, now entering into the spirit of the game.

'I can see you're going to have some unexpected fun,' exclaimed one of Henry's friends. 'Well we must leave you and find our own car – are you sure you've got one waiting for you too?'

'Yes, thank you, so much,' said Henry.

'Well, I'll give you a ring tomorrow and see if we can meet on our boat,' said his friend's wife.

'That would be fun,' said Henry. He was ignoring me completely now.

At last we left.

'If you'd like to come with me,' said Henry formally as if still speaking to a stranger. 'I should have a man waiting for me with the car that I usually hire.'

I dutifully followed him outside. It was a hot warm night.

There was a distinctive Mediterranean smell. I could hear the noise of crickets in the airport flower beds. The stars seemed strangely bright after England. I was thrilled.

'This is a lady I've just met at the airport who would like a lift to the island,' I heard Henry explain to a young man with his car.

Henry signed some papers. The young man left. Henry lifted up my suitcase and put it in the boot. He held open the door. Was he never going to kiss me? Was he never going to feel my nakedness under my dress? I felt like screaming.

But he said nothing as we drove off in the darkness.

I had no idea where we were going, but finally I saw the outline of a castle-like medieval town outlined against the moonlit sky. We drove up to it. We crossed a draw-bridge and found ourselves in a maze of very narrow unlit streets. Tall darkened houses, built of stone, towered over the car as Henry expertly found his way down the twisting streets.

'This is the old capital,' was all he said in explanation. 'It's deserted at night and full of tourists by day.'

We came out into a cobbled square, dominated by a large darkened church, with a line of old cannon in front of it.

'The old cathedral,' said Henry as he parked the car in the deserted square. He got out and held my door open for me. Silently I followed him across the square and down into an even narrower darkened lane than the one we had just driven down. There was no sign of life, just the occasional chink of light behind shuttered windows.

Suddenly we reached the raised high stone battlements. Henry led the way up some stone steps. We could see for miles. We were at the top of high walls. The moonlit countryside was laid out below them. I found it breathtaking.

'For hundreds of years,' Henry suddenly said, 'this was the centre of the fight against the Barbary Pirates. Many of their ways of life were adopted here – including slaves. Captured young women would be sold here on the battlements.'

Was it true, I wondered, or was Henry just making it up? Either way it sounded rather exciting.

'Now just imagine yourself, a young married woman, captured at sea and brought here. You're standing up on this narrow stone platform, one of a line of pretty frightened women, your hands tied behind your back, looking straight ahead and not daring to look down at the man who is coming to inspect you.'

I found myself assuming the position he described. I was indeed now standing higher than Henry on a raised platform – the firing platform of the battlements now behind my back.

'The slave dealer shows off your body to the man whose eye you have caught,' went on Henry, reaching up and unbuttoning my dress. Nervously, and yet very excited, I looked around. There was no one about – just the darkened houses and battlements. I raised my head and looked straight ahead again. I felt my dress falling open from my breasts to my knees. I felt Henry jerking the top of it back over my bare shoulders. He put his hand gently on one of my breasts, as if weighing it. I gasped.

'An interesting young creature,' I heard Henry say a little below me, as if talking to the imaginary slave dealer. I strained to keep my head raised, still looking straight ahead. 'Married, you say? All the more interesting.'

I felt his fingers running down to my belly, kneading it, knowingly.

'Turn round!' ordered the slave dealer's voice. Obediently, I turned round and faced the battlements. What a game! 'Legs apart! Now bend your knees! Lean forward! Hold up your dress! Head up and keep looking at the wall!'

What a game indeed.

To keep my balance, I found that I had to thrust back with my buttocks. I blushed at the thought of the way I was now having to display myself.

I felt the would-be buyer's hands between my legs, exploring deeply, and finding the wetness of my arousal. I bit my lips as I strained to hold the humiliating position, humiliating indeed but also terribly exciting. Would real slave girls also have been betrayed by their natural sensuality as they stood still, whilst being felt on the block by a good looking stranger?

'Touch your toes!'

A finger already wetted and made slippery by my own arousal now penetrated me from behind. I gave a little moan.

'Even more interesting!' the buyer commentated, his finger still inside me. 'I'll take her!'

The finger slipped out.

'Now turn round and kneel down – on all fours!'

I felt a collar, a sort of dog collar, being fastened round my neck. A lead was fastened to it.

'Now pull your dress around you, but don't button it up again. And follow me back to the car. Understand, slave?'

'Yes,' I answered.

'Yes, what?' demanded Henry.

'Yes, Master.'

Desperately embarrassed lest some one might see my half nakedness, I tried to hold my dress closed in front of me, as I stumbled along behind Henry, pulled by the lead attached to my collar.

We arrived back in the deserted square.

'Crawl back to the car at my side – on all fours!'

'No, please! Not here,' I implored him.

'Slave girls do what they're told, or they get beaten!'

Horrified, I saw that Henry now had a little dog whip in his hand. I fell to my knees and crawled painfully at his side over the cobbles.

'Get into the car, but keep your dress unbuttoned,' Henry ordered.

Not until we were about to drive down into the car deck of the well lit ferry half an hour later were the collar and lead removed, and I was allowed to button up my dress again.

Henry took me up onto the upper deck. It was a warm night. I longed to be taken into his arms, but I knew that we must now behave almost as strangers again, strangers sharing a car.

The sea was quite rough as the ferry made its way across the channel to the island, passing several little fishing boats with acetylene lamps to attract the fish. I saw the high cliffs of the island outlined against the moonlit horizon. I saw the outline of the doomed churches and old watch towers. It all seemed a new world, and the presence of Henry was both reassuring and challenging . . .

Another half an hour later, we were driving down a twisty road leading down between high cliffs to an inlet of the sea, lit up by the moon. The inlet, too, had high cliffs on either side, and then at the end, which we were approaching, was a small village – once just a tiny fishing village. Right on the water's edge, separated from the sea only by a narrow promenade, was our small hotel.

Henry drove up to the back of the hotel.

'I'll drop you here and go and park the car. You go in and pretend that you've come by taxi. I'll come in later. Remember we don't know each other. My room is next to yours. In exactly one hour's time, knock on the door, and then come in and drop to your knees. Then crawl to the bed, and crawl up it under the bedclothes, making sure that your head is kept hidden under the sheets. Then please me!'

My head was in a whirl as I checked in. The hotel seemed empty – everyone was in bed. I was still highly aroused. How much longer would I have to wait to be kissed? To be cuddled and told how beautiful I was? And then . . . would I, at last, be allowed relief, allowed to climax?

My room was tiny – as I had expected. But I could hear the sea breaking on the narrow strip of sand in front of the hotel, for the wind was getting up.

I heard Henry go into the big room next door. I looked at my watch. I must wait another forty five minutes. Why? For God's sake, why? I longed to burst into Henry's room and fling myself into his arms – alone at last! Then I remembered the little dog whip. No, I must do as I had been told, and wait . . . and wait . . . thinking all the time only of Henry.

Never had time passed so slowly. I unpacked and hung up my clothes one by one, taking as much time as possible over each one. Still half an hour to go! Slowly and methodically, I re-packed everything and then equally slowly and methodically unpacked again. Still fifteen minutes to go! I changed into my most exciting night dress. I brushed my hair, and made up my eyes. Still another five minutes to go! I was so excited that if anything had happened now to stop me going into Henry's room, I would have died – I really would, I told myself. Two minutes to go! I tried to tell myself a little story. Anything to make the time go by ... I looked at my watch again ... Oh no! I was two minutes late!

I crept out of my room. Timidly, I knocked on Henry's door. It was ajar, obviously left open for me. I tip-toed in and shut the door behind me. I fell to my knees. I crawled across the darkened room, over the hard tiled floor, towards the bed. The big French windows were open. There was a little balcony. I could hear the sea. I put my head under the bedclothes, between Henry's outstretched legs. Then inch by inch I wriggled my way up the bed. I felt Henry reach down and grip my hair, holding me in place. Silently I began to do my duty ...

I will never forget the noise of the sea that accompanied my silent ministrations. Nor will I quickly forget the way I was desperately wondering whether I, too, was going to be allowed any relief. Secretly, I feared, I already knew the answer. No! Henry, that selfish swine, would certainly enjoy making me wait, on tenterhooks, until the next day.

But I was wrong, quite wrong. Soon I felt Henry's hand pulling me up, right up level with him. Oh, the sheer joy! The bliss! But my excitement was soon even greater, for although he was still holding me by my hair with one hand, with his other he was slowly reaching down past my breasts, past my tummy, over my smooth hairless mound, down over my beauty lips and then ... and then ... he was touching my beauty bud.

'Darling,' he said with a laugh, 'what a lark it's all been!'

2

I remember, I remember

It was four days later.

I was sitting having breakfast on the terrace in front of the hotel. A few feet below me the sea of the long inlet was slapping at the foot of the low sea wall. Further out in the deserted inlet I saw the figure of Henry swimming. He would shortly be coming back to the terrace, still in his swimming things, to have breakfast – but not at my table. In the hotel we had kept up the charade of not knowing each other, and he would, I knew, sit down at the next table, give me a courteous nod, and ask if I had slept well.

Slept well! My God, I thought, ever since that first wonderful night I had slept like a log in his arms, satiated with love and waking up only to the noise of the sea lapping below our window.

As I stirred my coffee, I thought back to so many of the other extraordinary meetings I had had with Henry, and how wonderfully exciting and arousing they had been. Did other couples, I wondered, have such fun – or know what they were missing . . .?

I remember the time I was sitting alone in the crowded stalls of the Coliseum, waiting for the opera to start. I looked, I knew, stunning, quite stunning. I glanced at the empty seat next to me, and then turned to read the programme.

Just as the lights were going down for the overture, a tall large figure slipped into the seat. Unknown to me he had been watching me from the raised balcony at the back of the stalls. He paid no attention to me until the interval, then he turned to me and smiled.

'Are you alone?' he asked with a smile. I saw that he was

a tall attractive middle aged man. He seemed very sure of himself. 'Can I invite you to come and have a drink at the bar.'

'Well, that would be very kind of you,' I replied formally. Henry rose from his seat, went into the aisle and followed me to the back of the stalls.

'Over to your left, I think,' he said indicating the bar. 'What can I offer you?'

'Are you alone, this evening,' he asked during the second interval. 'I know we don't know each other, but perhaps you'd like to have dinner with me?'

I paused as if in thought.

'Well, I don't know you,' I lied prettily with a smile of intrigue, 'but I think I'd like that very much.'

It was not until later that night, when Henry reached over in bed and pulled me to him, that I could give up playing the role of a casual pick-up.

'Oh what a lark you are,' he said with a grin.

On another of our secret weekends together, Henry had given me strict instructions as to what I should do in preparation for his arrival at my boudoir. Henry gave a warning knock at the bedroom door, waited a moment and then entered. The room was dark behind the drawn curtains.

'Come along in, Your Excellency!' I heard him say, mysteriously.

He must have smiled to himself as he saw the little hump in the bedclothes at the bottom of the bed and the chain that lay on the pillow, leading down under the bedclothes to my collar. I was playing my part properly.

'You see, Your Excellency!' he said, 'the girl is waiting for you. Don't hesitate to use the whip to make sure she does what you want.'

'Thank you,' came the slow reply in a heavy African accent. 'Don't worry, she'll soon learn to do as she is told.'

'Very well, I'll leave you to it,' replied Henry. He went over to the door and shut it. Then he pulled a rubber mask over his head. It was a very realistic mask. It was a mask of a cruel and terrifying looking black potentate with a shaven head.

'So, little white slut,' came the deep African voice. 'You're terrified of having to please a black Master are you?'

I recognised the sounds of a man slipping on a silken robe. He picked up a long whip with a short handle, and cracked it. There was a noise like a pistol shot.

'So, just you make sure you really do please your Master – or this whip will be waiting for you.'

From under the bedclothes I let out a whimper of genuine fear. Behind the mask, the man smiled.

Naked under his robe, he slid into the bed and picked up the chain, holding it in his left hand. In his right hand he now held a long whippy cane. Slowly his legs reached down to the bottom of the bed until they lay on either side of my hidden crouching form.

For a moment or two he lay quite still, savouring the feeling of terror that he knew was gripping me.

Then he gave the chain a jerk – the agreed signal. Instantly he felt my soft little tongue silently licking first one foot and then the other.

He gave the chain another jerk and, as he lay back enjoying the sensation, my little tongue slowly moved up his legs. Then it stopped – just short of his groin.

He gave the chain an angry jerk.

'No! No!' came a whisper from under the bedclothes.

Still holding the chain, Henry sat up slightly, put down the cane and slowly reached down to lift up the foot of the bedclothes to reveal my bare little white bottom. He picked up the cane again and brought it down across my white bottom. I gasped with pain from under the bedclothes. He repeated the stroke. Instantly he felt my tongue again. He threw the bedclothes down and once more lay back.

Moments later he put down the cane and still holding the chain in his left hand, put his right hand down under the bedclothes. His manhood was becoming increasingly hard. He gripped my hair and guided my mouth to it, holding my head firmly in place . . .

Several minutes passed – minutes of exquisite pleasure for the man.

He glanced under the bedclothes. He saw a river of honey coloured hair, rising and falling. Then he raised his knees.

'Get your tongue down!' ordered the African voice. 'Right down!'

'No! I couldn't!' came my little plaintive voice. 'No, not that.'

'Oh, yes, little slut . . . that!'

Again he slowly raised the bedclothes.

'All right, Sir! All right!'

My little tongue dropped obediently, down between his legs. But it was too late. The cane fell once . . . twice . . . three times.

Not until the tongue was desperately busy, cleaning, sucking and probing were the bedclothes thrown back again.

Another five minutes of exquisite pleasure passed. Then Henry jerked the chain again and pulled my head up over his belly.

He pushed down the top of the bedclothes.

Holding the chain taut, he ordered 'Look up!'

From under the cascade of my blonde hair, two beautifully made-up blue eyes glanced upwards.

I screamed in genuine terror as I saw the black mask and the cruel eyes looking down at me.

But it had, I knew, been one of the most exciting moments of my life.

I recalled the time Henry had said we were going on a mystery tour. Unable to see where we were going, I felt the car suddenly stop. I heard the door slam shut and the noise of footsteps going away. Had we arrived at his house?

I was kneeling naked under the cover in the boot of the big station waggon. I longed to look out but the heavy plastic cover was drawn taut and with my hands chained there was nothing I could do except anxiously wait and wonder what was going to happen. The weight of the six foot length of heavy chain, fastened to the ring at the front of the metal collar locked round my neck, was a further constant reminder of my helplessness.

I heard footsteps returning, the heavy footsteps of a man. I trembled with fear and excitement.

Suddenly the back door of the car was flung open. It was dark outside. A hand grabbed the end of the chain and gave it a tug.

'Out!' ordered a man's voice.

I felt another tug on my collar and stumbled out. It was a warm summer evening.

'Get down!'

I fell to my hands and knees. I could feel the wet grass. Vaguely I could recognise the buildings in the half light. Embarrassed I looked around to see if anyone else was watching, but I could see no one – just him, just my Master.

'Come!'

I felt the sharp tap of a dog whip on my buttocks and a tug on the chain. Crawling on my hands and knees, I scuttled along behind him over the grass, obeying the pull of the chain. In the darkness I saw that we were going through an opening in a tall hedge and on into a remoter part of the garden.

Suddenly I saw bars in front of me, black metal bars. I heard the squeak of a small metal gate and watched as the bars were opened.

'Get in!'

I crawled past the small barred gate. It was immediately closed and locked behind me.

I heard the noise of the end of heavy chain being locked round one of the bars. Then I heard the man's footsteps going away. I was alone, chained and naked!

Anxiously I looked around. As my eyes gradually got used to the darkness, I saw that I was in a small outdoor cage – like a little dog run. I tried to stand up but my head hit more bars. I would have to remain on all fours – like an animal.

I started to crawl round the little cage, over its grassy

bottom. The heavy chain hung down from my neck. With its far end now fastened to one of the bars, the loop of the chain dragged after me and restricted my movements.

I made out what seemed to be a little wooden kennel in the corner. I found that the chain just allowed me to reach it. I crawled through the little entrance to the kennel. The floor was covered with straw. There was also an old blanket. The chain became taut and stopped me. I came out of the kennel and crawled in again, this time backwards. I found that I could lie down, curled up in the small kennel, but the chain would keep my head and neck near the kennel doorway.

I found that there was a sort of shutter above the small entrance to the kennel that could be lowered and fastened shut. There was a little gap on the bottom, as if for a chain. My God, I thought, am I going to be shut into the little kennel by day so that the odd passer-by would not see me?

Leaving the cage I explored my little domain, crawling in the darkness, and always aware of the heavy chain fastened to my neck. Level with my head I found a little gap in the bars. On the other side, hanging from the bars, was a bowl. Water! I put my head through the gap and lowered it into the bowl. Eagerly I began to lap the water up.

Feeling refreshed I then saw another little hole in the bars with another bowl beyond it. It held a bone. I was feeling ravenously hungry. With my chained hands I retrieved the bone. There were little bits of cooked meat sticking to it. Holding it in my chained hands I began to gnaw it – just like a real dog, I realised. It was delicious!

But how long would that damn swine keep me here in this cage? Knowing him, it might be for the whole weekend. Would I get any more food? If I was going to be shut up in the kennel by day, how would I get at the food bowl? Perhaps I'd better save the bone for the next day. Like a real dog hiding a bone, I concealed the meagre nourishment under the straw of my kennel, where I could find it again later.

After the long journey I was not surprised to feel a growing need to spend a penny. But where? I had found that there was a sandy patch in one corner of my cage. Was this intended for . . .? Goodness, how shame-making! But needs must! I crawled over to the sandy patch, with the heavy chain once again dragging along behind me. Like a real bitch, I parted my legs and thrust back as I emptied myself onto the sand.

Then I crawled back to the barred entrance gate. With my chained hands I checked that it really was locked. It was!

I found myself gripping the bars of the cage in desperation. I looked up at the stars. I listened for any signs of human life. There were none. I imagined my Master sitting down to a delicious dinner in a warm well furnished room. And I meanwhile was chained naked in a cage with just a bone. It was so unfair – and so typical of him. I hated him! I hated him!

Was I going to be kept here all the weekend? Supposing a real dog was put in with me? My God!

It was beginning to get cold. I crawled back into the kennel and pulled the old blanket over me. I began to doze off.

I awoke to a scuffling noise. I saw two little eyes in front of me just outside the kennel. A rat! Attracted by the smell of my precious bone! I gave a cry and shook my chained hands. The rat ran off, disappearing between the bars of the cage.

Scared, I tried to keep awake, but I could feel my eyes glazing over . . .

'Come, little bitch. Come to your Master!'

I awoke with a start. My Master had returned!

'Come here!'

I scuttled across to the now open entrance to the cage. I felt the chain being unlocked from my collar.

'Out!'

Grateful to be free of the heavy chain, I crawled out of the cage.

'I want my little bitch in my bed for the night. But if you don't behave you'll go straight back into the kennel!'

I felt thrilled, excited, aroused. He was a man, indeed.

He bent down and flung my slight body over his shoulders. He strode off towards the house.

'Oh, Henry!' I heard myself crying out happily. 'Oh, Henry!'

Driving with Henry!

So often it was quite an experience. He liked me to sit alongside him quite naked, with a fur rug handy to pull over myself if we stopped at traffic lights.

My hands would be chained and in his hand, as he drove, he would hold another chain that led back to my collar.

If it was already dark, he would be looking for a certain large 'P' sign that he would have already noticed on his way up to meet me.

'This one looks very suitable,' he would say, as he swung off the road and into a long deserted lay-by that was separated from the road by a hedge. Stopping the car, he would lower the back of his seat and lie back.

'Work!' he would order.

For me the 'P' sign now meant something quite different from before, and as I would later pass several more of them, I would smile to myself . . .

Driving for Henry!

I would have to wear my smart Navy blue suit and he would give me a stiff little cap, rather like the hats that airline hostesses wear. I would hold the back door open for him and then, getting into the driving seat, ask: 'Where to, Sir?'

It was a smart fashionable wedding at St. Margaret's in Parliament Square. The traffic was appalling, but Henry, immaculately dressed in his morning coat, had taken the precaution of making sure that he had a chauffeur.

I, wearing my chauffeur's cap, had driven carefully up to the church entrance, stopped, got out and opened the door for Henry – watched by numerous tourists coming out of Westminster Abbey.

Later I had driven round and round Parliament Square

until I saw the guests coming out. I waited for the bridal party to drive, and then, my excitement rising, I spotted Henry. I drove over, stopped and once again opened the door for him . . .

The reception had been held in a magnificent house looking out onto Green park. Having dropped my Master, I had parked amongst the other chauffeur driven cars behind the house.

'What's your boss like then?' one of the chauffeurs had asked with a grin.

'Oh a pretty good selfish bastard,' I had replied.

'They all are,' he had said. 'But why's a pretty girl like you working for one.'

I thought of what was going to happen when I picked Henry up, of the exciting arrangements we had made to spend the night together.

'Oh just love,' I had replied with a laugh, 'just love!'

Strangers!

I always found that meeting up with Henry as strangers was very exciting – particularly if, as was so often the case, we had not seen each other for a month or so. Oh, the sheer excitement of all the anticipation!

Boots!

I could not resist the sight of a man, particularly Henry, in riding boots and spurs. The mere thought of him striding along in them, or standing imperiously with his booted legs astride, his tight white hunting breeches gleaming whilst holding a riding whip in his hand was enough to arouse me.

Silence!

For days before the meeting we would not ring or contact

each other, heightening the excitement and eager awaiting, and avoiding the chance of a silly row over an unconsidered remark which would spoil everything.

For days before the meeting I would go through my clothes to make sure that I would be dressed perfectly for whatever role Henry had ordered – or I had suggested. Days before the meeting I would secretly pack for it. As the excitement and anticipation grew and grew, I could think of nothing else.

Some women, I knew, were only really turned on by physical caresses and touches. But for me the mental side was equally important, imagining that I was Henry's humble little slave, about to be beaten for his pleasure.

Instructions!

And if, on top of everything else, Henry sent my instructions well before the meeting, then my cup, or rather my juices, would indeed be overflowing. In my office I would read and re-read them until my excitement and imagination made me almost burst with desire, and until I knew them by heart. I would lie awake at night in my husband's bed, going over them in my mind again and again.

I well remembered in particular one set of instructions, and the sheer thrill and excitement of carrying them out, in full: –

'Slave! You are to be in the foyer of the hotel at six sharp. You are to wear your smart red coat, and stockings and shoes. But under your coat you are to be naked, stark naked, with your beauty lips freshly smoothed clear of all hair and carefully painted to match your lipstick. Your nipples are to be outlined in black and, again, painted in matching red.

'I shall be sitting in a quiet corner having a drink. I will appear to have just come in from riding, wearing breeches and boots and carrying a whip. You are not at first to pay any attention to me, and act as if I were a stranger. You are to read a magazine, occasionally looking round the room as if looking for someone.

'After a few minutes I shall get up, fetch a drink from the bar, and go back to my quiet seat. This is to be your signal to get up and slowly walk towards me. As you pass me, you are to turn momentarily and discreetly open your coat and, in a way that no one else can see, slowly display your naked body to me. If I flick my fingers, as you will be desperately hoping, then you are to close your coat, settle your bill and go out and wait for me in my car.

'In the glove pocket of the car you will find a pair of self locking handcuffs. Having first slipped your arms out of your coat and put it over your shoulders, you are to put the handcuffs on your wrists and wait for me.

'When I arrive you are to keep silent until spoken to and even then you are at all times to call me "Sir".'

And on another not-to-be-forgotten occasion: –

'You are to be in the park at five, walking up and down. You are to be smartly dressed, but naked under your frock. When you see me you are to pay no attention but to go on walking slowly up and down. When I sit down on an empty bench you are to approach it, and appear to accidentally drop something by my feet. You are then to get down on your knees as if looking for it, but in fact you are to lick the soles of my shoes, first one and then the other, carefully and humbly, until I click my fingers. You are then to get up, pretend to put what you have dropped into your bag and continue your walk.

'I shall then stand up and you are to move so that you are exactly three yards behind me. You are to remain this distance behind me, like a little dog, as I walk through the park and down the streets. If I go into a shop you are to wait outside, standing at attention. If I speak to a friend you are to remain behind looking away.

'When I enter my hotel, you are to appear to be a tart that I have picked up. I shall give you the key of my room. You are to go up, undress and get down into the foot of the bed under the bedclothes. When I come up, five minutes later, you are to keep quite still. When I get into bed, you are silently to start licking me, hidden anonymously

59

under the bedclothes. Not until I reach down and pull you up by the hair are you to show your face.

Reconciliations!

And the sheer impudence of the man!

I remember how my Mistress, Ursula, had persuaded me to have nothing more to do with men. She had stood over me as she had made me burn everything that Henry had given me. She had then made me write and tell him what I had done, adding that I now had a new and much more exciting life, and so I never wanted to see or hear from him again.

It all was, I knew, the most hurtful thing I could possibly have done to him. Over the next few days I tried to put him out of my mind, as I enjoyed the thrill of being my Mistress's slave: a slavery that was far deeper, and far more continuous and satisfying, than any man would have bothered to subject me to. But even so, I was sad at what I had done.

It was a week later that I had to attend a private seminar in a town a hundred miles away. My head was full of what I was going to learn and say, and the questions I was going to ask. I entered the room and sat down, greeting several old colleagues.

Suddenly Henry entered, looked around, and without a word, sat down next to me and began to read the programme. My mind was on fire! How had he learnt that I was going to be here? How had he been able to get an invitation? What would my Mistress say if she ever heard about it? She'd thrash the living daylights out of me!

My heart was beating fast. I glanced up at him. He had done all this, just to see me! And after what I had done to him!

He had turned to me and, speaking as if we were complete strangers, had calmly asked me if I had come far to hear the speakers. Somehow I had managed to stutter out a reply, my mind in a whirl.

Then the speaker had begun.

Shyly and nervously, I had touched Henry's hand.

When the speaker asked for questions, Henry had asked a most pertinent one, although he could have known nothing about the subject. I saw the other people present turn and look at him. I felt so proud.

Coffee break! Still Henry maintained his distance and anonymity, going off to talk to the speaker.

The seminar resumed. Again I touched his hand. Had he noticed?

At the buffet lunch he politely offered to get me some food. Gratefully I accepted. My mind was in far too much of a turmoil for me to have done anything. He looked so commanding and dominant as he brought it to me. He made all the other people look so mediocre. My heart was melting. My thighs were wet. Damn my Mistress! Damn her!

Then suddenly he had turned to me.

'I'm leaving now, say goodbye to everyone and come down and join me in my car!'

I had done so, and as we drove happily off to make love, I had leant over and kissed him.

'Oh, Sir!' I had cried, tears of happiness running down my cheeks. 'Oh, Sir!'

3

The romantic adventure

Henry has just phoned.

'Listen!' he said. 'I've just booked tickets. Be ready by 28th December. Returning next week on the 5th.'

I was already committed to doing several other things over the New Year, but it was no use saying to Henry, 'Sorry I can't go', as he'd already faxed the money to the hotel in Switzerland.

What was I to do?

Well, I thought, just cancel other plans and do as Henry says – he's taken such trouble and actually bought the tickets and organised everything. Full marks to the Brute, the Bounder, he's certainly won this round. I'll just enter into the spirit of the adventure . . .

I had no time to think before Christmas. We would be spending Christmas itself with some of John's rather grand cousins. But it has still all been last minute shopping, organising food for John for when he comes back to the house, and arranging for the gardener to look in occasionally when John is away. I certainly didn't want to come back to burst pipes. I had to race around after the gardener to check that he really would come in – he's half a lush, and at Christmas he goes on the bottle and disappears. He's most unreliable, but he has a brilliant sense of humour and so we keep him on – but every year I say this is the last one and he must go.

Eventually I got around to throwing in some ski clothes and John and I agreed to take two cars to his relations as I would have to go and appease Mark on the 27th before joining Henry on the 28th. John of course knew nothing of all this. He just thought I was going on an innocent short holiday with a girl friend.

62

Christmas with the cousins was always the greatest fun, and as everybody was busy after Christmas, either shooting or racing, no one, not even John, was the least surprised when off I went on the 27th. They all knew I was going skiing and it just looked as though I was going a day earlier.

Mark, however, was not appeased. I shouldn't have bothered to go and see him.

'All I get is just one day of your precious time,' he kept saying.

So all the 27th it was row after row. Early in the morning of the 28th we made it all up, but then I had to get up and drive off to Bounder-land.

I arrived to a tumultuous reception from the Bounder. There he was like the cat who had swallowed all the cream, with the bed still warm from his other mistress. He didn't even give it time to cool off before he was ready for Number Two. Where he gets his energy from, at his age, Heaven only knows. But of course I was also hot footing it from the bed of Mark!

His housekeeper had left us the most delicious lunch, and then, just as I was about to start, I was told: 'Dogs don't get fed at table.'

Instead, I, now 'Fido', was given some scraps from a bowl on the floor and told to lick it all up without using my fingers.

So like a good little dog, I obeyed my Master and ate up all the lovely scraps. Then it was time for Fido to be taken out by her Master on a lead for a little run in the garden. But it was still daylight and there were too many people about. So my Master took his little dog off to a dry ski centre to limber up and get fit for Switzerland – and for himself to do a bit of showing off amongst the local rather dull people who, like me, were simply trying to stand up on the slope.

The dog was brought home and made to wash and clean herself properly – the way this little dog has been trained to do – so that her Master could make passionate love. It was a very humble little Fido that crawled into the big bed, licked her Master's toes and feet and then higher up, remembering all the time that Fido was just a little dog who had been taught to bark by her Master.

Then Fido was allowed to wash again and have a little supper, before it was off to Portsmouth to catch the boat.

Soon Henry was onboard, doing all his Admiral stuff, pointing out to Fido this destroyer and that carrier, with its span and length. There was no doubt that he had an amazing knowledge, and with his commanding air little Fido began to feel like a spoilt puppy . . .

Then we went down to our little cabin, and next morning at seven thirty Fido and her Master were really off on the Big Adventure.

Henry was in supreme form – driving down the A13 to Paris as if he was in a motor race. Foot on the pedal and at a safe hundred miles an hour we flashed through Caen and past Deauville and Rouen. Fido would have liked to stop in Rouen to see its splendid Gothic churches, old houses and excellent museums, but Henry merely replied: 'Stop! Don't be ridiculous, we must get to the Alps by daylight.' – So no stopping! We had a brief stop at Aire de Vironvay and then Fido had to drive. But although she was doing a moderate seventy or eighty miles an hour, Henry pushed Fido out of the driving seat, saying: 'A hundred or nothing!'

So on and on we raced, not stopping to draw breath. The Adventure was in full swing.

Soon Paris was looming. It was scarcely ten in the morning and Fido hoped that she could perhaps ask Henry to stop in the centre and maybe allow her to catch a glimpse of Isabella. She was still so much on Fido's mind. But Fido knew that Henry would want to be part of it if they met. So she kept quiet.

Versailles Nord was flashing past. Henry flew into the tunnel and out again. Round the outskirts of Paris they rushed, with little Fido longing to shout out: 'Isabella – I am here!' I could see the Eiffel Tower in the distance . . . So near and yet so far! But Henry pressed his foot down even harder. Brrm . . . Brrm . . . Fido could hardly bear it.

I desperately wanted to blurt out to Henry: 'I want to stay in Paris!' But there was no time.

On towards Lyon, past Fontainebleau, and then a quick stop at Aire des Chatâigniers for the little dog, and for Henry to eat his housekeeper's delicious picnic. Then onto Dole, Besançon and the lovely ancient town of Pontparlier with Henry pointing out the Jura Mountains as they descended into Neuchatel.

Just before Neuchatel, Fido was made to bare ber breasts and be manacled. The Swiss were so impressed to see a blonde woman racing through the town topless. There were a few unbelieving looks from lorry drivers, and one almost crashed into Lake Neuchatel, doubtless thinking that his wildest fantasy had suddenly come true. So Henry made Fido cover up.

Excitement was now mounting as, at about two o'clock, we approached the sign for Bern. Henry informed Fido in a knowledgeable way that Bern was the political capital of Switzerland – perched high above the River Aare. And, of course, already there had been numerous history lessons. Fido had to admit to herself just how much she admired Henry – his brilliant driving, his outstanding knowledge ... It all fuelled her secret love of the Slave-Master relationship.

Soon sheer bewilderment hit Fido as we turned up a narrow valley. It was still day but in front of me was the most wonderful view of a huge white-capped mountain. Soon I could see the most amazing frozen waterfalls.

Henry went off to park the car and the final stage of the most dramatic day in Fido's life was just about to start. We got into a little Alpine train which went slowly zig-zagging up and up. Fido could not believe it, but it was no dream, for when we alighted from the train in the twilight, it was all real – lovely little snow-covered Alpine wooden chalets with the towering mountains gleaming white all around. It was just amazing.

A fantastic eight hour drive had ended at the most romantic little hotel that Fido had ever experienced.

Henry was indeed Doctor Zhivago and in the next few

days he was to be better than the hero of any romantic film. He really came into his own, and Fido felt passionately in love with this romantic figure.

Each night a sleepy little Fido curled up in her Master's arms and licked him to sleep in gratitude for all her happiness.

Oh my Bounder! My Brute!

4

Jealousy, hatred and love

I have just had a spell of festering – festering over Henry.

It is so destructive and ghastly. The horribleness of Henry a year ago floods back and I tell myself: 'Stop it all now. You must stop seeing that ghastly Bounder, that awful Brute. Stop!'

It eats away at me like dry rot or woodworm, slowly gnawing away. If someone else told me this, I would tell them to get rid of the rot, or whatever was causing them to fester, or tell Henry straight out. But he wouldn't see. He'd just laugh and say that Emma is jealous again. Damn right I am!

How I detest people who fester. So I hate myself. After all, I have no need to fester. My life has never been better. So this festering is self inflicted.

But the truth is that I am so angry that I could run my car into the back of his and smash it up. I long to scream: 'I hate you. Go away!' but I feel his selfish big head is too stupid to comprehend why I am so annoyed.

He rings and gives me a message for Fido but, instead of enjoying it, I am secretly outraged because I think that that is a game which should be played by two people who have a very unique relationship. And ours is all over now, because one minute we are deep into games, into fun and making little plans – and the next minute he acts as if I was just a plaything whilst he plans his weekends with other women. He expects me just to turn up on the 30th as slot number 2, 3, 10 or whatever.

Well, that just doesn't suit me! I don't want to be some number. God knows I want to scream, to break a window, to knock everything over, to . . .

'Pick up the phone and ring the bastard,' a voice tells

me. 'Tell him you think he is a devious underhand bastard who is just using you when he feels like it, and then cuts you out when it suits him. Tell him you want to get away. Tell him he can have all the bloody slots or sluts that he wants. But you just want to get right away – live a different life.'

The phone rings again.

It's Henry!

I try to conceal my rage, my anger. I think I will just stay quiet and just never turn up again. Let him plan what he likes. Just say yes, but don't go.

So here I am meekly saying: 'Yes ... Yes ... I see ... Good idea ...', when suddenly, like a pneumatic drill, I feel my whole body shake. I think I am having a seizure, and I suddenly know I must tell him: 'You're missing the whole point, you idiot, you slimy bastard.'

I really do think now he still hasn't realised how much annoyance and anger he has caused me.

I am annoyed that he has just assumed that I no longer want to go to anything in his part of England. He has got his other female role players for that – and I am delegated to another role. I resent this – not because I want to attend some dull old Conservative meeting or a Burns Evening, but because it's his assumption now that everything is cut and dried. Well, it bloody well isn't!

He's not married, so the relationship can't be the same as when his wife was alive. So he can just forget that!

The stupid thing about all this is that I am not hankering after his world. I feel established in my own – and possibly also a little bit in Mark's too, partly because I love his area of England. So why do I get so cross? Because suddenly Henry is excluding me from his part of the country as though I smelt like a bad fish.

I accept that the woman he hopes to marry comes first in his part of the world. I like her enormously, and I do not want to exclude her from anything. But what I do not accept is that now that he has his little local clique, Fido is just brought out for his amusement only when it pleases him.

Anyway all this seems utterly stupid. So what do I want?

I just want him occasionally to say: 'Emma, this is happening down here, would it interest you?' In this way I am given the choice – not just kept out.

Nine times out of ten he will be safe in asking me as I won't be able to go. But if he goes back to this style of a year ago, of trying everyone else first, and then, only when they have refused, trying me – well I won't be there either. That sort of thing might suit some people, but I am far too busy to be bothered. So there!

Now that I have said everything I feel a new person!

I simply couldn't go on writing about our lovely Adventure with all that pent up anger in my head.

Oh those gorgeous, gorgeous Alps. How I loved it there! And loved Henry too. I long to write about it all.

Life in the Alps – those very special Alps. The mass of ski lifts and mountain railways. The joy of seeing Henry skiing. I wonder whether I prefer him in ski boots or riding boots. I had visions of him meeting me at our secret rendez-vous in England in ski boots and of having driven a hundred miles in them, and then not being able to take them off. So we make love with his boots on. Visions of Henry, tall, athletic, whirling down the slopes, instantly make my heart beat and beat, and the manly way he walked with his skis, took control of all the travelling, and even arranged a 'Special Emma Day' for me to go tobogganing!

How could I suddenly be so cross and forget all that loveliness together?

Come on Emma! See it from Henry's point of view. He's not tied to any one woman, and anyway I'm married and live a long way away. So stop being jealous!

Come on Emma, admit that you were getting things out of perspective. Don't be so sensitive and stupid. Think, woman! Think of all the fantastic fun you can have with Henry – before you throw it all away. Admit all that and don't spoil everything.

Don't let it be like a lovely summer's day and then Bang! – a flash of jealousy, like a clap of thunder, and the lovely picnic and party's over.

Instead let's go on picnicking together – loving and being generous to each other. I am not asking for anything, nothing at all. I just don't want to be put into an exclusion zone.

Woof! Woof! I just want to be his little dog again, his foot cushion. I want to remember the hotel in the Alps, shopping at the Co-op with stupid Fido separating the bananas before taking them to be weighed. 'You can't even shop!' Henry had said scornfully.

Watching the curling and the ice hockey, go-carting, sitting on my Master's knee on the terrace at the end of the run back to the village . . . Oh it was all so lovely, so lovely. Please, please don't be afraid to tell Henry how amazingly exciting and extraordinarily wonderful the whole Adventure was, even down to his mastery of the sudden and terrifying onset of black ice on a long steep hill near Paris on the way home.

Admit that not only is he 'A Nice Little Boy', as one of his local girlfriends described him, but also 'A Clever Little Boy' too. And all little boys are naughty at times. So don't be jealous, just laugh!

Yes, Henry's laughing little Fido is back again! Woof! . . . Woof!

Part III

THE COUNTESS

1

The Countess comes to stay

For weeks I have been doing up my studio-cum-dressing room in the lovely 17th century old rectory that my husband, John, has recently inherited.

I have beautiful muslin curtains, a chaise longue, a little cupboard with my erotic dressing up clothes as I like to call them, some of my old dolls, a little table and chair, and lots of exotic pictures on the walls – nearly all of women and young girls. Off this girl's room is my bathroom.

I met the Countess, as I always think of her, at a party given by Sebastian, a rather effeminate interior decorator.

The Countess was tall, nearly six foot, with big breasts, a masculine face, cropped hair, very long legs, and a cold distant look. She spoke good English with a rather French sounding accent. I gathered that her family came from Romania.

She was quite dismissive of me at Sebastian's until she heard I had been a girlfriend of Ursula's, and then she became less cold. However, I couldn't say that she warmed to me.

But I was fascinated by her. In fact her aloofness made me want to be noticed by her. However, she was also quite cold with Sebastian, so I presumed that was just her manner, and plucked up my courage.

'You must come to the country sometime,' I said rather casually.

To my amazement she replied: 'I'd love to.' Then she added: 'When?'

I instantly thought of my girl's room. Would she like that?

It was clear from the conversation that we had during the evening that she enjoyed women, but she made no sign of it towards me. I knew that John was going to be away one night, so I said: 'Why don't you come for Wednesday night – I could meet you off the train.'

She looked in her diary and, although she was pretty busy, she said that she could fit that in but would have to leave after lunch on Thursday as she had a meeting in London at four. She also said that she was flying to Romania on the Saturday or Sunday.

On the Wednesday I was in a fever of excitement. I was still feeling like the little slave of my wonderful master, Henry, and was wondering whether being with a woman again would enhance my feelings for him. Naturally, I was also wondering if she would really be interested in me.

I picked her up at the station at seven. It was a most beautiful evening, with the countryside looking simply lovely. The local castle in the distance impressed her and she loved our old house, particularly its yellow stones and the setting, looking out onto the castle. I was amazed by how receptive she was, but she is very artistic and paints a lot, particularly in oils. She doesn't exhibit though.

We had drinks outside and to my surprise she proved to be amusing and fun. I suddenly felt a hand on my leg. It moved up a bit, and then she quietly whispered into my ear: 'I like your legs!'

Her hand rested there for what seemed to be hours. I was tantalised. We drank our drinks quietly. Soon she had her hand inside my little panties. It was fantastic what she was doing.

'I've brought a special little case,' she whispered. 'Would you like to see inside it?'

I was very curious. I wasn't at all sure what she was going to show me, but when she opened the case I was astonished to see a little girl's cotton dress, all smocked. Then under layers of tissue paper she showed me a schoolgirl's gymslip, and then a little cane.

'I think you'd look very pretty in these. Is there a room where we can go?'

I took her upstairs to the guest room, showed her the

bathroom and said I would be ready in my studio in twenty minutes. This would give her time to bath.

'Take the case, little girl,' she said, 'and put on the dress first. It may not fit you, in which case try on the gymslip. Either way, I think you'll make a very nice little schoolgirl!'

I was tingling with excitement. It all seemed too wonderful to be true. I had been wondering whether this beautiful and sophisticated woman would bother to take any notice of me, and now here she was asking me to be her little schoolgirl. Of course, after all my experiences with Ursula, I knew exactly how to be the perfect little schoolgirl and I felt sure that the Countess would be very excited when she found me.

So I quickly bathed and dressed up. I then arranged the studio with the little desk and chair and sat there until my Mistress came.

The time seemed to pass very slowly. I was partly scared stiff and partly very excited. I wondered what she would think of me. It is always a little alarming at the beginning.

Then suddenly a long naked body appeared in a mask – the mask of a black woman. She looked terribly fierce. I was very frightened – but also excited at not quite knowing what was about to happen.

'What's this I find?' she screamed from behind her mask. 'A naughty little schoolgirl . . . Have you written out your lines?'

Then down came her cane across my legs – a stinging sensation left me feeling numbed.

'Write,' she shouted. I started to do so, but within seconds I had the cane across my hands. She was really brutal. I could not write as my hands hurt so much.

'You're just being silly,' she shouted.

I started to cry a little.

'Oh,' she rasped, 'how I hate snivelling little girls. Go and stand in the corner! And put your back to the wall.'

I stood there, genuinely and deliciously scared. The mask made her seem even more frightening. Quickly she tied my hands and then she made me part my legs.

'Hmm! Nice!' she said putting her hands between my hot

75

little beauty lips. But I was wet not from passion, but from fear. 'That's what I like to see, child – real fear. And you're going to be really terrified whenever you're with me.'

Then she put a blindfold on my face and left me tied. She told me not to move. I must have been there for fifteen minutes, anxiously wondering what was going to happen.

Finally she came back. She put some cream on my little bottom. I could feel her probing. 'This is nice, but I want you spotlessly clean. And now I'm going to thrash you just to make you remember next time. Bend over!'

'No!' I cried. But blindfolded and with my hands tied there was nothing else I could do.

She gave me ten strokes – slowly and deliberately. It seemed to go on for ever. I never knew when she was going to stop. I was getting really scared, and I was reeling with the pain. It was all too shocking. I hated her and wanted to throw her out of my house. I had made a frightful mistake, I thought.

Then she led me, still tied and blindfolded, to the bathroom. She made me bend over again, and I felt something penetrating me. Then I felt a slimy liquid jetting up inside me . . . I felt so demeaned and so degraded as she stripped off my blindfold and untied my hands, but I could see that she was very excited. She told me to have a quick bath and then, when I went back to my room she met me at the door, replaced the blindfold and tied my hands again. All the time she had been shouting obscenities at me and making me feel awful.

I could see nothing as she led me into my girl's room, but she made me bend over the chaise longue and then within seconds I heard myself scream as this big dildo went up inside me. It must have been strapped onto her, as I could feel her body heaving as the dildo moved inside me. Soon she started to cry out that she was reaching her climax. She was screaming and then I was pushed to the floor and made to lick her juices. Even as I licked she was still climaxing.

She freed my hands and made me rub her juices inside me and excite myself. Then, keeping me blindfolded, she excited me even more. I felt I was going somewhere I had never been before, and we both collapsed into a heap on the floor.

It felt like the most exciting thing that had ever happened to me. It was a mixture of hate and of being completely overcome against my wishes. It was like a fantasy come true.

What would my Master say? I could feel myself getting excited again just thinking of him and of how he would react, when down came her cane.

'That's enough!' she said. 'Now I want dinner and I want you to serve it to me.'

That night we slept together in one amazingly tranquil sleep. I hung onto her like a bear clinging to its mother. We slept until ten the following morning.

When she awoke, she was cold and business like. We had a quiet breakfast. She did not talk much. I was longing for her to talk about the previous evening, but she did not say a word. She just wanted to talk about her rather mysterious activities in Romania – half charitable, but also, it seemed, half business.

I took her back to the station. I longed for her terribly to tell me when we could meet again, but she said not a word except that she wanted to take me to Romania fairly soon. She would let me know. What's so special about Romania? I wondered.

I felt in a haze. I longed to ring my Master, Henry, and tell him all about it, word for word, but alas, as usual when I need him, he was away.

2

A strange meeting

I haven't taken ecstasy but I am on such a high!

Can it be a sex high, or is there no such thing? There must be, for I am desperate for Henry, desperate to be licked, to have him drink my juices, to have him spank me twenty times, to be his naughty little slave girl – or his equally naughty little niece – and to have to perform in front of him.

The Countess has telephoned again. I am amazed, as she left very cool. I thought I would not sound too enthusiastic, despite feeling a longing for her whip. But her voice literally made me melt. Indeed she is so soothing and nice that I feel I would agree to anything she suggested.

She gave me some orders down the telephone and I find I am doing exactly what she tells me. It is almost hypnotic.

We decided to meet in London. I had told her about meeting Henry on the bridge in St James' Park and she had loved it. Now she has suggested that we should meet there and she would send me instructions.

The instructions came in the post, completely cold, just like a shopping list:

1. Go to the hairdresser and manicurist.
2. You are to look extremely glamorous, a sophisticated business woman with high heels, carrying a brief case. You will wear a smart coat.
3. Underneath that coat there is to be nothing on but suspenders and stockings.
4. You will walk up and down the bridge as if you were trying to pick up a man, and remember that I will be there watching. If possible you are to pick up a man, but only an Army officer or equivalent, and you will be followed.
5. If you are unsuccessful after half an hour, your angry

Mistress will appear and you are to follow from a distance. She will get into a taxi, so you will need to be on the ball and have your taxi follow immediately after hers.

6. Just ask the taxi driver to follow the taxi in front – and, if you lose us, then telephone the number at the bottom of this page and you will be given details on where your taxi is to take you.

Three days later

I was not too keen on these instructions. I knew I certainly could not possibly go through with picking up a man in the middle of St James' Park, of all places. And yet I also knew that I would get my Mistress's cane if I did not make some attempt to do so.

On the day, I knew I looked smart as I had my hair done and so on, and so all that was in order.

I was also terribly excited, and actually felt that it might be rather fun to pick up a man and see what happened. But it could be dangerous and Mark would have a fit if he heard about it, and so would other people. This really was playing with fire. I decided that it was better as a game to play at a party, where you know people a little. At least you know the background is all right.

Flushed with excitement, I walked up and down the bridge and to my amazement I got some very good glances. One very smartly dressed man, perhaps an Army officer, actually brushed by me and then said: 'Oh, I'm so sorry, I think I've made a mistake.'

This should have been my cue to say: 'Oh no!', and to start a conversation. But I was too nervous, and it didn't help to remember I had nothing on underneath my coat, and only some little things in my brief case.

I was feeling very frightened and, after what seemed ages, my tall Mistress finally appeared, ignored me and started to walk off very fast. In my high heels I could not keep up. It was terrible, I had to make little runs and felt so foolish. She seemed to walk for ages. And then

I suddenly saw her stop at a taxi rank. This was my cue to get into the second taxi and follow.

We went all the way to Richmond, and stopped at a tall Georgian mansion with a garden. It looked lovely, but I had no time to think. I got out of the taxi, paid him off and, still following my Mistress, rushed up three steps to the front door. I was now very close behind her but she still ignored me.

The door was opened by a very ugly man. She brushed past him and screamed at me to get upstairs and into the second room on the right. Again I found myself making little running steps.

The room was very bare except for mirrors, a few small tables and lots and lots of cupboards. In fact it could have been a small ballroom for it had some lovely chandeliers and candlesticks and a parquet floor.

I sat there looking at my pathetic self in the mirror. Where had all the confidence gone? Or the gloss, or the smart business woman? I now looked like a frightened little girl.

I could hear my Mistress bellowing downstairs, and I almost wished she did not come up, and yet in some strange way I was physically so excited that I was wet, and my breasts were almost bulging out of my coat.

Moments later she stormed in with her cane. She ripped off my coat.

'So the slut couldn't even get a man!' she yelled. 'No man would want you! . . . Come here little slut!'

To my astonishment I now saw, not far from the beautiful chandeliers, that there was the most enormous big hook. With a long pole the Countess put a rope tackle over the hook.

Then she strapped leather manacles, joined by a short chain, onto my wrists. The chain was hooked onto the tackle and I found myself being hoisted up towards the ceiling and left swinging. It was the most ghastly sensation. But this all excited my Mistress so much that she peeled off my stockings and, with almost savage sexuality, started to lick my beauty bud, and to suck the wetness that was now flowing. In fact the sheer fright of hanging from the hook had made me wet the floor, but even this did not deter her.

'What a spectacle you are,' she cried. 'I think I'll leave you there for my friends to see. What a laugh that would be!'

She was now laughing and screaming, and almost demented – sex crazed. She had undressed and was playing with herself, looking at me, and making me look at myself in the mirrors. Soon, she screamed that she was having a huge orgasm. I simply could not believe it, but she was screaming obscenities, laughing and exciting herself even more.

After what seemed hours, she lowered and unhooked me. By this time I had become excited from seeing her in such a state.

'So the little slut would like to climax too,' she teased. 'But she isn't allowed to, is she?'

I was now begging. She made me stretch out on the floor. Then she pounced down on top of me. It was too much, and I started to climax without any help. But then she lashed me with her hand so hard that I stopped.

'Oh, please,' I begged, 'please!'

'Yes, go on begging . . .'

She went to one of the cupboards and I was astonished yet again to see that it held whips of all sorts and harnesses. My God! I thought. But then she produced a little make-up case and in it was a huge artificial manhood, a black one. She strapped it on her thighs, and turning me over she slowly forced it up me from behind.

So there I was, on the floor with my face now downwards and this black manhood beginning to penetrate deeply into me.

I screamed and cried, and she said: 'If you make any more noise you will be sent to the punishment room.'

Again I was very frightened. I did not say another word. I just bit my lips and went very quiet.

'That's a good little girl!' she said.

Then, as the manhood penetrated more deeply, it seemed to open. After the initial terrible shock, I felt I was suddenly floating. Again I screamed. I felt I was bursting. Amazingly she held it in place and then, at the same time, she put her other hand onto my beauty bud, so that I was squirming from both sides. She was also holding my body rigid, and this had the effect of making me climax even more. My Mistress was loving every minute of it. In the end I just collapsed in a heap.

'There, there, little girl,' she murmured. She was now really nice to me. She wrapped me up and carried me to a little cot and gave me a little sip of milk.

I slept for I don't know how long – until I heard a voice purring: 'My little girl doesn't need men, does she?'

I was suddenly wide awake and there was my beautiful Mistress kissing and caressing me.

'I think you can be trained,' she was saying, 'to be a very exciting little plaything for certain of my friends.'

'Oh, please, no!' I cried. 'I just want you. I don't want anybody else.'

'Then, no more men, Emma, is that understood?' I wondered if this was the time to tell her all about Henry. I wanted to share Henry with her. I knew he would be excited by her and it could all be a great deal of fun.

'I have something to tell you,' I blurted out. 'I'm in love with a wonderful man!'

Suddenly there was the most terrible scream. 'What's our dirty little slut talking about?' She lashed me across the face. 'Now stop all this nonsense.'

'But it's true,' I cried, 'and you would like him too.'

She was in no mood to listen. Furious, she stormed out and left me alone for the rest of the night.

The following morning I had to leave very early to get back to my office in the country, and so I sneaked out of the house, through the conservatory – I guessed that alarm bells would not yet have been fitted there, for it was so new.

What would Henry have to say about all this, I thought, as I struggled against the rush of morning commuters to get the train back home.

What indeed?

82

3

The Countess baits the trap

'I'm coming to stay for the weekend.'

It was the imperious voice of the Countess. I was in her office when the telephone suddenly rang. The Countess was back! I had thought that she was still in Romania. She remembered how angry she had been about Henry. Then with a thrill she remembered how exciting it had been when she had stayed last time. Then a black cloud of disappointment came over her.

'But you can't, not this weekend . . . my husband will be there.'

'All the better. You'll find it all the more exciting, knowing that you belong to me.'

'But . . .'

'No "buts", Emma! You'll be deceiving your husband under your own roof – and because I'm a woman he'll not suspect anything. Men never do – they're such idiots. But we shall know better, shan't we Emma?'

'Yes,' I agreed rather hesitantly. It did sound very exciting. I remembered all the exciting things that had happened every time I had met the Countess. And it was true that John, that great booby, would never in his wildest dreams have imagined that his wife and the Countess were lovers – or rather Mistress and Slave.

'And then I shall be taking you away with me to Romania,' continued the attractive foreign sounding voice.

I caught my breath. Henry had particularly warned me not to accept any such invitation. Thank Heavens I had a genuine excuse for refusing!

'But I can't. We've arranged to go to Ireland next week,' I stammered. It was true. 'We're going to stay with relations.'

'That's all right. I shan't want you in Romania until the next weekend, and so I'll come to Ireland for a day or so too – just to make sure you aren't really seeing some man! Then you can join me in Romania a few days later.'

'Oh but . . .' I wailed. But it all sounded so exciting and she knew it wouldn't matter if she was away from her office for a couple of weeks.

'Don't argue with me, Emma!' came the cool reply. 'Just do what you are told. You know you like decisions being taken for you! I shall be arriving tomorrow evening, Thursday.'

'But I must go to my office on Saturday morning to clear up a few things.'

'That's all right. I'll come with you. I've got some shopping I want to do.'

'Oh!' I said. The Countess seemed to have an answer to everything.

'When are you flying to Ireland?'

'Monday' I gasped.

'Monday what, Emma. Haven't you forgotten something?'

'Monday, Mistress!' I whispered.

'Yes, indeed. And don't you forget it. Now book me a seat on the same plane to Ireland and if I can't stay with your relations, then book me into a nearby hotel.'

'Oh, they've a large house and I'm sure they'd be thrilled to meet you . . . Mistress.'

'Good! And by the way I shall be bringing something that you'll find rather interesting . . .'

'Oh!' I said, intrigued.

'But make sure you are quite naked under your dress when you come to meet my train – and make sure you're quite smooth. I don't want to see a single hair, do you understand.'

'Yes, of course, Mistress.'

I was overcome with excitement – an excitement that, she knew, would build up with every passing hour until the Countess finally arrived.

* * *

84

The moment for which I had been so desperately waiting had arrived.

Feeling madly excited I rushed along the platform to where a tall distinguished looking woman was getting out of a First Class carriage.

Silently the woman coldly handed me an old fashioned chauffeur's cap to put on, pointed to her luggage and walked off to my car. Now wearing the humiliating cap, I followed her, staggering under the weight of her cases. I opened the back door for the Countess, and put her cases into the boot. Then I got into the car and drove off. I did not dare speak.

'Stop at the next secluded lay-by,' said the Countess. It was the first time she had spoken since getting down from the train.

'Yes, Mistress,' I replied, wondering what was going to happen. 'This one's very quiet.'

I stopped the car.

'Now come into the back of the car, little girl, lift your dress right up, and stretch out over my knees, little girl.

I felt very embarrassed as I lay back. Thank heavens, I thought, I had carefully removed any hair. I felt rather like a baby girl being changed, but it was not Pampers that the Countess then produced from a plastic bag.

'Look!' she said, with a triumphant smile.

I raised my head. Hanging from the Countess's hand was a metal chastity belt. It had the usual shiny metal waistband, this time fastening at the back, and the usual protected front piece – protected to prevent the beauty lips, held tightly together by the inner slot, from being touched by a finger or by a vibrator. But at the back, instead of the usual two chains going up to the waistband, there was a single thin curved metal rod.

But what caught my attention, even more, were two metal rings that were each attached to the waist band by two chains. The two rings were joined by another but much shorter chain.

'Put your feet through the rings,' ordered the Countess.

I did as I was told and the Countess pulled the rings up

over my knees. The rings now fitted tightly round my thighs, just above the knees. I was shocked, and yet also excited, to find that, because of the short chain linking the two rings, I could not now part my thighs by more than a few inches.

The Countess now pulled the band up to my waist.

'Turn over!'

I now lay on my tummy. I could feel the Countess pulling the metal protective piece down over my beauty lips and then pulling the metal rod, to which the protecting piece was attached, up between my buttocks. I could feel my beauty lips now being held, tightly closed, and I could feel the metal rod pressing against me, from behind. I heard a click as the Countess snapped together the two ends of the waist band and the end of the curved metal rod. I heard a lock being turned.

'Now, that's better,' said the Countess with a smile. 'You can turn over again now.'

The Countess examined the fit of the belt. Then, apparently satisfied, she said: 'You're going to wear this, my little slave, until you arrive safely in Romania. It's a very effective purity belt – much better than an ordinary chastity belt because you won't be able to spread your legs to try and get your finger under it to touch yourself. It was specially designed for use in Middle Eastern harems where the shortage of black eunuchs makes it difficult these days to ensure that the girls are kept pure for their Master. With these belts on, they're kept pure as the driven snow, utterly frustrated, and desperate to catch their Master's eye. I'm soon going to have you desperate to catch my eye too!'

'But, it'll have to come off at night, Mistress,' I wailed. 'My husband . . .'

'No! You'll just have to tell him that you're not well – and then come and please me in the spare bedroom.'

'But how do I go to the loo, with this rod . . .?'

'Oh, you'll soon find that won't stop you. It's just a little awkward. But you'll have to learn to keep the rod clean – as well as yourself. And I mean spotlessly clean. The rod must be shiny and bright at all times. Do you understand?

And of course if you want to spend a penny then you easily do so through the covered slot on the front. No, little girl, you're going to keep the belt on until you join me in Romania in a week's time.'

'Oh, no!' I cried.

'Oh, yes, little Emma,' said the Countess, adding with a little laugh, 'unless, of course, I decide to slip it off temporarily when you come and visit me in my bed!'

'Oh, yes!' I cried out.

'But I warn you, I don't want you bothering me by begging me to take it off the whole time. It will be my decision, if and when I ever, in fact, take it off. If you ever ask for it to be taken off, then you'll be beaten. Do you understand?'

'Yes,' I murmured aghast at the thought.

'Oh, little Emma, it's all going to be so exciting and you'll feel so much more my helpless little slave! I shall enjoy the feeling of total power over you!'

'Oh!' I gasped, feeling quite overcome.

'Now get back into the driving seat, keep quiet, and drive me to your house. And just remember that I shall want plenty of respect and obedience.'

As I stepped out of the back of the car, I could feel my thighs being held together by the short chain, whilst my knees and feet were free. I found that I could walk normally, provided I took short steps. I could also feel my beauty lips being held pressed tightly together under the metal slot, and I could also feel the metal rod going up tightly between my buttocks.

It was all very exciting, I had to admit. It all made me feel that my body was now completely in the power of the Countess.

At dinner that night I felt quite excited as I sat, apparently serene and self controlled, surrounded by several couples – old friends whom my husband and I had invited to dinner before they knew the Countess would be staying.

They, and my husband, all found the exotic Countess quite fascinating with her fund of stories about her sophisticated international jet set life, and of her concern about what was now happening in Romania.

But for me, sitting quietly at the top of the table, it was all quite different. As instructed by the Countess, I was stark naked under my long dress – except for the astonishingly exciting, if rather uncomfortable, belt. I was aware of it the whole time. My lower body was compressed between the covered slot at the front and the curved rod at the back, and my thighs were kept close together by the little short chain.

How I longed for the dinner to be over, for the guests to leave, for John to go to bed, and then to be able to slip away to the Countess's bed. Then, I thought, surely the Countess will at last take off the belt and allow me a little relief. It was a relief that I seemed to need so much more now – because, I realised, of the frustration caused by the cruel belt.

I thought back to when I had gone to the spare room to help the Countess bath and dress.

'We'd better have a little practice run for you going to the loo with the belt on,' the Countess had announced taking me into her bathroom off the spare room. Then very embarrassingly and very explicitly, the Countess had made me practise using one hand to hold the rod slightly to one side, behind me, as I sat on the loo. Then I had to practise cleaning and washing myself under the shiny metal rod, before cleaning and polishing the rod itself.

'Tomorrow, I shall want you to come and show me that everything is perfectly clean – after you've done your little morning duty. And woebetide you if I find one little spot of dirt,' the Countess had warned.

Then under the Countess's very chic, long flowing, French dress I had to strap onto her an artificial manhood. One part of it went up inside the Countess, exciting her with every step and movement. The other half, the half that I simply could not get out of my mind, secretly stuck up under the front of the dress. The Countess had embarrassingly made a point of brushing past me frequently, so that I could feel the erect artificial manhood. And, before dinner, whilst waiting for the guests to arrive, she had smilingly told me to put on a little smooch music.

'In Romania we never miss a chance to dance!' she had laughed.

Then, saying to John that she was sure he didn't mind her dancing with me, the Countess had held me tight to her. It had been a secretly very exciting moment for me. The Countess had not said a word as our lithe slim bodies swayed against each other. I could feel the Countess's hand holding the belt, in a proprietary way, through my dress. I could also feel the artificial manhood probing up against me and against the front of the belt.

I had become very wet and excited under my belt and now, sitting silently at the table, was wet again at the memory. It was all so frustrating – excitingly frustrating. Oh, when would this dinner party end? I wailed to myself in frustrated despair.

'I'm just going to my room to look for something,' I whispered to my half sleeping husband, as I slipped out of his bed. I had kept well to my side of the bed to prevent him from feeling the metal belt under my nightdress, and had anxiously pushed aside his hand if he ever reached for me. 'I'll be back in a moment.'

I tiptoed along the corridor, and knocked quietly on the spare room door.

'Come in, little girl!' I heard the Countess murmur.

Moments later, we were in each other's arms. It was so exciting. The artificial manhood had disappeared, and instead the Countess was wearing a sort of leather corset. I saw that two strange looking rings had been sewn into it low down, one on either side. Below the corset I could feel my Mistress's naked beauty lips, wet and excited. I knew mine were too – under the belt. But whereas, by order of the Countess, mine were quite smooth and hairless – like those of a little girl – the Countess retained her hair and kept it neatly shaped.

I could feel the Countess's large hard breasts pressing against my own soft ones. I felt ready to explode when the

Countess began to squeeze my nipples whilst kissing me passionately on the mouth.

I was about to whisper to the Countess, urging her to unlock the belt, when I remembered the Countess's warning not to do so.

'Now, little Emma, I think I'll use your tongue tonight. Go to my suitcase and bring me a little leather bag you'll find in it.'

Wonderingly, I handed the bag to the Countess, who opened it and pulled out a small leather harness.

'Put your head down, Emma,' ordered the Countess.

I felt the harness being fastened round my head. One strap went round my forehead and was fastened at the back of my head. Another went over my head and down under my chin. The two straps were fastened to each other where they met at my temples. A ring, rather like the rings on the Countess's corset, hung from each of these joins, and from each ring hung a leather rein. I did not understand their purpose, but it was an exciting feeling, wearing the harness.

'Now put your hands behind your back,' instructed the Countess. She tied my wrists together. 'Now, you're nice and helpless! Lie down on your tummy.'

The Countess then led each of the reins through one of the rings on the sides of her corset. She pulled the reins taut. I felt myself being pulled by my head harness, pulled up between my Mistress's now outstretched legs. As the Countess continued to pull on the reins, I felt my head being pulled down onto the Countess's beauty lips. The position of the two rings on the side of my head harness and those on the side of the Countess's corset cleverly ensured that my mouth was positioned just right – just right to give my Mistress exquisite pleasure.

Desperately I tried to raise my head, but my Mistress gave the reins a jerk, and my mouth was pulled down again. Then the Countess, holding a rein in each hand, gently pulled one rein and then the other, making me move my mouth from side to side. With my hands tied behind my back, I now felt completely under my Mistress's control. I felt utterly servile.

The Countess now put both reins into one hand, and picked up a whip.

'Now, my girl,' she said bringing the whip down across my backside and giving the reins a jerk, 'let's feel that little tongue!'

For the next fifteen minutes, my mouth and tongue were tightly controlled by the mixture of the reins and the whip, as the Countess used them to bring herself to a series of screaming climaxes. They were climaxes probably made all the more profound and exciting by the thought that the owner of the mouth and tongue was herself being allowed no pleasure and that John might hear what was going on.

Finally, a replete Countess let go the reins and unfastened my head harness.

'Now get out and crawl back to your husband's bed!' she ordered.

'Oh, no!' I cried, mad with desire. 'Don't send me off like this. Please take off . . .'

Suddenly I again remembered the Countess's warning. I fell silent, biting my lips. I saw the whip still in the Countess's hand.

'I'm sorry, Mistress. I didn't mean it. It won't happen again.'

'It had better not!. You're lucky that I'm feeling so satisfied. Now get out – on all fours! And don't forget to come and show yourself to me tomorrow morning, nice and clean again, after you've done your morning business!'

Back in my sleeping husband's bed, it was a long time before I was able to fall asleep myself. For what seemed hours I tossed and turned, desperately trying to get at myself under the belt and give myself the relief that my body was screaming out for. But that damned little chain, keeping my thighs together, made it quite impossible to move the belt at all.

Never, never, had I felt so frustrated.

It is next morning.

I'm alone in my small office. The Countess has gone out to shop, secure in the knowledge that I would not be able to misbehave in her absence.

I'm trying to clear my desk. But, in fact, I'm feeling far too frustrated and excited to be able to do anything except, once again, put my hand under my skirt in yet another vain attempt to touch my beauty bud and give myself much longed for relief . . .

Just now I reached for the telephone. At least I could share my frustration.

For once Henry was in. His cheerful voice boomed back at me as I described all that had happened and the awful belt into which I was locked.

'Serves you right, you silly bitch, for getting into the hands of another woman when you could have come here and be having fun and games with me!'

The bloody man!

The belt was only ever removed once before the Countess flew off to Romania, and that was whilst in Ireland. Several times I had had to creep along the passageway to the Countess's bedroom to be fitted with the degrading head harness and satisfy my Mistress. Every time the whip was there to remind me not to ask for the belt to be removed. But then on one occasion it was! I was so thrilled!

But to my dismay, it was put back on again before I was allowed proper relief. My frustration was now even greater!

The Countess had smiled as she saw my desperately disappointed little face. She knew that there would be no doubt now that I would follow her to Romania – no matter what warnings Henry might have given me. Frustration is indeed a powerful weapon!

4

Arrival at the castle

It was getting dark as my plane landed at Bucharest.

I had been so thrilled at the thought of seeing a new country and of seeing the Countess's work there at first hand. Above all, I had been excited by the thought of that awful belt being taken off, as the Countess had promised. How wonderful it would be to spend a couple of weeks with the glamorous and dominant Countess – and without that damn belt!

Now, however, I was feeling very lonely and far from home, and was delighted to see, waiting at the barrier, the tall figure of the Countess. She was looking as groomed and chic as ever, in a long swirling fur-edged skirt with a tight fitting fur-edged coat and black boots. On her head she wore a smart looking black fur cap. She smiled at me but then looked away, as if also looking for someone else.

Carrying my suitcase, I rushed up to the Countess and fell into her arms.

'Oh, my darling Mistress,' I cried, 'I'm so glad to see you!'

'Now little Emma that's quite enough,' the Countess said, rather coldly, in her attractive French-sounding accent, pushing me back. 'Now give me your handbag and your tickets and passport ... Good! ... Now I want you to stand here and not move. I've got to meet some other people just arriving on another flight and I'll be back in a moment.'

A little hurt, I watched the Countess go up to a large, rather Latin looking man in a flashy blue striped suit. He looked grim and unsmiling. Two burly men were with him. They kept looking round the large arrivals hall. Were they bodyguards? I wondered.

Then rather to my surprise, I saw that he was also accompanied by a black lady dressed as a nurse, or, rather, a child's Nanny. How strange, I thought.

He and the Countess were deep in conversation. Idly, I had wondered if he had just made his money trading internationally in some underhand way in drugs, arms, or even women. Perhaps, I had thought, he was a member of the Mafia – a real life Mafioso! Mentally, I secretly termed him the 'gangster'.

What on earth, I wondered, had the Countess got to do with this sinister looking man. Then I saw the Countess pointing to me, and they came over towards me.

'Yes,' I heard the Countess say to the gangster in English. 'She's a married woman. It's always interesting for my clients to see an older married girl being put through it, as well as younger ones!'

I did not understand what the Countess was talking about. The gangster nodded and I saw the Countess usher him and his party towards a large car waiting outside.

'I'll see you there later this evening,' I heard the Countess say. 'You'll find your suite very comfortable and we can discuss your programme then. Everything is ready for you, just as we agreed. And if you hurry you'll be in time to see the arrival and processing of the new prisoners – something that my clients always like to watch.'

Clearly, thought I, he may be a gangster but he's also an important and wealthy man. But I was completely mystified by the Countess's talk of programmes and prisoners. What prisoners? What processing? And what did she mean by clients? Did the Countess have a tourist business she had not told me about?

Then the Countess came back to me. She made no reference to the gangster, nor to my chastity belt, and instead, rather brusquely, said, 'Now Emma, I told you you would have an exciting time here. But you must promise me that you'll keep yourself to yourself and not talk to anyone. Simply do exactly what you're told and you'll be all right. Do you understand?'

'But aren't I going to be with you the whole time,' I

wailed. 'I thought I'd come here to have a lovely holiday with you!'

'I won't be far away, darling, and you're going to find this weekend a rather exciting surprise. But just remember that it's all a little game, and soon there'll probably be an even more exciting surprise in store for you! No! No questions, and remember what I said about not talking to the other girls and doing just what you are told.'

'Other girls?' I wailed again. 'And the belt . . .?'

But the Countess ignored my questions as she led me outside. It was bitterly cold and there were signs of snow on the ground. She took me over to an unmarked van.

She opened the door of the van. Inside it was like a simple mini-bus with a wooden bench along each side. Several blankets were lying on the seats. There were no windows. The contrast with the limousine that the Countess had produced for the gangster and his friends was marked.

'Up you get, Emma,' said the Countess. 'Hurry up, I've got to meet another plane.'

Before I could ask any more questions, the Countess had shut the door with a bang, leaving me alone with my suitcase in the starkly furnished and darkened van. There was a little light in the corner and a rather strange mirror in the partition that completely cut off the driver's compartment.

In the half darkness, I groped for a handle to the door. I wanted to get out and run after the Countess. But there was no handle. I was locked in!

I sat down on one of the hard benches, left to my own thoughts and wondering what was going to happen. The Countess had promised me, back in England, an exciting and unusual trip. Well it was certainly starting in a strange way! I could not help finding it rather exciting too!

After what seemed hours, I heard girlish voices and laughter. They were talking in German, and I could not understand what was being said. I recognised the deeper voice of the Countess.

Suddenly the door was flung open. Light blazed into the van, half blinding me. Three girls climbed into the van.

They all seemed surprisingly beautiful and vivacious with sparkling eyes. Before I could cry out and ask the Countess what was happening, the door was shut again with a bang, and almost immediately the van moved off.

The girls sat down on the hard benches and looked around. They seemed surprised to see me, and several of them said something to me in German. I did not understand them. Anyway, remembering what the Countess had said about not talking to other girls, I just shook my head. The girls then ignored me.

For over an hour the van swayed and jolted over what seemed to be mainly rather bad and twisting roads. Then it slowed down, as if climbing up a hill. Soon the noise of the tyres changed as if the van was driving over cobbles. Then it stopped.

Abruptly the van door was flung open.

'*Heraus! Schnell! Heraus!*'

A man was shouting in a mixture of broken German and English, punctuated by what I recognised, horrified, as the crack of a whip.

He repeated his orders in English. 'Out! Quickly! Get out! Move!'

Scared stiff, I and the other girls tumbled out of the van. We were in some sort of a courtyard. It was brightly lit. Beyond the lights seemed to be a large building, like an old castle. Shadowy figures were pointing down at us from a balcony. I thought I glimpsed the striped suit of the gangster whom I had seen at the airport.

But my attention was taken by the shouting man. With one hand he was holding back a fierce and snarling dog. He was wearing a black uniform with a leather belt over one shoulder and a peaked cap. With his other hand he was cracking a long thick black leather whip. He seemed quite young but his grim face had a cruel look.

'Pick up the suitcases! Line up!' he was shouting, cracking his whip and bringing the terrifying dog closer to the cringing women. 'Get into line! Properly! Hurry!'

It was a scene that reminded me of pictures of the arrival of new women prisoners at a Nazi concentration camp, with the terrified women stumbling out of cattle trucks, and shouting black uniformed SS guards, with dogs and whips. I remembered what the Countess had said to the gangster about being in time to see the arrival of the new prisoners. My God! What had I let myself in for? I joined the line of scared looking girls.

'Stand still! Stay in line! Stand up straight!'

Still holding the snarling dog back, the terrifying young man in the black uniform walked down the line of us frightened girls. He pointed at an open doorway some way across the courtyard.

'When I crack my whip again you will turn and run through that door. And you will stay in line!'

There was a pause. I looked at the door nervously, wondering what lay beyond it.

Suddenly, the whip cracked.

'*Rennen*!' the young guard shouted. 'Run!'

With the dog snapping at our heels, we turned and ran towards the doorway, carrying our suitcases as best we could. I heard laughter, both male and female, from the balcony.

Once through the doorway, the young man used his dog and his whip to drive us fast down a corridor and into a large tiled room. A big bath was situated in the middle of the room and standing by it, arms akimbo, was a big powerful looking woman. She was dressed in a long severe black dress, with a leather belt from which hung a big bunch of keys. Her greying hair was pulled straight back into a bun at the back of her neck.

She looked, I thought with a fright, like a prison wardress.

Behind her stood a similarly dressed, stocky, young woman, obviously the wardress's assistant. She might have been a peasant girl, I thought.

The black uniformed male guard had disappeared. The wardress gave an order in German and then, for my benefit, repeated it in good English but with a heavy German accent. 'Put your suitcase in the corner. You will not need it here.'

Wonderingly, I put my suitcase on top of the other girls'. The Countess had said it was all going to be an exciting surprise. Well it was certainly a surprise all right, but it was all too frightening to be exciting.

The wardress gave another order, and again repeated it in English for my benefit. 'Line up! Tallest on the right, shortest on the left. Hurry!'

One of the girls was hanging back, smiling contemptuously. The wardress and her assistant went up to her. The strong looking wardress's assistant grabbed the recalcitrant girl's wrists and held them behind her back. Immediately the wardress smacked the girl hard several times across the face. Then she stepped back and repeated her order. Crying, the girl scuttled into the line. We all hastily sorted ourselves out. I found myself in the middle of the line.

A man came into the room. He was dressed in white like a male hospital nurse. He looked sinister and cruel.

My God, I thought, what next?

5

Indoctrination procedure

The wardress was shouting more orders.

'Strip to the waist for inspection! Quickly! Naked to the waist! And stay in line!'

No! No! thought I, not in front of this man. It was all too awful. There were also cries of protests from the other girls. But the wardress raised her hand and the protests died away.

'I said strip, you slut!' she shouted to me, raising her hand. I saw that the peasant girl was now behind me, reaching forward as if to hold my wrists.

'Yes, I will, I will,' I whimpered, beginning to unbutton my coat.

'Silence!' shouted the wardress. 'Here you speak only with permission. Understand?'

She gave me a sharp smack on the cheek, and raised her hand again. 'Understand?'

Scared stiff, I nodded.

'Then strip to the waist!' said the wardress grimly, walking slowly up and down the line of frightened women. 'Hurry! I want to see your naked breasts and naked navels in ten seconds.'

She started to count slowly in German. '*Eins . . . Zwei . . . Drei . . .*'

I and the other girls were now tearing off our coats and blouses in sheer panic, fear overcoming our sense of shame in the presence of a man.

'*. . . Sechs . . . Sieben . . . Acht . . .*'

With a little cry of despair, I joined the other girls in pulling down my chemise and in tearing off my bra. I pulled my skirt down a little to bare my navel, but I then covered my breasts with my hands to hide them from the watching man.

'... *Neun* ... *Zehn* ... Now hands on head. At once. And look straight ahead! Shoulders back!'

I felt desperately shy. I hesitated about taking my hands away from my breasts. Suddenly my arms were gripped firmly from behind by the wardress's assistant. The wardress came slowly up to me. I looked at her, terrified. Slowly she raised her hand and proceeded to smack my face ... once, twice, three times.

Then she stood back. I was sobbing as my hands were released.

'Hands on head! Stand up straight and look straight ahead!' she shouted at me again.

This time I rushed to obey. Never again, I resolved, would I be slow to obey this terrifying woman. I remembered the Countess's strange warning about doing what I was told and I would be all right. I certainly would do so in future! At the same time, however, I also thought that if this was just a game of the Countess's, then it all seemed to be going a bit too far.

The male nurse now passed down the line, feeling each woman's breasts and nipples carefully, calling out, apparently in Romanian, to the wardress as he did so. Out of the corner of my eye I had seen her take a notebook out of a pocket in her long black tunic. Now she was writing in it.

The breast inspection apparently over, the wardress closed her notebook with a snap. She shouted something in German and then turned to me.

'I count ten again – and you stark naked. Understand? Completely naked – or else!' She paused. 'Now go! *Eins* ... *Zwei* ...'

I and the other petrified girls were now tearing off our skirts, our panties and stockings, and stepping out of our shoes.

'*Acht* ... *Neun* ... *Zehn. Gut.*'

Like the others, I was now standing naked, looking ahead and with my hands on my head. But I still had the wretched chastity belt on.

The man in white came over and he and the woman walked up and down the line, pointing to each of the

100

women in turn and discussing them in what sounded like Romanian. They kept pointing down at my chastity belt and then at the other girls' bellies. I had noticed that, unlike me, the other girls still had their pubic hair.

Then out of the corner of my eye, I saw the wardress turn and give a little nod towards a large long mirror set high in the wall of the room, alongside a small balcony. It looked somehow strange, rather like the one-way mirrors that I had seen in some Mistress's houses in London.

Goodness, I thought, horrified, were people looking at me, naked, from behind the mirror? Perhaps that awful gangster was there? Was this what the Countess had meant when she had told him that he would be in time to see the processing of the prisoners. My God! This was too awful! And to be seen locked into that awful chastity belt! I wanted to run away and hide. But I did not dare move.

Then suddenly the man in white came back to me. He had a key in his hand. It was the key to the chastity belt. He walked behind me.

'Step forward one pace!' shouted the wardress. 'Stand still! Keep your head up and part your legs a little.'

Scared, I did as I was told. The chain linking my thighs prevented me, of course, from parting my legs more than a few inches. I felt the male nurse unlock the belt. The rod between my buttocks fell away, as did the slot holding my beauty lips and the rings round my thighs. Eagerly I stepped out of the belt. At last! I felt my beauty lips open like a flower after spending all that time compressed together.

The man picked up the belt and gestured to me to get back into line.

The wardress turned back to the line of naked women. She pointed to me and to the girl standing next to me.

'You two, into the bath!' she barked. 'We get rid of lice! Move!'

Quickly I ran to the big bath. It was full. It had a strange smell.

'In!' shouted the wardress, pushing us both down into the bath.

The water was warm. Horrified, I saw the peasant girl

push my companion's head under the water and hold it there. Suddenly the wardress pushed my head under the water. It tasted horrible. Lysol! I tried to come to the surface to breathe, but my head was firmly held down. I struggled desperately, but to no avail.

It felt like I was going to drown! That awful gangster and the other people whom I had seen on the balcony outside had paid the Countess to watch a girl being drowned!

Suddenly I was released. Spluttering I came to the surface. Immediately the peasant girl began to rub a pumice stone over my arms, my shoulders, my belly . . . whilst the wardress and the male nurse watched smiling.

'Out!' shouted the wardress. 'You clean now. Lice dead!'

She flung a towel at each of us. We dried ourselves gratefully, rubbing our hair. Two more girls were now pushed into the bath.

'You go with male nurse!' the wardress now shouted at me and my companion.

Feeling very ashamed at my nakedness, I silently followed the white clad man through the open double doors into the annexe off the bathroom. It was like a massage parlour with several couches in a row in the middle of the room. There was a brazier in the corner with several pots bubbling on it.

Again there was a curious mirror set high on the wall. Was it really a one-way mirror? I wondered.

The male nurse spoke to the other girl in German. She lay down on a couch. The man pointed to another couch and indicated to me to do the same. He came over and quickly strapped my wrists to the side of the couch. Then he strapped my ankles wide apart and slipped a hard cushion under my buttocks. My legs were towards the strange mirror. I blushed as I realised my beauty lips were being displayed, but I could not move now.

Approvingly, he ran his hand over my smooth mound. Then, glancing up at the mirror on the wall, he slowly parted my beauty lips.

I felt his fingers probing between my beauty lips. He

began to examine me expertly, caressing me gently. To my embarrassment, I felt myself begin to respond. Then he began to squeeze the bud itself, tantalisingly. I could feel it growing, becoming more prominent as he went on. How awful!

Again I heard him call out something in Romanian to the wardress, who came over from the bathroom. I saw her take out her notebook. She started to write in it. Looking up at the mirror, she called out in a loud voice as if reading what she had written. It sounded like the report that the male nurse had made about my intimacies. I could have died of shame – but what was so strange about me? I wondered.

I saw him go over to the other girl. He bent down over her. Then he called out something in an excited voice. The wardress rushed over. She too bent down over the girl. I heard the wardress question the girl in German. I heard the girl answer in a sobbing voice.

The wardress stood back and began to write in the notebook. Again, glancing at the mirror, she read out what she had written. She laughed happily and went back to the bathroom.

Now I began to wonder what on earth was so strange about the other girl.

I saw the male nurse walk over to the brazier. He examined the various pots and returned with one of them. In it was melted wax. Then he again ran his hand over the down of my mound. It was two weeks since I had last been treated in London and some little blonde hairs had begun to show again.

The man was smiling cruelly. Then with a wooden spatula he began to spread the wax over my mound and down over my beauty lips, holding them apart so the wax covered all the little hairs.

Then leaving the wax on me to solidify, he repeated the process on the other girl, first cutting her long pubic hair with a pair of scissors.

Then he returned to me. He bent down. I gave a little cry as he ripped off the wax – it was far more painful than when a beautician did it in a beauty shop in London. But it was even more painful for the other girl with so much more hair when, a few minutes later, he ripped the wax off her intimacies.

The man then ran his hand through my hair and then through that of the other girl. Horrified I saw him pick up a pair of clippers and put them down on a little table, together with a razor, some soap and an old fashioned shaving brush.

He stroked the other girl's hair and said something in German to her. Immediately she started to scream her head off.

'*Nein! Nein!*' she was shouting, her eyes starting from her head as she struggled in vain to get free from the couch to which she was tied.

The wardress came in from the bathroom to see what the noise was all about. She smacked the girl's face. The girl stopped screaming, but she was still whispering, '*Nein! Nein!*' The wardress said something to the male nurse, who stood back, his razor still in his hand.

Then the wardress came over to me.

'All prisoners must have heads shaved,' she said. 'He now going to shave yours.'

'No! No!' I heard myself screaming just as the other girl had screamed. 'No! Not that! Please!'

The wardress smiled.

'Very well, but you will be punished. Soon you will both be begging to have head shaved.'

She again took out the notebook. She started to write in it, looking up at the mirror and calling out slowly as she did so, 'Refused to have head shaved. Ten strokes! Both girls.'

Then the man picked up a set of thick marker pens. Carefully he painted a broad red strip across my belly just under my navel, and under that he painted a blue one. He then painted a broad yellow strip across the belly of the other girl and below that a green strip.

The wardress came over and looked down approvingly. She said something in German to the other girl, and then turning to me said in English, 'And your name here now just "Red and Blue". You remember your name!'

I wanted to protest. My name was Emma! But I did not dare open my mouth. Anyway, I thought, it might be rather deliciously degrading to be just called 'Red and Blue'!

It was a scene that was repeated with the other two girls as they were brought in from the bathroom and tied down on couches. Their body hair was also removed, and they screamed blue murder when they were threatened with having their heads shaved. Instead they had two coloured bands painted on their bellies: black and yellow on one girl and blue and green on the other.

We were now released and made to line up again in order of height. The wardress gave each of us a long, shapeless, black and white striped, thick, serge smock and told us to wear them. I thought it looked like a prison uniform. The sleeves were extra long and covered the hands. A bag-like glove held the fingers and thumbs helpless, and a rubber band around the wrist prevented the fingers and thumb from being removed from the restraining bag.

The smock fitted tight across the tummy and had a cut-out through which the coloured bands painted on each girl's belly could be seen. A matching strip of coloured cotton had been sewn onto the back of each girl's smock for further ease of identification.

I remembered our arrival at the castle; the guard brandishing a whip and a snarling dog; it had all reminded me of pictures of prisoners in a concentration camp. These striped prison smocks also reminded me of them . . .

Goodness! What was the Countess up to? Was she re-creating in the castle one of the women's concentration camps of the recently overthrown Communist regime? Had the castle been the centre of one? Had the large bathroom and this room been real processing rooms?

My God! I thought. Was the Countess now charging rich men, like the gangster, to come and stay at the castle and watch it being used as it had been? Had she tricked me and the German girls into coming to stay – and then treated us as prisoners, for the amusement of her guests? Were they the clients she had mentioned to the gangster at the airport? Was all this what she had meant when she had said at the airport that it was all going to be an exciting surprise? Well, it was certainly a surprise all right . . .

'Right turn!' the wardress shouted. The girls were now in a line, standing one behind the other. 'Hold out right arms.'

The male nurse and the peasant girl now passed down the line of women and snapped their right wrists onto a common chain.

The girls were now held by the wrist, each closely behind the girl in front. But the wardress wasn't finished.

'Hold out left legs!'

As the girls balanced on their right legs, the male nurse and the peasant girl snapped each girl's left ankle to another common chain. The girls were now even more firmly held chained behind each other.

It all seemed so expertly done that I wondered if the wardress, the male nurse, the young guard with the fierce dog, and the fat peasant girl had done it all many times before. My God! If the castle had been a sort of woman's concentration camp during the Communist regime, then had they been involved in running it? Had they terrified, stripped, scrubbed, depilated and shaved the heads of numerous batches of frightened young women, students and newly-weds, sent here for trying to escape from the country with their lovers or husbands, or for criticising the regime? Had they also been marked with an identifying colour or number and been given only this coarse striped prison smock to wear?

My mind was racing, and so was my imagination. But was it all just fantasy – just an exciting game, as the Countess had said at the airport?

I remembered how the Countess had spoken to me of getting back her old family castle, complete with its retainers. I remembered now that the Countess had said something about it having been used before the fall of the

Communist regime as a prison or interrogation centre by the dreaded Secret Police.

At the time the significance of that remark had not registered. But now it did! My God! Had these terrifying people worked for the Secret Police? Had the Countess kept them on when she got back her castle – kept them on to repeat what they used to do in exchange for refuge from justice? Had she kept them on to earn her money by repeating, for the amusement of wealthy men and women their treatment of young female political prisoners? Now the girls were innocent, like me – or perhaps they were girls whom her lesbian friends had sent here for disciplining?

I looked up again at the strange mirror set high on the wall.

If it was a one-way mirror, had high-ups of the old regime come here to enjoy watching newly arrived young women being humiliated? And what had happened next? What indeed! What would now happen to me and these German girls? My God! What had I let myself in for? I must have been mad, I thought, to have fallen for the blandishments of the Countess . . .

'March round the room!' shouted the wardress. 'Heads up!'

Their chains clinking, the girls stumbled round.

'Keep in step!' warned the wardress angrily. 'Properly!'

The wardress looked up at the mirror and smiled as if showing off the girls under her control.

The male nurse opened a door. It seemed to be leading down some steps. A blast of cold air entered the room, making me shiver under my serge smock. The man beckoned the chain of girls towards him.

'What are you going to do to us now?' I longed to demand. But remembering the power of the wardress's hand, and what the Countess had said about simply doing what I was told, I kept quiet.

Again the man beckoned the line of shrinking girls forward, a nasty smile on his face.

6

The dungeons

Suddenly behind the line of us women, running, stumbling in our chains and heavy serge prison smocks, a man appeared.

It was the same cruel faced young guard, uniformed in black, who with his whip and his fiercely barking dog had driven us into the castle when we arrived.

He still had both with him, and again he was shouting.

'*Heraus!* . . . Out! *Schnell!* . . . Quickly!'

He was angrily pointing to the large door in which the white clothed male nurse was standing beckoning to the line of us closely chained young women. The guard cracked his whip. It made a terrifying noise like a pistol shot. He made as if to let the snarling dog get at our heels.

Once again I glimpsed the wardress smile up at the mirror set in the wall. If the mirror was a one-way one, I thought, then it must be an erotic sight – a line of terrified chained women being driven on by a young man with a whip and an angrily snarling dog.

Frightened and stumbling in our chains, we ran hesitantly towards the door.

'*Schneller!* . . . Faster!' the young man shouted.

The male nurse led the coffle of running girls down a long corridor. It was bitterly cold. But with the dog barking menacingly at our heels, none of us dared even to pause for breath.

The corridor led to a winding stone staircase set in a tower. The guard and his dog drove us down and down.

Finally we came out into a wide stone corridor with a heavy wooden door with iron bars set across it. The male nurse opened the door. The young guard drove us through it and immediately the male nurse locked the door behind us. There would be no escape from here, I thought.

Along one side of the wide corridor was a line of small wooden doors, apparently leading into cells or dungeons. Each door had what seemed to be a small circular peephole closed by a wooden disc held in place by an iron catch. There also seemed to be a rather large circular hole in each door, also covered by a wooden disc closed by an iron catch.

The male nurse gestured to us to halt. Puffing and out of breath, we stood nervously and closely chained, one behind the other.

'Keep eyes fixed ahead! Don't look round!' ordered the young guard in German and then in English. He cracked his whip to emphasise each order. 'Heads up!'

I heard a rattle of chains from behind me. I was aware that the girl behind was being unchained from the coffle. I heard footsteps, the barking of the dog, then a little cry and the slamming of a door.

My own wrist was now seized by the male nurse and unfastened from the chain, followed by my ankle. He gripped me by the arms and led me to one of the wooden doors. I saw that the next door now had a black and yellow chalk mark on it. The name of the girl who had been chained behind me! He unlocked my door with a large key, thrust it open and gestured to me to go in.

I hesitated, but the young guard let his snarling dog leap forward towards my legs. With a cry of fear, I ran through the door which was immediately locked behind me. I was in pitch darkness. I heard a scratching noise as if the male nurse was marking the outside of my door with the colours of my name: red and blue.

Soon I heard the clinking noises, as the remaining two girls were unfastened from the chains, and the slamming noise as they were shut into cells. Alarmed, I started to grope around in the darkness.

Suddenly the cell was filled with light. I blinked up at a bright electric light high up, out of reach in a corner. It must have been switched on from outside. I looked around. I saw that I was in a dungeon with bare stone walls and a stone cobbled floor.

The dungeon was empty except for a heavy wooden plank cot set against one wall and fastened to the floor. There was no mattress. On the planks folded in a pile were two dark brown blankets and a stained striped pillow.

In the middle of the dungeon was a solid looking table, also fastened to the floor. Alongside it was a wooden stool. There was nothing else, no sheets, no pillow case, no shower, no loo, no hand-basin, no towels, no mirror, nothing!

Suddenly a little red light appeared high up in one corner. There was something black behind it. There was a slight whirring noise. The black thing seemed to be turning slightly. Suddenly I recognised it: a remotely controlled television camera. I remembered Ursula had had one in the maid's room in which I had so often been shut up and which she had controlled from her bed. Goodness! Was someone else watching me now! But who? The Countess? Or that awful looking gangster?

Well, I thought, a joke was a joke and I, too, certainly enjoyed a bit of fun. But this terrifying dungeon was too much. I'd show the Countess, or her guests, what I thought of them! Slowly and deliberately I put my tongue out at the camera and made a face.

Seconds later I heard a telephone ring outside in the corridor. I heard a woman's voice answer it.

Then I heard a key being inserted into the large old fashioned lock of my dungeon door. In strode the wardress. She was looking furious. She walked slowly up to where I was cowering, petrified, against the wall. She seized my hair and then pointed up to the camera.

'You stupid girl!' She smacked me hard across the face.

'In future you show respect!' She smacked me again across the face. Then she pushed me down onto the floor, onto my knees. With her booted foot she pushed my head down onto the cobbled floor.

'You stay like that until I give you new order,' she shouted. 'You not move! Camera watching!'

Then she strode out of the room again, locking the door noisily behind me.

I was left sobbing, kneeling on all fours, my head still reeling from the wardress's heavy hand. My thoughts were in a turmoil. My God! I thought. I really must do what I am told – as the Countess had warned me. I had thought that the Countess was just joking. Clearly she wasn't. But just what was going on?

Five minutes later the eye-hole in the door was opened from the outside.

'Get into bed!' shouted the wardress.

I wondered whether I should take off the thick prison dress. But the clever way in which the lining was strapped round the wrists of my helpless hands made that impossible. Anyway, it was so cold!

Shivering, I lay down on the hard bed. I saw that the television camera had followed me. I felt scared. I pulled up the blankets.

On the wall by the bed was a framed notice. It looked as though it had been there a long time. Was it, I wondered, a relic of the days when the castle had been a woman's prison? Something was written in Romanian and then in German and English.

'It is forbidden' I read 'for prisoners to put their hands under the blankets. Penalty: ten strokes.'

Like a naughty child, I hastily put my wrists onto the top of the blankets.

Despite the hard planks of the bed, I soon felt sleepy. I was physically and emotionally exhausted. I longed to put my gloved hands down and to lift up the heavy serge smock, but with the bright light still lighting up the dungeon, and with the television camera still trained on me, I did not dare to do so.

Soon I was fast asleep . . .

A touch of prison camp discipline

I stirred in my sleep. It was quite late, and the early morning sun was already streaming in from behind a small barred window set high in the bare stone dungeon wall. I could hear footsteps in the passageway beyond the locked wooden door.

I saw that the bright light had been switched off, but that the little red light from the front of the television camera was still shining. Who, I wondered, would be looking at their screens so early in the morning? Then I remembered how Ursula's maid Rafaela, had also had a monitor screen in her kitchen so that she could keep an eye on what I was up to, even when Ursula was asleep. Similarly, was there also a monitoring screen here? Perhaps in the corridor outside?

I longed to put my hand down under the blankets and try to give myself a little pleasure from my heavily gloved fingers. But with the television camera pointing straight at me, I did not dare to do so.

I glanced about the bare dungeon. I was wondering about this when suddenly there was a rattle of keys and the door was flung open. The white clad male nurse entered. He was carrying a large bottle and a large spoon together with a metal bowl. With him was the fat, sturdy, peasant girl.

Silently the girl pulled me off my wooden bed, and pushed me down to my knees in front of the grim faced male nurse. Quickly she bound my wrists behind my back with a strip of cloth. Then she gripped my head from behind and bent it back so that my mouth was raised towards the man, who had put down the bowl, and who was now pouring something out from the bottle into the spoon.

Then holding the full spoon in one hand, he pinched my nose with the other.

I felt as if I was suffocating. I saw him smile cruelly as I tried to push his hands away and shake my head free. But with my hands bound behind me, and my head tightly gripped by the peasant girl I was helpless. Terrified, I was forced to open my mouth to breathe. But as I did so, the male nurse expertly thrust the contents of the spoon down into my mouth.

He stroked my throat to make me swallow it all, like a kennel man does when making a dog swallow a dose. It tasted horrible and slid down my throat like a heavy oil. I never learnt what it was, but already I could feel it sliding down into my stomach.

Horrified I watched him pour out another large spoonful from another bottle. The male nurse said something to the girl in Romanian and they laughed as if sharing some private joke. Then before I could gather my thoughts the man gave a nod to the fat peasant girl who pulled by head back again. Then he again gripped my nose. Again my mouth was forced open. Again he thrust the spoon's contents down my throat. This time it tasted bitter.

He stood back, apparently pleased with having given me two large doses of medicine so effortlessly. He smiled up at the television camera, which I saw to my horror had turned and was pointing down at me as I knelt at the man's feet. Someone, or perhaps some people, were enjoying watching a helpless girl being dosed by a brutal man!

The male nurse turned to the metal bowl. It seemed to be full of a sort of thick grey porridge. He scooped a large spoonful out of the bowl and nodding once again to the peasant girl to hold my head tightly back, he thrust the spoon into my mouth. He repeated the process several times, obviously anxious that I would not have a completely empty stomach for the medicine to work on.

Then, as he and the peasant girl silently turned towards the door, their task apparently completed, the wardress entered.

'You stay standing in front of camera, until I come to

let you out,' she grunted, before also turning towards the door and locking it.

I did not know how long I was left standing there. Slowly I could feel the medicine having its way. Soon I was twisting awkwardly in front of the watching television camera. It was awful! And so humiliating.

Soon I was desperately wondering how much longer I could hold out. I looked around the bare stone dungeon for some sort of receptacle. There was nothing! Could I hold out until the wardress returned? I remembered the wardress's painful way of smacking a woman's face . . . I must hold out, I must, I told myself, as I writhed and grimaced in front of the camera.

Suddenly the door opened again. It was the black clad young guard. He cracked his whip and the dog snarled.

He unlocked a little door low down in the wall to reveal a small continental type loo. He gestured to me to go to it, and then left me. I could hear him repeating the process in the next dungeon. The relief!

Minutes later the guard returned.

'Out!' the young man shouted once again, holding back the barking dog and cracking his whip menacingly. 'Hurry! At once!'

Quickly I ran out into the passageway. I noticed a television camera – just like the one in my dungeon. It was training up and down the corridor. The two leading girls of the chain were already there, one standing behind the other. Quickly I took up my position as third in the line. Dumbly I held out my right arm and my left leg to be attached to the chain gang.

But this time we were chained differently – by the neck! The peasant girl fastened a metal collar loosely round my neck. Some three feet of chain hung from a ring on the front of the collar. The fat girl attached the end of this to a ring at the back of the collar round the neck of the girl standing in front of me. We were made to stand well apart so that the chains linking us all were taut.

Then, when I had been duly chained by neck to the back of the collar of the girl standing in front of me, I let myself relax. What a mistake! Prisoners, as I was soon to learn, were never allowed to relax in this awful prison.

'You! Red and Blue!' I heard the young guard shout. He cracked his whip, frighteningly, just behind me. 'You always stand at attention here!'

He came over to me and brutally pulled my head back by my hair. I saw that the television camera was now trained on me.

'Head up!' he again shouted. Then he raised his hand and slapped me hard across the face. I gave a cry of pain. 'Hands to your side! Look straight ahead!'

Terrified, I kept my eyes rigidly fixed on the wall ahead – looking over the back of the head of the girl in front of me. But I was aware that he was standing back looking at me from the side, tapping his whip impatiently against the palm of his hand. I held my breath as the moments passed.

'Shoulders back!' he suddenly shouted, cracking his whip again. I shivered in fear as I strained to obey his orders. 'Suck your belly in!'

He put his hand onto my straining belly and felt it through the serge material. I gave a gasp but did not dare look down. I strained to pull in my tummy.

'More!' shouted the young man, still feeling my belly. 'You want whip? Pull in belly more! That's better! You stay like that! You now think only of being in correct position for standing at attention! Strain shoulders back more . . . Harder! . . . Belly in! . . . Head up! . . . Eyes front! . . . Heels together!'

He paused.

'And now . . .' Again there was a pause. I felt like a mouse being played with by a cruel cat. Then, suddenly he cracked his whip again and shouted: 'Up on your toes! . . . Up! . . . Right up! . . . And keep your belly in and your head up . . . Properly!'

It was an almost impossible position to hold. I started to totter, biting my lips to as I strained to keep upright.

'Careful!' he shouted. 'Keep up on toes, with shoulders back and belly in, or you'll get whip again.'

Again there was a long pause. He watched me closely as

I desperately tried to hold the position of attention. I was aware that the camera was still trained on me. How many other people, I wondered, were enjoying watching my degradation as they lay back in their beds, enjoying a delicious breakfast.

'Better!' he shouted. Pleased, I again made the mistake of relaxing slightly and glancing at him. 'No! You silly bitch! Eyes front! . . . And keep chin in! . . . And stand up straight!'

Again he slapped me across the face.

'Get back into position!' His shout of anger drowned my own screams of pain.

Then, greatly relieved, I saw that he had now moved down the line, making each of the other girls strain to hold the position of attention. But now I did not dare to relax for one moment.

Somehow I managed to concentrate on straining to remain on tiptoe and at attention. I heard the young guard go back to the line of wooden doors. I heard one being opened.

'*Heraus! Schnell!*' I heard the young man shout.

Standing rigidly at attention, I heard the girl, Black and Yellow, being chained behind me, and then she too was put through her paces and made to take up the proper position of attention.

The horrible young guard now came to one side of the line.

'When I crack my whip – and not before – you will all turn to your right and face me – but keep standing up on your toes with your ankles together as you turn, or you'll get the whip.'

Again there was a long pause. Desperately I wondered how on earth I was going to turn whilst keeping my ankles touching – and remain standing on my toes at the same time.

Then the dreadful young man slowly raised his whip. I could hear the other girls sucking in their breath. Suddenly the whip cracked, and, tottering on my toes, I somehow managed to turn slowly and face the young guard. As I did so I could feel the loose collar being pulled round my neck so that the two rings and the taut chains that attached me to the girls on my left and right, were now also on either side of me.

But the young guard still had not finished with us. He cracked his whip yet again and his wretched dog snarled at us.

'Pull up dresses!' he shouted.

We all hesitated. He cracked his whip several times. Scared stiff, I followed the other girls in lifting up my dress. I felt very ashamed at having to do so in front of this young man.

'Right up! Hold dress right up over shoulders!'

Four young naked female bodies were now on display. Display? I noticed the young guard looking up, smirking, at another balcony with a strange looking mirror alongside it. Oh, no! Were we again being watched? An early morning erotic display for those of the Countess's guests who were up and about?

Below the balcony the television camera was trained on the line of girls. It was slowly moving left and right and then zooming in on one of us. Was it being used to amuse and titillate those of the Countess's guests who were still in bed and not standing behind the mirror?

Either way, was it all just an amusing display of enforcing strict but humiliating discipline on poor innocent girls? My God! I thought. How degrading it all was.

I jumped as the guard tapped my naked tummy with his whip.

'Bellies in!' he warned. 'Eyes front! Keep position of Attention. Silence!'

For a full minute we were left, our bodies bared, silently straining as we stood at attention, barefoot on the cold stone floor. Only the grimaces on our faces showed our growing discomfort.

'Up on toes!' he shouted. 'Heels together! Now we want to see you properly. So bend knees! Yes, bend knees!'

I could hardly believe it. Quite apart from this being so difficult to do without losing one's balance, it was also degrading. I could feel my beauty lips parting.

Then the white garbed male nurse now came down the line. He was carrying a sponge in one hand and a bucket of tepid water in the other. I gasped when he got to me and ran the wet sponge under my arms and over my breasts. I began to shrink and cower.

'Position!' shouted the watching young guard.

Hastily I stood up straight again.

The sponge was moving down over my tummy. I didn't dare look down.

'Clasp hands behind neck!' was the next order.

How shame-making it all was, I thought. But I was quickly brought back to my senses by a series of shouted reprimands. The fact that they were being given by an obviously virile young man made them all the more humiliating. His manhood, constrained by his tight breeches, was obviously reacting to the stimulus.

'Chin up! ... Keep belly in! ... Legs apart! ... Keep knees bent!'

I could now feel the sponge between my legs. The camera was trained on me as the male nurse cleaned me after I performed my morning toilet.

'Here you will learn,' the young man was shouting, 'that you always only perform together and to the crack of my whip – like trained animals in a circus!'

My mind was in a turmoil. Never had I felt so frightened. The periodical crack of the young guard's whip was indeed terrifying. Yet I must admit that being drilled and groomed like a performing animal was unbelievably thrilling.

Minutes later it was all over. Not only had we been washed but our hair had been combed and brushed. We were now standing, still at attention, in a line facing the strange mirror. The remotely controlled television camera was still trained on us. Our prison smocks hung down again, our heads were up, our shoulders back, and our eyes were fixed on the wall facing us.

The young guard bowed towards the mirror, as if his part of the performance was completed. Then, leading his dog, he left.

Once again we were marched down the corridor. One at a time we were unfastened from the chain and put away in our cells.

'Half an hour's rest!' said the wardress to me as she shut and locked the heavy wooden door.

Thankfully, I flung myself down on the hard wooden bed, scarcely able to believe that the humiliating performance in which I had just participated had not been some awful dream. But there was nothing dreamlike about the dungeon in which I was imprisoned, nor about the red marks across my face.

It was, I was to learn later, a performance that would be repeated every morning, partly for hygiene, partly as a way of imposing discipline, but also partly because it was popular with the visitors as a spectacle.

8

More prison discipline – and a special parade

A bell suddenly rang from the corridor. A circular hole in the door opened.

'Come to door!' I heard the wardress order. Remembering how hard the woman could smack a girl's face, I jumped off the bed and ran to the door.

'When bell rings twice,' I heard the wardress say, 'you run to door and put head through hole. Now go back and wait!'

Nervously I waited, wondering what was going to happen.

Suddenly the bell rang twice. I ran to the door and, still wondering, bent over and put my head through the hole. Instantly a wooden clamp came down over my neck, holding my head. Looking up and down the corridor I saw that the heads of the other three girls were also pushed through their doors.

Just below each girl's head was a small metal feeding trough.

The fat peasant girl passed down the line of doors, pouring a mixture of soup and vegetables together with lumps of boiled potatoes into each trough. I was feeling very hungry but this mixture did not look exactly appetising – especially at breakfast.

The wardress shouted something in German, and then turning to me said: 'When bell rings three times, it is signal for prisoners to lower head and start eating – quickly! You will have two minutes to eat it all up. When bell rings four times you stop eating instantly.'

There was a pause and then without warning the bell rang three times. I saw that the other girls put their heads

120

into their troughs and started slurping the food. How I longed for something solid – not this liquid mixture. Suddenly I gasped as the wardress pushed my head down into it.

'I said eat, eat quickly. I want to see the inside of the trough really licked clean, and shiny.'

I was soon gulping the stuff down like the other girls.

'Fifteen seconds to go!' the wardress shouted. The girls were all now desperately trying to finish the food and clean their troughs.

The bell rang four times. I looked down with dismay at my still half full trough.

'Stop!'

The wardress came down and inspected the line of troughs, making notes as she went.

'Not bad – three strokes! . . . Bad – five strokes!'

She stopped at my trough. 'Bad – five strokes!'

Moments later she released the catches above the girl's necks.

'Heads in!' she ordered. As I pulled in my head, I heard the sliding wooden cover being secured again over the hole in the door.

Reeling from the experience, I sat down on the stool, my head in my arms. I heard the door being opened.

'When anyone comes in, Red and Blue, you stand up – jump up!' the wardress said menacingly. As I hastily rose to my feet, I saw that she was carrying several sheets of writing paper and a pen, which she put down on the table in the middle of the dungeon.

'Come here!' she said to me. Then she put her hand up my right sleeve, freed the band round my wrist, and pulled off the stiff glove that prevented me from using my fingers properly.

'You sit and write letter to Countess, thanking her for bringing you here for disciplining. Hurry! I come back for letter in five minutes.'

The heavy figure of the wardress turned and left the dungeon, locking the door behind her. I sat looking at the paper. Thank the Countess for bringing me here indeed!

What should I write? Anyway what could I write in only five minutes? I picked up the pen.

> *My darling,*
> *What is going on? I love fun and games together, but this is all too much!*
>
> *Who are these awful people in charge of me? I thought we were going to be together here. But you seem to be using me merely as a humiliated woman prisoner to show off to other people. What other people? Surely not that awful gangster-looking man I saw you with at the airport? And I'm not a prisoner – I'm your little girl friend. Or I thought I was!*
>
> *And this awful dungeon is also too much. So is that terrifying black uniformed guard with that equally terrifying dog. And as for the scene this morning – well, really!*
>
> *Darling, please release me and let's go off together to see something of Romania. I'm sure it's beautiful, but all I've seen is a dungeon, and . . .*

The wardress came in. She snatched the pen from my hand, and picked up the letter. She read it carefully – twice, and then put it down.

She turned back to me and silently put my right hand back into the imprisoning glove and fastened it again to the the voluminous inside sleeve of my serge prison dress. I was nonplussed by her silence and foreboding expression, but I was completely taken by surprise by what now followed.

The wardress picked up my letter again, and then slowly and deliberately tore it up. Then she turned and smacked me twice hard across the face.

'You silly girl! You never learn! Countess not want to read that rubbish. She want to read thanks for bringing you here as prisoner. She want to read how you enjoying it! You want more punishment? You get more! You get ten strokes for impertinence – this impertinent letter!'

With that she strode out of the dungeon, taking the

122

paper and pen with her, whilst I reeled under the shock of seeing my letter being torn up, of being yet again at the receiving end of the wardress's strong arm, and of once again having my fingers imprisoned in the stiff gloves.

I staggered to the hard wooden bunk. But hardly had I laid down, when evidently alerted by the watching television camera, the wardress stormed in again.

'It is forbidden to lie down on bed during day!' she shouted, raising her hand menacingly. Hastily I rose to my feet. How I had longed to lie down. The wardress left, locking the door behind her, leaving me alternatively walking up and down the small dungeon like a caged beast, and sitting motionless on the hard stool at the table, sobbing into my crossed arms.

'*Heraus! Schnell!*' I heard the wardress shouting out in the corridor. My door was unlocked. 'Red and Blue! Out! Quickly! Time for Daily Punishment Parade!'

Punishment Parade! I was terrified as I ran out into the corridor and quickly took my place in the line of girls.

I longed to run away and escape. But I saw that the heavy door at the end of the corridor was firmly closed. Anyway, I thought ruefully, even if I did manage to get out of the castle, where could I go dressed in this awful and distinctive striped prison garb. And the Countess had my handbag, with my airline tickets and passport, as well as all my money, my credit cards, cheque book and diary. So I would be helpless. No, there was no escape from what was now going to happen to me.

'Hold out right arms!'

The male nurse and the peasant girl were coming down the line of women fastening each one's right wrist to a chain – and this time the chain was much heavier. Then, instead of being told to hold out our left legs, we were ordered to hold out our left arms, so that we could be attached to another heavy chain.

I was now standing helpless in the chain gang. My legs were free, but both my wrists were pulled down by the weight of the heavy chains.

'Open mouths!'

The wardress came down the line thrusting a ball gag into each girl's mouth. It was held tightly in place by a strap that fastened behind the girl's head. I found my mouth was held wide open. I could not now say a word. I longed to pull the gag off, or at least ease it a little. But with both my hands chained down to my side, there was nothing I could do.

Then I saw the male nurse was holding what seemed to be several blindfolds. He slipped one over the leading girl's eyes and tied it around her head. He came on down the line, repeating the process. I was scared stiff when he put one of the blindfolds on me and I found that I was in total darkness.

I heard the big door at the end of the corridor being opened.

'Quick. March!'

The line of girls stumbled forward – but where to, I wondered anxiously, the words 'Punishment Parade' going round and round in my mind.

9

Punishment and the whip!

Chained together by both wrists, we stumbled along the corridor, a line of gagged and blindfolded young women, up the spiral staircase and along another stone corridor.

'*Halte!*'

I heard the noise of a heavy door being opened and then shut and locked behind us. Security is certainly very tight, I thought.

I heard voices. Some people were laughing and chatting. I recognised the voice of the Countess. How awful to be seen by people like this. I longed to call out in protest but, of course, could not do so.

Then I heard the leading girl's wrists being unfastened from the heavy chains and something being done to the girl. I heard the wardress apparently reading something out, and then creaking noises as if something wooden was being turned. But of course, thrown into darkness as I was, I could see nothing.

Suddenly there was a whistling noise, and the noise of a whip on flesh, followed by a choking grunt from the girl and cruel laughs from the people apparently watching. The noises were repeated. A muzzled girl was being whipped!

I counted ten strokes. Ten strokes! I was terrified.

Then I heard a noise as if a sobbing girl was being reluctantly led across the room to something else. Scared almost out of my wits, I heard a noise as if something wooden was being closed. The wardress called out something. Again I heard laughs, and again a whistling noise, followed by a little grunt. The girl was being punished again!

The beating continued and then I heard the girl being re-fastened to our chain gang. Moments later I heard the girl immediately ahead of me being unfastened. I heard more laughter and the girl's own little grunts of pain and protest as the whole process was repeated. Horrified, I realised that I would be next. I waited trembling with fear.

Eventually I heard the girl's wrists being re-fastened to the chains just in front of me. Then my own were gripped and unfastened. I was led forward. I felt the wardress unfasten the securing bands around the wrists of my heavy prison dress. Suddenly it was pulled off me. I was now stark naked, but still in darkness and gagged. It was a humiliating and terrifying feeling.

I felt myself being pushed backwards against something curved. I wanted to cry out in protest, but could only give a little grunt. This was greeted with laughter. My wrists were raised high above my head and fastened back to a ring. The curved apparatus behind me was now turned.

I was lifted off the ground by my wrists, but my back and buttocks were still resting back on the strange machine to which I was attached. I felt my ankles now being pulled down and similarly fastened. I was now arched right back. My breasts, belly and thighs must be well displayed, I realised with a blush.

Suddenly the whole apparatus to which I was attached turned again. I felt my head rising and then begin to fall. My whole weight was now on my ankles. I tried to scream. Again my little grunts were greeted with laughter. I was now held upside down, with my arms pulled back below my head. It was a strange sensation.

Then, I felt the blindfold being unfastened by the wardress. I blinked in the bright light as it was removed. I saw that I was strapped, upside down, to a large wooden wheel.

It took me a little time to see things straight, but I could not miss the figure of the young guard standing right in front of my naked and exposed body with a terrifying looking long black whip in his hand. He was stripped to the waist, his muscular and well oiled torso glistening. He was playing with the whip, flicking it so that it gave little cracks. Terrified, I could hardly take my eyes off it.

Again I tried to cry out. Again my little grunts were

greeted with laughter, coming I now saw, from a gallery overlooking the bare room. There seemed to be half a dozen people there, seated comfortably and drinking coffee. I saw the Countess, dressed immaculately as ever in a well cut blue suit. She was talking animatedly to the man I had seen her with at the airport – the gangster.

She was pointing at me as she talked. I felt very ashamed, both at being naked and at the inhuman appearance that, I realised, the large ball gag in my mouth would give me.

Suddenly I heard the voice of the wardress, reading out aloud from a notebook with red and blue markings.

'Red and Blue. Aged thirty. Irish. Married. Her husband thinks she is on a holiday with a girl friend. Not yet used for breeding. Ten strokes of the whip for refusing to have head shaved!'

I shivered with fear.

The grim faced wardress nodded to the young guard. He raised his whip. The spectators stopped talking, their eyes gleaming. I gave a little whimper of fear from behind my gag, my eyes staring at the whip. Then he brought it down – but cunningly pulled it back so that it simply cracked menacingly, just in front of my naked body. I caught my breath. The young man now had the complete attention of the silent spectators.

Again he raised his whip, and again he pulled it back, appearing to bring it hard across my body. Again I was left without a mark physically, but mentally I was in a turmoil of fear and dreaded anticipation.

For the third time he raised the thick black whip. A strong man, like this young guard, could half kill a girl with a few strokes of a whip like that, I thought, and I was by now almost paralysed with fear.

This time he delayed pulling the whip back by a split second, and it caught the undersides of my breasts as I hung there upside down. It was a relatively gentle stroke, but it hurt terribly and left a long red mark. I was screaming my head off from behind my gag, and the spectators were eagerly pointing to the stripe across my breasts.

'One!' called out the wardress in a loud voice.

Oh no! I tried to cry out. Not another nine! But a second later the next stroke caught me unexpectedly across the front of my thighs. It was a slightly harder stroke and it too left a clear mark.

'Two!' called out the wardress.

The guard now came up and felt the soft belly that was so invitingly displayed in front of him. He raised his hand slightly to feel the hairless mound.

'Yes,' he said in heavily accented English to the enthralled spectators, 'a ladder of five red stripes would look very pretty here – and show off my expertise and accuracy with the whip. I will place the first across the top of the girl's beauty lips, the next across the mound just where the beauty lips end, and the next three equally spaced up to the navel.'

Ignoring my suppressed screams of pain, he carefully and accurately carried out his self appointed task, earning with each stroke a little round of applause from the enthusiastically watching spectators.

Then he gestured to the wardress for the wheel to be reversed again so that I was now hanging from by wrists again, no longer upside down.

My ankles were then unfastened and I was turned round so that, still hanging from my wrists I was now facing the wheel with my back exposed.

Then the wheel was again turned, so that once again I was hanging upside down. The last three strokes would be across my now exposed back and shoulders. He raised the whip. Scared almost out of my mind, I tried to look back over my shoulders. I saw the whip raised. Again he played with me, pulling the stroke back twice before it hit me, but still letting it make a terrifying crack.

Once again it was the third stroke that was for real: the first in a neat ladder of red stripes across my shoulders.

'Eight!' called out the wardress, shortly followed by 'Nine!' and then 'Ten!'

Sobbing, I was taken down from the terrible wheel. I staggered back towards my place in the line, desperately seeking to ease the pain in my breasts, across my tummy and across my shoulders. My God! I was thinking. How long can I hold out about not having my hair shaved off. Would I and my companions be beaten daily on the wheel until we begged to have our heads shaved?

'Oh no, Red and Blue,' cried the wardress, seizing me by the arm. 'We haven't finished with you yet. You haven't had the cane yet – only the whip!'

She dragged me over towards a wooden stocks, whilst the spectators laughed gloatingly at the sight.

'Bend over!' the wardress ordered. 'Put you head down in this cut away part and each wrist in the smaller ones on either side.'

I looked askance at the wooden stocks. Poor me!

'Move!' shouted the wardress, picking a long thin whippy cane.

Hesitantly, I bent over and lowered my head into a half moon shaped cut-out on the top of the stocks.

'And your hands!'

The wardress then lowered a thick hinged piece of wood, like a plank, which was also cut away in three places. It fitted neatly down onto the top of the stocks, imprisoning my neck and wrists. The wardress locked together the two halves of the stocks with a bolt.

I was now held bending over tightly with my knees bent.

'Knees straight!'

I straightened my knees. Since my head was now slightly lower than my hips, my buttocks were now raised and well thrust out.

'Legs apart!'

I felt the wardress strap my ankles to the bottom of the wooden frame.

'Head up!'

I was now looking straight at a large mirror in which were reflected the Countess and her comfortably seated guests in the little gallery. I blushed as I realised that my raised buttocks and beauty lips would be prettily exposed to them, and in the mirror they would see every contortion of my face as I was slowly flogged.

The wardress read from her leather bound book.

'For impertinence to the Countess, ten strokes!'

Impertinence to the Countess! That's not fair, I wanted to cry out. But gagged as I was I could only shake my head – something that produced a round of laughter from the cruel spectators. How could I have been impertinent to the Countess when I hadn't even seen her until just now? Then I remembered my letter being torn up and the wardress's threat – a threat that I had little thought would be carried out like this.

The wardress now picked up a long thin whippy cane. She came to the front of the stocks so that I could see her. She flexed the cane several times, bending it into a semicircle with her powerful hands and then releasing it again. I caught my breath as I watched her every movement. She made several practice strokes through the air and brought it down with a crashing noise onto the padded top of the stocks, making me jump with fright.

The cane was too thin to really mark or hurt a girl, but it could certainly still sting. Certainly my eyes were on stalks as, once again, petrified, I watched the wardress and the cane.

The wardress made a little bow towards the spectators. She came behind me and began to measure her stroke with the cane, tapping my trembling little bottom, and making me flinch. I was now watching her every movement in the mirror.

'Wait!' came the clear incisive voice of the Countess. 'I think it would amuse my guests to hear the slut scream. Take off her gag. And if she says one word before her caning starts, give her another six strokes!'

The wardress unstrapped my gag. I stretched my mouth with relief. I longed to beg for pity but, remembering what the Countess had just said, I did not dare to say a word.

The wardress went back behind me. So the Countess wanted to hear some screams, she must have been thinking? Well, by God, she'd soon make poor little me, a mere chit of an English girl, scream all right – from sheer fear as much as pain. Perhaps she was also thinking that it would soften me up for herself. In the mirror I was horrified to see the wardress stand back to take a little run. A run!

Seconds later the room echoed with a terrible scream.

'One!' the wardress announced. 'Nine more to come!'

The spectators had a real ringside view as my neat little bottom was striped – though not so exactly, or prettily, as the young guard had done to my belly and back. The fact that she was taking a run for each stroke, spoilt her aim – even if it put the fear of God into me. In the mirror they could see my face twisting and writhing with the pain of each stroke and could watch as scream after scream escaped from my lips.

Minutes later, now crying and rubbing my bottom with my hands, I was marched back to the chain gang of waiting women. Once again I was chained by each wrist to my companions. Once again I was gagged and blindfolded.

Then once again I had to listen to a girl, this time that last girl in the line, being flogged. This time, however, I could follow just what was happening without having to see it, and sympathise with the young woman in her pain and distress.

As I listened to the last girl being thrashed, I realised that the beatings had produced more fear and noise than real pain. We had been used in an erotic spectacle for the Countess's guests, but hadn't been seriously punished. Clearly our bodies were being saved for something more. What? I wondered anxiously.

'A half hour break, for a mid morning schnapps,' I heard the Countess announce, 'and then you can watch these sluts being put through their paces in the gymnasium.'

10

Circus animals and a cruel race

Inside the large gymnasium was a circular ring surrounded by iron bars, just like the cages you see set up in a circus when the lions and tigers are being put through their tricks by the whip carrying lion-tamer.

The cage was open at the top, but the bars curved back inwards with sharp spikes, making it impossible for any animal – or any human – inside the ring to get out.

The covering of sawdust on the floor made it all the more realistic.

The cruel-faced guard, smarly dressed in his black uniform, was the lion-tamer. In one hand he carried a long circus whip and in the other a prodlike cattle goad with two short projections which gave a mild electric shock. Just as a lion-tamer has to rely on his whip and the occasional shouted command to make his animals do what he wanted them to do, so the young guard relied heavily on his whip and goad, as well as on shouted orders, to make us girls perform the tricks we were being taught.

We were uncomfortably perched, kneeling up on little high pedestals like those on which lions and tigers in circus acts are made to sit on when not being put through their tricks by their tamer. The pain of our beatings had now worn off but each of us was now looking at the goad with terrified eyes – each of us had already half jumped out of our skin when the guard had touched us with it.

We were all dressed in tight fitting shiny cat suits that covered our heads and the tops of our bodies. We were effectively muzzled by a zip fastener over our mouths, and the cat suits just had little slits for the eyes, tiny holes under the nostrils, and cut-outs for the breasts. Each cat suit was striped like the skin of a real tiger.

But we were only half dressed in these realistic cat suits, for below the waist we were naked – something which made us even more open to the terrifying touch of the guard's goad. It also enabled each girl to be identified by the coloured strip painted on her bare belly above her now prettily painted beauty lips. The marks of our beatings were still visible on our buttocks, thighs and bellies.

In a ring around the cage, the Countess and her guests were seated comfortably, enjoying the erotic scene as they munched little biscuits and sipped glases of Champagne.

'Now, you, Red and Blue!' The guard pointed at me with his long whip. '*Aufstehen!*'

It was a word of command that I had learnt to recognise – and obey. Quickly, I assumed the same position that, one by one, the other girls had been made to take up: balancing up on my toes, with my knees apart and my hands held up level with my breasts, like the paws of a dog that had been taught to beg. Terrified, I saw the guard coming over towards me with the goad outstretched in his hand. Hastily I parted my knees even more. I had to strain to hold the position. I was frightened that I might topple over. To help keep my balance, like the other girls, I kept my eyes fixed straight ahead.

I would, I realised, be making an erotic picture of a well disciplined strange creature, half woman half animal, being put through her paces by a terrifying young man armed with a whip and cattle prod. To my shame, it made me feel very excited. I could feel my hairless beauty lips becoming moist. I blushed under my cat-like mask as I realised that the spectators would see them to be glistening. I could smell my arousal.

Satisified, the guard turned away.

The girl-cats had already been made, one at a time, to jump on and off a leather covered wooded gymnasium horse, and to roll off it onto a thick rubber mat. Now out of the corner of my eye, I saw the fat peasant girl open the door into the cage and carefully bolt it behind her. She was carrying what seemed to be several different types of hoops.

She held up one, high on the far side of the wooden horse. The guard barked an order. He cracked his whip.

Immediately the girl, Yellow and Black, jumped down from her perch and stood waiting stiffly at attention, her eyes fixed ahead. The guard cracked his whip and immediately the girl ran towards the wooden horse. Just as I had already been made to do so several times, she bounced on the wooden springboard, and did a somersault onto the wooden horse. But this time she hesitated for a moment, looking at the hoop with a mixture of alarm and shame. The guard raised his goad and touched her naked buttocks. With a cry the girl flung herself neatly through the hoop, landing with a neat somersault on the mat.

I felt scared. Some of these young girls were trained gymnasts – used to doing this sort of thing. But I was older and had not done it since my school days. But, I realised, making me perform like the younger women made the spectacle even more arousing for the cruel spectators.

The other two girls followed the first one, jumping back onto their pedestals, like well trained circus animals, after each had been made to jump through the hoop.

'Now, you!' barked the guard again pointing at me and cracking his whip.

I tried to overcome my fear as I jumped down from my perch. I, too, stood rigidly at attention waiting for the crack of the whip. The guard deliberately kept me waiting. I shivered as I felt the sawdust beneath my bare feet. I had indeed been reduced to the level of a performing animal.

Suddenly the whip cracked. I tried to look as graceful as possible as I somersaulted onto the horse. I wanted to go on, but the hoop seemed so high! I simply couldn't somersault through that!

Suddenly I was hit by an electric shock. The goad! With a scream I flung myself through the hoop, and landed untidily on the mat.

'You! Do it again!' shouted the guard angrily, pointing with his whip back at the wooden horse. Scared, I ran back and stood at attention again, obediently waiting for the crack of the whip.

Three times I was made to jump through the hoop, until I found myself doing it more fluently and gracefully. Then, gratefully, I jumped back onto my pedestal, out of breath and breathing hard.

The peasant girl how held up a large hoop of paper.

The guard barked an order and the first girl repeated the trick, but this time jumping through the hoop, curled up in a little ball, and breaking the paper. I remembered, as a girl, seeing a tiger doing the same trick at a circus.

The audience clapped. The young guard bowed with a smile and ordered the next girl to do the same trick through a fresh hoop of paper.

I was very frightened when it was my turn. The idea of having to jump through something I couldn't see through was very unnerving. How frightening it must be for an animal, I thought. But a touch of the goad soon made me overcome my fears.

As I stumbled back to my perch, I saw the young guard acknowledging the applause for my performance.

Then something awful happened. The peasant girl put a match to one of the hoops. Instantly it burst into flames. the girl held it up, just as she had held up the other hoops.

'You!' the guard shouted pointing his long whip at me.

This time I was to perform the trick without the benefit of watching the others doing it first. I looked at the flames. They seemed huge! I was scared out of my wits.

'No!' I cried out under my cat suit. 'Not me! Please, not me!'

'You!' cried the guard coming towards me with the goad.

Terrified, I jumped down and stood at attention, my breasts rising and falling with agitation, my eyes on the flames. The whip cracked. I somersaulted onto the wooden horse. The flames seemed even larger. I would be burnt to death!

It took two touches from the goad before, with a shriek of fear and pain, I flung myself through the flaming hoop . . .

* * *

The whip cracked.

'Down!' shouted the guard.

Four little half naked figures, their backs and legs making a perfect straight line, slowly bent their elbows. Then in unison, their bodies held rigidly stiff, they lowered their bodies until their bared hanging nipples just touched the sawdust on the floor – making a perfect press-up.

I bit my lips under my cat mask as I strained to hold the excruciating position. Twice before I had felt the whip across my bare bottom when I had collpased onto the floor. Twice the whip had made me resume my position. I would not risk the whip again. I could feel the sweat running down my back as I strained to hold the position.

At last the long circus whip cracked again.

'Up!'

Slowly, four panting little bodies were raised until their arms were straight.

Oh God, I wondered, how many more times will this frightening guard make us do this. But, I realised, it must be yet another exciting sight for the silent spectators.

The whip cracked again.

'Down!'

'You! Knees more up!'

The long whip caught my bare buttocks as I ran, my hands clasped behind my neck round the cage, my naked breasts bouncing with each step. Quickly I raised my knees even higher in the air in a perfect prancing step. I was panting with the exertion as, driven on by the whip, I ran round and round, making sure that with every step my upper thighs were raised to the horizontal.

I saw the fat peasant girl put two little wooden jumps onto the well worn track around the inside of the bars.

'You jump!'

I had seen the other girls being schooled like horses over the jumps. Now it was my turn. I knew that I must not slow down or falter before each jump – or the whip would land across my rump. I must not alter my fast stride as I jumped. I must not look down, but keep my head up. I must not drop my hands to my waist to get better balanced, but keep them clasped behind my neck.

The first jump was coming up. Clumsily I touched it with my foot. I felt a sharp crack across my naked bottom as I stumbled to regain my footing, my hands in front of me. Somehow I managed to avoid falling. I resumed my position and my prancing stride. The second jump was coming up. It seemed higher. Desperately I flung myself into the air, cleared the jump and landed gracefully on the other side.

I smiled happily as I heard the applause. But it was not for me, it was for my trainer . . .

The whip cracked.

'Mount!'

Quickly we four girls mounted our exercise bicycles. They were fixed to the floor, and did not have saddles – just handlebars, pedals and a rear wheel.

'Up!'

We stood up on our pedals, our buttocks raised.

The guard came down the line fastening each girl's wrists to the handlebars of her machine and her ankles to the pedals. We would not now be able to dismount.

Then the guard came down the line again, this time holding in his hand several long electric leads that led back outside the cage to where the spectators were sitting. Several were holding little control boxes to which the leads were attached. There was a little handle on the side of each box which could be turned.

The spectators were excitedly placing bets amongst each other, and glancing up at the big clock-like distance meter above and in front of each bicycle. This showed the distance that each girl had been deemed to pedal. The girls, however, could not see these large dials.

I felt the guard part my buttocks. I felt so humiliated for this to be done by a man. But with my wrists strapped to the handlebars and my ankles to the pedals I was helpless to prevent him. I looked round and, horrified, saw that he had a curiously shaped, metal vibrator in his hand. It was attached to one of the long electric leads. I saw him grease

137

it carefully, and then I felt it being inserted slowly up into me. Desperately I tried to clench my buttocks, but the guard just laughed and went on slowly driving it up me. Then he gave it a little pull to make sure that it would not slip out.

The guard went on to the next girl. I wriggled my buttocks, trying in vain to expel the device. There were laughs from the watching spectators. I blushed with shame. I realised that the curious shape would ensure that once inserted, my own rectal muscles would keep it in place.

Moments later I felt a strange little tingling feeling inside me, coming from the vibrator. What was being done to me?

I was then horrified to hear what the Countess was saying to her guests.

'The race will be over five kilometres. The dial above each girl will show how far along the course she has gone. The three red stretches on the dials at Kilometres One and Three, and in the final stretch leading up to Kilometre Five, represent hills. The pedals will then automatically become harder to turn. As the girl's driver, you can control your girl's speed by turning the handles on your control boxes slower or faster. The faster you turn them the greater the series of shocks the girl will receive. They'll soon learn to pedal harder when they feel the shocks! By comparing the position of your own girl on her dial with the other dials, you can see how she is doing. I know that you would rather drive your girls with a whip, but remember that they have already been well thrashed for your amusement, and this scheme is just as exciting – and leaves no marks!'

The Countess paused.

'Remember,' she went on, 'that to win the prize, it's no use exhausting your girl too early – she's got a lot of heavy work to do before finishing the course! A good driver will alternatively conserve his girl's energy and then drive her on fast again, so that she does not become utterly exhausted until the final hill up to the finishing line! ... So ... Are you ready? ... Go!'

I felt the tingling feeling build up to a series of shocks. I longed to put my hands back and pull out the vibrator but, of course, strapped as they were to the handlebars, I was quite unable to do so.

I saw the other girls beginning to pedal. As I followed suit I felt the vibrations decrease. Then just as I slowed right down, they increased again. Quickly I turned the pedals more quickly, panting with the exertion. The shocks eased again. But this time I kept on pedalling at the same speed. I had learnt to obey the intrusion inside me – just as the Countess had said.

. I saw that the other girls were all pedalling away at different speeds. Were they too being controlled? But who by? By different spectators? I looked back quickly at the guests seated comfortably outside the cage. I saw that the awful gangster-looking man whom I had seen at the airport was there. He was looking at me and his eyes were gleaming. He was holding a black box in his hand. It had a handle. I saw him give the handle a quick turn and immediately I felt a tingling shock. He was the one who was controlling me! He was my driver! That awful cruel looking gangster! Oh no!

But before I could think any more about him, I suddenly felt the pedals becoming much harder to turn. I had to slow down. It was like cycling up a hill on a bicycle that had no gears. I felt a warning tingle inside me. I tried to keep up the same speed as before, but it was just too much hard work. Then came a nasty shock, then another and another. Desperately I struggled to pedal faster. It was such hard work! I was panting hard, as I was driven on and on by the gangster. What a cruel swine he was!

I could feel the sweat running down my back. I saw that the other girls were also struggling. The shocks were coming fast and furious, making me strain my guts out to keep going faster and faster. I was becoming more and more exhausted.

Then suddenly the pedals became easier to turn again. The shocks eased. Gratefully I slowed down and began to get my breath back. I saw that two of the other girls, however, were being kept hard at it by their drivers. Was my gangster being cunning? Was he allowing me to take it easy in preparation for another burst of fast pedalling?

Indeed a few moments later, the vibrations started again, and I found myself forced to pedal again faster. But whereas I was feeling a little rested, with my energy partially restored, the other girls were showing signs of distress.

But I was allowed no further respite. For God's sake, I wanted to scream, how long is this awful race going on for? I had no way of knowing, and with the zip fastener closed over my mouth, I couldn't call out.

I felt the pedals again become much harder to turn as, unknown to me, I approached the second hill, the one at Kilometre Three. This time my cruel driver really made me keep going. It was awful. I felt I was going to die of exhaustion as the pitiless shocks drove me on and on.

I felt at my last gasp when the pedals suddenly eased. Again, unknown to me, the dial above me showed that I had breasted the top of the hill.

The race continued with each driver keeping his hand on the control box and his eyes on the dials above each girl's head.

Although I did not know it, I was lying second as I hit the final hill. The gangster showed me no mercy now as he drove me hard up it. There was no point, he must have reasoned, in sparing me now to conserve my energies. All that mattered now was to drive me really hard, but cleverly, to the finishing line and so win the prize.

I saw the gangster looking anxiously at the various dials behind me. Evidently his girl, me, must be catching up on the leading one with only two hundred metres to go!

I saw him turn the handle hard. He must have seen my buttocks jump up in the air as the shock hit me. With my ankles strapped to the pedals I had to keep going. Again he turned the handle hard. Again he saw me jump. But I pedalled all the faster!

One hundred metres to go. The leading girl was flagging! She was younger than me, but her driver had made her peak too early. Again the gangster turned the handle, determined to get the last ounce of energy out of me, even if he half killed me.

Moments later I won – by a mere second!

The gangster put down his control box, and turned to receive the congratulations of the other spectators. Ignored by my victorious driver, I was in a state of complete collapse, slumped across my bicycle, gasping for breath.

The wardress paid no attention to me for a couple of minutes. She had seen this bizarre sport too often to be seriously worried about me. Finally she entered the cage and, coming up to me, pulled back the zip over my mouth. She poured a little reviving brandy down my throat. Then she closed the zip back again.

'You'll be all right soon. Now get back into line again!'

She unfastened my wrists and ankles, and somehow I staggered over to where the other girls, all panting heavily, were allowing themselves to be chained up again.

'Lunch!' I heard the Countess say to her guests. 'You'll find it delicious. Follow me!'

The guests departed, chattering amongst themselves.

The guard's whip cracked.

'Back to dungeons – *rennen!*' came the order.

11

A strange encounter

Back in my dungeon, I lay down on the hard wooden bunk, recovering from the morning's exertions.

We had all been given a little slimming, but nourishing, soup in our feeding troughs, and now were resting.

There was nothing to do, nothing to read – and anyway with my hands immobilised inside the sleeves of my smock I couldn't hold anything.

I thought back over the horrifying events that had taken place since my arrival in Romania. What a fool I had been to accept the Countess's invitation.

Idly, I traced the line of bricks in the wall by my bunk. Suddenly I noticed that one smaller brick looked rather loose. Curious, but unable to use my hands properly, I managed with effort to prise it loose with my teeth. At least it was something to do! Astonished, I saw that there seemed to be a little hole behind the brick and in it I could see several pieces of paper.

I caught my breath. Had a previous inmate used to hide writing materials? Had she then used it to hide what she had written? I wondered if I could somehow extract them without the watching television camera seeing what I was doing?

Nonchalantly, as if I was just turning over, I moved so that my body, dressed in the loose prison smock, would hide my head. Then, carefully and gently I put my mouth to the little hole and with my teeth pulled out one of the pieces of paper. I saw that there was writing on it, writing that seemed to have been written quite recently. I saw that there was also a little pencil in the hole.

Carefully, so that any one watching the television display would not notice anything untoward, I awkwardly, but secretly, smoothed out the crumpled sheet of paper. The handwriting was tiny as if the writer wanted to write as much as possible on each precious sheet of paper. Astonished, I saw that it was in English! In a woman's handwriting. I began to read.

Thank God I've managed to steal a little paper and a pencil, and found the secret loose brick. It must have been made by a previous prisoner to hide something. Well I'm going to use it to keep a secret record of what's happening in this terrible place.

Next day
I'm so worried. Because I speak a little Romanian, I was able to understand a strange conversation I overheard between the young guard, the terrifying one with the dog, and the awful male nurse. It all sounded so odd that I'm writing it down before I forget it.

'Are any of them being done soon?' the young guard asked.

'Yes,' replied the male nurse, 'the Countess wants that new foreign girl to be done the next time the film director comes. She says she's got a suitable partner for her and that several dealers might well be interested in her.'

'Good!' said the young guard. 'I think she'd make a very suitable reluctant star. It's making it really professionally that attracts them and their friends to come here and see them for themselves.'

'Yes,' went on the Male Nurse, 'they say their clients really seem to enjoy our girls – even if they are reluctant.'

'But it's exactly that which gives their clients the pleasure and excitement! Knowing that the girls have been forced into it. It gives them such a wonderful feeling of power over a woman!'

'But surely it can't be much fun making love to a girl who doesn't want to respond,' objected the younger man.

'On the contrary, these cruel men get their kicks from the fact that the girl is hating it all whilst having to give them exquisite pleasure.'

'But why should the girl bother?'

'Because, just like here, she's terrified of the whip! She's terrified of the man who has bought or hired her. She knows that the whip awaits her if she doesn't strain every nerve and muscle in her body to give him pleasure. So these rich men really enjoy having a girl who doesn't want to do it but who has to. But, of course, it's not easy for them to find such a girl.'

'Yes,' agreed the young guard, 'no girl is going to agree to make love to some of these men voluntarily – not these days!'

'And that's why the clients are willing to pay so much to use a pretty girl who is being forced into it.'

'Or,' interjected the guard with a nasty laugh, 'to hire, or to buy one from the Countess to take away in their private planes, knowing that the girl is most unlikely to get away – she'll be far too well guarded.'

The male nurse also laughed. 'Yes,' he said 'and the agents say that being able simply to hire one from the Countess for just a couple of weeks for their best clients makes it all so easy – and financially rewarding . . . The funny thing is, the agents say, that at first they just don't realise what's happened to them. But you should see their faces when they finally do!'

The conversation went on in this mysterious vein for some time. I don't quite understand what they were talking about.

Just what do they mean by making it professionally? Making what? And just what is it that a girl is being forced into? Is this something to do with why I have been tricked by the Countess into coming here? Is this why I'm being kept in this awful dungeon? My God! Am I that foreign woman that they were talking about? And if so what did they mean by being done and by being a very suitable reluctant star?

Oh, I'm so frightened.

Just then I heard the rustle of a key in the door. Quickly I thrust the piece of paper back into the hole with my teeth and pushed the brick back with my mouth.

The door opened.

'Out!' ordered the wardress.

Quickly I ran out into the corridor, my hands clasped behind my neck, just as I had been taught to do.

I saw that the other girls were already in the corridor.

'Line up!' shouted the wardress. Hastily I and the other girls formed our usual line. Now what was going to happen, I wondered anxiously.

'Time for a shower!' snarled the wardress in German and then in English for Emma's benefit. She pointed at two little alcoves off the corridor each with a rubber waterproof curtain hanging over its entrance. 'Two girls to each shower, and make sure you wash each other well. But no talking!'

Then the wardress went down the line of girls taking off our thick smocks. We were now all naked.

'You two!' the wardress shouted, pointing at me and one of the other girls. 'Go into first shower.'

I saw from the coloured mark on her tummy that my companion was Yellow and Green. She smiled nervously at me as we entered the shower. I remembered the strange excitement this girl had caused when she first arrived and was being depilated and inspected by the male nurse.

The wardress turned on the shower. It was nice and warm.

'Now get under shower, both of you, and start washing each other – all over properly,' she ordered, handing Yellow and Green a piece of soap. She turned to supervise putting the other two girls into the other shower, and drew the rubber curtain to prevent water from wetting the corridor floor.

'We must . . . obey,' whispered Yellow and Green conspiratorially to me in broken English, as she started to rub the soap all over my now wet body, and then handed it to me for me to wash her in turn, 'or we get punished again.'

I was thrilled to find that one of the girls spoke a little English. I had often noticed Yellow and Green. There had seemed something strangely gentle and almost childlike about her – childlike and yet very attractive. I remembered the Countess's instructions at the airport not to talk to any of the other girls. But what harm could there be in exchanging a few whispers with this delightful girl?

Soon both our bodies were covered in soap lather as we

laughingly washed each other. I could not help feeling excited as she rubbed the soap playfully over my nipples and down between my legs. Our bodies touched continually. We were like little girls bathing together, I thought.

We could hear the wardress busy down at the far end of the corridor. We were alone behind the rubber curtain and naked! As if seeking mutual consolation after all our terrible experiences, we found ourselves kissing each other, our soapy breasts pressed together. I could feel Yellow and Green's hands reaching down and tickling my hairless mound and beauty lips and then my beauty bud itself. She was obviously an experienced girl.

I was gasping with pleasure as the girl started to roll my nipples and beauty bud gently between her fingers. It was a secret and stolen moment of pleasure, made all the more exciting by it all happening behind the wardress's back.

Seeking to return the pleasure she was receiving, I tried to part the girl's own hairless beauty lips, seeking out her beauty bud. But, strangely, she pushed my hands away. Mystified, I looked enquiringly into the girl's eyes. Tears were forming.

'What's wrong, darling?' I whispered, my fingers still seeking the elusive centre of the other girl's pleasure.

'Please forgive me, I'm just so nervous about what's going to happen to me that I can't do anything,' whispered Yellow and Green in a frightened voice as she gently went on pushing me away.

'Do you know then what this is all about?' I whispered back.

'Yes, I think so, but I'm not certain. It's all too awful. You see . . .'

Further explanation was stopped as we heard the wardress approaching. She pulled back the curtain.

'Out!' She handed us towels and then went onto the next shower. Soon all four girls were dressed again in their smocks. But this time their fingers were free.

The wardress took them all up to a long table.

'Now you do some embroidery,' she said, handing them each some needles and threads, and a piece of half completed embroidery. 'You make pretty pieces to be sold in castle shop to guests. Now start!'

I sat down next to Yellow and Green. My head was reeling from what had just happened. What was the poor girl's story? I was longing to ask her, but the wardress, walking up and down behind the working girls, made us keep silent and concentrate on our work.

Then at last the wardress had to answer the telephone that hung at the far end of the corridor from the work table. It was a long conversation. I looked at her. Her back was turned! I turned to Yellow and Green.

'Tell me,' I whispered sympathetically, 'what do you think is going to happen to us? How did you discover? By accident?'

'No, not by accident,' replied the girl speaking English with difficulty. 'My lady friend . . . How you say? My Mistress, she very jealous of my boyfriend. She warn me not to see him again. But I could not break it all off. I loved him – and my Mistress also. But she find out I go to stay weekend with him. She furious. She say she punish me and make sure I give no more pleasure to him. She say she send me to special place in Northern Africa or Italy. I not understand what she means. But now when I see that horrible man I think can guess. Is he from the Mafia? Is he perhaps . . . what you say in English? . . . a white slave dealer?'

'What you mean he's been attracted here by the prospect of finding girls for high class brothels in Italy or North Africa?'

'Yes, my Mistress so angry with me that she say she just wants to make a lot of money out of getting rid of me! She also says that just the video would earn her a lot. But what video?'

'But who was your Mistress – this cruel woman?' I gasped.

'The Countess!'

'Oh no! No!' I cried, hardly able to keep my voice down.

'Oh, yes!' came the whispered reply. 'And I learn that she has punished other girls in same way. She like her girls only to give her pleasure and like stopping them having boyfriends.'

147

'Yes, that's true,' I said. I was remembering the dreadful scene the Countess had made when I had stupidly blurted out, in that strange house in Richmond, that I was in love with Henry. I also remembered the long period of frustration when I was kept locked up in that awful chastity belt. I turned back to Yellow and Green.

'But why are you here, if you are one of the Countess's girls?'

'I don't know,' the girl replied. 'Why are you here?'

'I don't quite know,' I murmured. 'The Countess was so persuasive. She said we would have such fun together. I never expected anything like this.'

'Nor did I!' whispered Yellow and Green. 'I'm so frightened because I heard the wardress saying something about that gangster man being very interested in me. What do you think she meant?'

'I don't know,' I replied, feeling more and more anxious. Doubts and questions were flooding through my brain. But before I could say anything more, the wardress had put down the phone and came striding back up the corridor.

'Silence!' she was shouting. 'The next girl who talks without permission will be flogged. You are here to work, not to chatter.'

12

A terrifying prospect

Back in my cell, my hands still free for once, and my mind reeling from what I had learned, I discreetly put my hand up onto the loose brick. I pulled out the sheaf of papers and read on.

It's now the day after I was taken into the room next to the bathroom – the one with the couches. I was so worried about what was going to happen, and asked the male nurse.

But he simply put his finger to his lips and said: 'Don't you worry your little head about that. The Countess will take good care of you. You're very valuable now!'

What did he mean about me now being very valuable? He simply wouldn't tell me. Instead he just brushed my hair and made me up as if I was a movie star.

Then the horrible wardress woman came in. She put me into a long satin negligée and my hands were tied behind my back. A collar was fastened round my neck and two chain leads were attached to it, one on either side, one held by the wardress and the other by the male nurse. I felt quite help-less.

In silence, I was then led along some passages and into another room. I was dazzled by a mass of bright lights, most of which seemed to focus onto a little platform with a cushion on it. Around the platform were what looked like several video cameras and another on the ceiling above it. A small bearded man was running round adjusting the cameras. An-other man was holding what looked like one of those long boom microphones that you see on television being used to record interviews.

Horrified, I then saw the awful young guard. He had a whip in one hand and was holding that terrifying dog with his other. Were they there, I wondered, to make me look scared stiff? If so, they had certainly succeeded.'

'You very lucky girl,' he sneered. 'We've found you a lovely fiancé.'

He turned to the bearded man. 'Ready, now?' he asked.

The bearded man nodded, and moved one of the lights so that it was shining straight into my eyes.

I was now standing up on the platform. The male nurse and the wardress were standing either side of me, holding me still with their chains fastened to either side of my collar. Behind me was the young guard with his whip and the slavering big dog. My hands were still tied behind my back. There was a silence and I could hear the cameras whirring. I must have been an erotic sight held there helpless.

Suddenly I heard a door being opened, and then I saw the most terrifying man I have ever seen. He was huge, like a Japanese wrestler. Indeed that was what he must have been for he looked Japanese and was naked except for a wrestler's white cotton band round his vast hips and belly, and down between his legs. His body was oiled and gleamed in the bright light. His face was fat and his small pig-like eyes were riveted on me.

I shrank back in horror, and tried to bolt for the door. But the laughing male nurse and the wardress held my collar chains taut, and the dog started to bark behind me. I could hear the cameras whirring as I struggled ineffectually to escape.

Then with a sudden cry the Japanese wrestler jumped up onto the platform and reached out for me. Despite his flabby body, he was immensely strong. With my hands still tied behind my back I was just putty in his hands.

Holding me with one hand, he ripped open my satin negligée with the other. He pulled it back to bare my tummy and gave another wild cry of delight. He put his hand down and touched my intimacies.

'No! No!' I screamed. I saw that the man with the boom microphone was holding it up towards me, as though anxious to catch my every scream of protest.

Then the huge wrestler pulled the negligée back over my

shoulders, baring my breasts. He gave another raucous cry of delight and ran his hands over them.

Again I screamed. Again I saw the man with the microphone holding it towards me.

The wrestler pushed me down onto my knees, gripping me by my hair. I was kneeling on the cushion at his feet, his white cotton wrestling loincloth only inches from my face. There was complete silence in the room, and again I could hear the cameras whirring, recording the well lit scene.

Then still holding me by my hair with one hand, he slowly untied his loincloth from between his legs, lifting it up and tucking into the part that went round his hips. The fact that he kept this part still wound round his waist only served to accentuate his nakedness.

I screamed and screamed as I now saw straight in front of my face, his hairy huge half erect manhood and the large heavy hemispheres that hung down below it.

I screamed even more, when with his now free hand he started to massage his manhood . . .

Still gripping my hair as I knelt at his feet, and still standing over me, he pulled my face towards his now hugely erect manhood.

'No! No!' I screamed. I tried to move my head away, but the taut collar chains held by the now grinning wardress and male nurse held me in position. To my shame I could feel my body beginning to respond to the nearness of this naked male.

'Go on!' I heard the young guard suddenly shout from behind me. I felt a line of fire across my bottom as he brought his whip down. Again I screamed. I felt the angry dog's breath only inches from my skin. Terrified, I lent forward and opened my mouth . . .

Controlled by my collar chains, and by sharp taps of the guard's whip on my bottom, I started to move my mouth backwards and forwards. The wrestler took his hand away from my hair and stood there with his fists now on his hips, his legs apart as I was made to pleasure him. Appalled I realised that the cameras were now capturing an even more erotic sight. Ashamed I could not help feeling yet more aroused.

Suddenly I felt the manhood in my mouth suddenly grow larger and begin to pulse. I felt the wrestler drop his hands to my head to hold it close to him. I saw the bearded man adjust one of the bright lights so that my face was even more brilliantly illuminated. It was too awful.

Seconds later a huge jet of bitter tasting slimy liquid shot into my mouth. I gagged. I could feel my eyes staring out of my head with horror. I tried to move my head away, but was quite unable to do so. I felt some of the liquid running down my chin. I felt the male nurse reach forward and stroke my throat, forcing me to swallow more of it. And I could see that on one side of my face, a camera was recording every moment.

The wrestler stepped back. His manhood slipped from my mouth. There was laughter and applause for the wrestler. I was ignored. The bearded man was looking delighted. He nodded to the male nurse and I was taken out of the room and taken back here to my dungeon, my mind reeling, and the vile taste of the Japanese wrestler still in my mouth.

I feel so ashamed. Not least perhaps because despite everything it had been really rather exciting. What strange creatures we women are!

A few days later
The wardress suddenly came to my dungeon. She said that the Countess had said I was to be prepared to be shown to a client.

'What client' I asked.

'Never you mind,' replied the wardress. 'Just someone who saw the video tape and is sufficiently interested in you to come all this way to see you in person. You're a valuable piece of merchandise now!'

I was washed and scented. My eyes were prettily made up. My hair was brushed back and a ribbon put in it. My mound and beauty lips were carefully inspected to make sure that they were as smooth and hairless as those of a little girl. Then I was dressed in the same satin negligée as before. My hands were tied behind my back, again just as before, and the wardress produced the same collar with its two chains. Clearly I was to be presented looking as identical as possible.

I glanced into a mirror. I saw a beautiful and sensuous young woman. But she looked appealingly frightened and scared.

Once again I was taken along corridors to the same room as before. I was made to stand up on the platform. But this time there were no bright lights and no video cameras. As before, however, the male nurse and the wardress held me helpless with the taut collar chains, and the young guard with his raised dog whip and the ferocious dog stood menacingly behind me. They were laughing and talking amongst themselves, and pointing at me, but I couldn't follow what they were saying.

What was happening? Why was I being displayed in this erotic way. With a little shiver, I remembered what the wardress had said about now being a very valuable piece of merchandise.

Suddenly the door opened. The Countess came in, followed by a short fat man. He had cruel looking eyes, which lit up as he saw me chained helplessly on the platform.

'Isn't she a pretty little girl,' said the Countess in English. 'And very reluctant and shy! Go and inspect her for yourself.'

The fat man waddled over to the bench. He stood back and admired my face. Then he came close. His face was level with my intimacies. He reached up and touched my breasts through my satin negligée. I looked down in horror.

'Head up and shoulders back!' ordered the young guard, giving me a sharp tap with his dog whip. 'And look straight ahead!'

Then the Countess came forward. I gasped as she jerked my satin negligée back over my shoulders, baring my breasts, just as the awful wrestler had done.

I felt the man's podgy hands weighing and feeling my breasts in an expert manner. Then he stood back and nodded at the Countess. She untied the satin bow round my waist, and pulled it away, leaving me looking half naked.

'Ah!' the fat man admiringly exclaimed. He came forward again and began to feel my body lips. I began to squirm with shame and embarrassment, but the wardress and the male nurse held me still by my collar, and the young guard raised

his dog whip warningly. Biting my lips I kept quite still as the man probed and felt.

'*Indeed, an ideal creature for my establishment,*' *he said. Then he ran his hand down over my slender waist and back up over my breasts. I did not dare to move or look down. '*A pretty young woman. She would indeed be most attractive to a jaded palate bored with too much willingness . . . But you are asking so much for her!'*

'*She is worth every penny!*' *replied the Countess cooly. '*And look at those voluptuous hips. She would also breed well, and with the market for blonde children for adoption being what it is, she could soon repay her purchase price. I would even take them off you as soon as they were born – provided they were blonde, of course.'*

I was horrified to hear what the Countess had said. So selling babies for adoption was another of her enterprises. My God! Or was she just continuing what had been a profitable little side line for the camp commandant of this former woman's prison.

'*Yes, that could well come later,*' *the fat man replied.*

I gasped in horror.

'*Bend your knees and thrust your belly forward!*' *ordered the Countess. The young guard simultaneously gave a sharp tap on the buttocks.*

I could feel the man's hand again on my intimacies. I could not help shrinking back.

'*No! Not there, please,*' *I burst out looking down at the horrible little man.*

'*Silence!*' *screamed the guard, bringing his dog whip hard down across my bottom. He pushed me in the small of the back. '*Get that belly thrust out . . . and keep you head up!*

My intimacies were now almost touching the man's face. I felt so embarrassed.

'*See how deliciously shy she is.*' *I heard the Countess say. '*Your clients will love that!'*

Moments later, I felt his finger exploring. But this time it stayed on my little beauty bud. He tickled it and grunted with pleasure at my reluctant but violent response.

'*Yes, I can see that we shall have to take care to keep her* always as pure and innocent as a little girl – and her natural sensuality strictly controlled!'

He stood back and out of the corner of my eye I saw him nod with approval towards the Countess.

'Oh, yes,' he cried in English with a strong Middle Eastern accent. 'This is indeed just as I like it. I think this one will give great pleasure to my clients . . . but there's just one more thing I would like to check.'

He came behind me. The young guard held out a pot of vaseline into which the man dipped a finger. Then he made me thrust back with my buttocks, and bend my knees. I felt my buttocks being carefully parted. I gave a little cry as I felt his finger penetrate me, exploring my tightness there. At last it was withdrawn.

'Yes, very good,' I heard him say. 'My clients often like to use a white woman there – they feel the shame so much more than a local girl.'

He came round to the front of the bench, wiping his hands and smiling. He handed the Countess a cheque.

'Please have her prepared for the journey. My servants will take delivery of her. My plane will be leaving this evening.'

'Of course! By the time we have had a fairly leisurely lunch, she will be packed up and in your car. But you'll be enjoying having her in your secret establishment, and I hope you'll soon come back for another one!'

The fat man and the Countess left the room. The wardress took me back to my dungeon. I was trembling with fear.

Hardly had she locked me up in my dungeon when the door opened again and in came the male nurse and the young guard. They were carrying a large trunk, which they left lying open on the floor.

'We'll be back in a couple of hours with the men who will be looking after you from now on. Then a little jab and it will be goodbye and sweet dreams. When you wake up it'll be . . . well, it would spoil the fun to tell you!' laughed the horrible male nurse.

I'm now alone in the dungeon, I'm terrified. I look with horror at the open trunk. I can see that the trunk contains a *little seat and several straps, together with several small air holes.*

I have written down what happened today in the hope that one day another girl might find this and be warned about what might happen to her. Obviously there is no hope for me now. I am just going to disappear.

Oh, my God! What a fool I was to trust the Countess . . . I can hear footsteps and voices in the corridor. They're coming for me! I must hide this . . .

I read all this with mounting fear and dismay. My God! I thought, was this why the Countess had inveigled me here?

I remembered poor Yellow and Green. Poor girl – and all just because she had a boyfriend! But so did I! Then I remembered, yet again, how angry the Countess had been about Henry. I also remembered the sinister gangster. And the large woman with him.

13

The party

It was about two days later, I think – there was no way of knowing which day it was in the awful prison with its terrifying regime.

'Knock on the Countess's door!' said the wardress, unchaining my hands from behind her back.

I nodded. A sudden feeling of exultation and freedom surged through me. I was dressed in my prettiest party frock – one that was a great favourite with the Countess and which I had specially brought with me – only, so far, I had only been dressed in that awful prison garb.

Then suddenly, without a word of explanation, the wardress had brought me this dress and all my make-up things, and a mirror, and told me to put it on and to make myself look as pretty as possible. The stern faced woman had not brought any other clothes, and I was deliciously naked under my dress. But when I had put on my dress, I saw that a little telltale strip of red and blue material had been sewn onto the decolletage.

'Just to help the clients staying at the castle to recognise you,' the wardress had said mysteriously when she had returned and unlocked the dungeon door. She had looked me over and then, satisfied, she had handcuffed my hands behind me and led me out of the dungeon.

In the corridor outside of the dungeons I had a glimpse of the other girls – all looking radiant and also dressed in party dresses, and each with a little strip of coloured material sewn below the bosom. No one looking at us would have guessed at the pain and humiliation we had suffered earlier in the day. But security was still tight – for the heavy wooden door at the end of the corridor was still shut and we were being lined up and chained together by our wrists.

'Come along, never mind them!' the wardress had said gruffly to me as she unlocked the heavy door before taking me upstairs to the main part of the castle, and to the Countess's bedroom door . . .

'Come in!' I heard the Countess call out.

Nervously I stepped into the room – and gasped. The contrast between this sumptuously decorated room and my bare stone walled dungeons was dramatic. And there sitting at a dressing table, idly brushing her hair, was the Countess herself dressed in a long scarlet and black peignoir.

'Darling Emma! How pretty you look,' She called out as she turned to face the hesitant younger woman. She laughed as she looked me up and down. 'I can see that the wardress's regime suits you very well.'

I wanted to protest but before I could do so, the Countess rose to her feet and swept me into her arms.

'Oh, darling,' she whispered. 'I told you it would it all be very exciting here! And hasn't it? What a lovely game!'

All my doubts and hatred evaporated.

'Oh, Madam,' I murmured bursting into tears. 'I thought you had abandoned me.'

'Abandoned you!' said the Countess with a lovely little laugh. 'On the contrary, I've really enjoyed watching you! It was all so exciting. Weren't you thrilled too?'

'Well . . . yes . . . but that awful young man with the dog? And the terrifying wardress! And that that dreadful male nurse . . . And those dungeons . . . And those awful daily beatings and exercises . . . And the the other girls?'

'Ah! But you're my favourite girl! That's why I've had you brought here now – to help me dress. And as for the guards and the dungeons, and the wardress – well just think how dull it would have been without them! And the beatings and exercises are all very good for you . . . But tonight we're going to have another excitment – a Cinderella Ball!'

'What?'

'Yes, a Cinderella Ball! Why do you think you are dressed up like that, you little goose? I'm having a party here in the castle for my clients and I've also invited the cream of the Diplomatic Corps. You and the other girls are invited too – just to look decorative. But just remember that at midnight a bell will ring, and you'll all have to run out of the room, back to your dungeons and back into your prison garb.'

'Oh no! How cruel!' I cried.

'Yes!' laughed the Countess. 'And you'll have to wear your chastity belt again, of course – just to remind you that you belong to me.'

'Oh no!' I gasped, secretly thinking how exciting it would be to be surrounded by men knowing that they were forbidden.

'Yes, little Emma,' said the Countess in a harsh voice. 'I don't want you disgracing me by behaving like a trollop.'

'Me behaving like a trollop! You beast!' I screamed, suddenly losing my temper. 'I let you do all those dreadful things to me here and you call me a trollop! Well, I'll soon tell all your high and mighty friends just what goes on here!'

'Oh no you won't!' laughed the Countess, evidently pleased by my sign of temper. How much more enjoyable it was for her to tame a spirited young woman! 'No, every word you say during the evening will be being recorded and listened to – to make sure you aren't telling anyone about the secrets of this castle.'

'Recorded?' I stammered, bewildered. 'Listened to! But how?'

'Ah!' said the Countess with a knowing smile as she held up a rather pretty pearl choker and fastening it with a little key round my throat. 'You see, you and other girls will all be wearing one of these pretty little chokers. They look quite innocent, but under the clasp at the front is a tiny little radio microphone. And, when I switch it on with this key, my people will pick up and record every word that you say – or even whisper. There won't be any British people here, but if you try and say one word to anyone about what's happened to you here, or ask them to help you escape, then immediately you'll be taken back to your

dungeon and thrashed to within an inch of your life ...
Simple isn't it, darling?'

'Oh!' I gasped. Was there no end to the Countess's cunning ruthlessness?

'If anyone asks what you are doing here, you simply say that you have come here for the weekend from London as my guest, and that you are having a lovely time. Say nothing more – or it'll be back to the dungeon in double quick time and then a very painful application of the cane to your backside. So just remember!'

I gave a little gasp of fear.

'But otherwise, if I give you permission, you'll be free to dance and flirt with all the handsome and cosmopolitan young men. But at the stroke of midnight it'll be back to the dungeons again and back to the discipline of the wardress! Won't that all be so exciting, darling little Emma? You'll be so longing to dance close to a handsome man, but terrified lest he feels your chastity belt! And you'll be longing to beg him to get you out of here, but too terrified to say a word! Oh, it will be such fun watching you!'

She laughed.

'So, now let's get that chastity belt on you and then you help me dress. And at the party I shall want you to attend on me like a Lady in Waiting. Just follow me about like a little dog until I say you can go off and innocently flirt with the man I choose for you – whilst all the time knowing that I have the key to your chastity belt!'

'Oh Madam, how exciting!' I gasped, genuinely thrilled at the thought of being secretly under the strict control of the Countess in such a setting.

'But, if you're going to be treated like a young girl,' said the Countess, 'you'd better give me your wedding ring and we'd better make sure that you're made up to look like a teenager!'

Three hours later I was standing dutifully behind the Countess as she, surrounded by her guests, watched a wild display of dancing by a troupe of local girls. With one hand, I was holding out a heavy glass ashtray in my hand

– into which the Countess was occasionally flicking ash from her long cigarette holder. With my other hand, I held a goblet of champagne.

Suddenly the Countess flicked her fingers and instantly I handed her the champagne. How I longed for even a little sip, but the Countess had made it clear that, like the other girls, I was only to drink orange juice.

Looking around I saw that the other three girls were each similarly standing behind the chair of one of the Countess's guests. Yellow and Green, I saw, was standing dutifully behind the sinister figure of the gangster. Poor girl!

I raised my nose proudly and sniffed disdainfully. I was the one whom the Countess had chosen to attend on her! I was the one who had to carry the Countess's glass of champagne as she moved round the room talking to her guests. I was the one whom the Countess had told to fetch her food from the sumptuous buffet. And now I was the one chosen to stand behind her during the display of dancing. I could see the other girls glowering at me jealously. It was a lovely feeling. I could even feel myself becoming excited by it all – under my chastity belt.

All the pent-up feeling of resentment at the way I had been treated had gone. But I could not help laughing to myself at the thought of what the rather smug man, now talking to the Countess, would say if he had the slightest inkling of what really went on in the castle. I was tempted to interrupt their conversation and briefly tell him the truth – just to see the expression on his face. But the knowledge of the little radio hidden in my choker, ready to transmit my every word to the hidden monitors, and of the terrible beating that would follow, quickly made me put any such ideas right out of my mind.

I felt I was being looked at, and turned. There, staring at me, expressionless, was the gangster. I saw him turn round and say something to a large, fat, dark-skinned woman sitting slightly behind him. She looked rather frightening.

Suddenly I recognised her as the black woman, dressed

as a nurse or nanny, who had travelled with him. The gangster pointed to Yellow and Green and then back at me. The black woman's eyes followed the gangster's fingers, and shifted from one of us to the other, as if weighing us both up and comparing us in a rather knowing way.

I blushed under the black woman's stare. Who, I wondered, was this terrifying looking woman who seemed such a confidante of the rich and sinister gangster – at least when it came to discussing women?

The Countess must have seen the dark woman's glance.

'Head up!' she murmured out of the corner of her mouth, whilst still apparently listening to the handsome diplomat at her side. 'Look straight ahead and puff out your breasts. That woman's in charge of the women in my guest's Establishment. His own clients like to watch her disciplining them. And I want them both to be really impressed by you. Now, do what you're told!'

What did she mean by Establishment? I remembered what I had read in my dungeon in the secret manuscript about a man buying women, perhaps for just such an Establishment. My God, the gangster must be another one. A white slaver? Did the Countess specialise in providing women for such men?

Feeling hugely embarrassed and yet strangely excited I obeyed the Countess. As the Countess had said, it was just a game. I could feel my nipples straining against the material of my dress. But then I saw that the gangster was now looking at Yellow and Green and whispering something to the black woman.

I remembered what I had read in my dungeon about the men liking reluctant girls – like poor Yellow and Green. I gave a little shudder of fear and disgust.

I turned away and met the eyes of a strikingly good looking young man. I could not help smiling at him in a coquettish way. When the ethnic dancers left the room and the music switched to more usual dance music, he came over to the Countess, and bowed.

'This is my protegée, Emma,' said the Countess, speaking in English. 'She comes from Ireland. Would you like to dance with her?'

I blushed at the way I, a married woman, was being treated like a young girl.

'I should be honoured,' the young man said. His accent might have been Italian, I thought. He was certainly very handsome.

'But no cheek to cheek or smooching, young man,' warned the Countess. 'Just remember that she's still very young and inexperienced.

For me the next half hour was a mixture of thrilling excitement and intense embarrassment. I could feel myself becoming more and more excited by the nearness of this charming young man and yet was terrified lest, if he held me too close, he would feel the belt under my dress. Oh what a clever ruse of the Countess's it all was!

I almost felt myself being carried away as the young man flirted with me, his hand becoming dangerously more daring. I was longing to see more of him. I had almost forgotten the tiny radio microphone and the threat of a thrashing, and was about to blurt out the truth and ask him to take me away, when suddenly a bell rang . . . It was midnight!

I saw the other girls hastily run from the room. I knew I would be beaten if I did not immediately join them. With a sob, I excused myself from the handsome young man, turned and ran out of the room too, not daring to glance back at him. Would I ever see him again, I wondered?

I heard the door close behind me. I turned and saw the young guard. He held his fierce dog with one hand and held a short whip in his other. The dog was snarling at me and pulling frighteningly at his lead. The contrast between the charming and civilised young man with whom I had been flirting only a moment ago and this terrifying young guard brought me down with a bump. How I longed to escape back to the sophisticated world that I had just left.

But I saw the young guard lock the door and pocket the key. There would be no escape back! I saw the grim faced wardress beckoning me. I saw that the other girls were hastily taking off their lovely party dresses. I saw that their heavy prison smocks were piled on a table.

'You! Take off dress!' ordered the wardress. I hesitated. The idea of being naked in front of the young guard still horrified me.

'Off!' repeated the wardress menacingly. I saw the young guard stride towards me, his whip raised, the snarling dog straining to get at me.

'All right!' I sobbed. Moments later I was naked – except for the tight fitting chastity belt. I saw that other girls were also wearing similar belts.

The wardress said something in German and then turned to me. 'You all wear belt all night – just in case being allowed to attend party gives you ideas above your stations. Belt make you remember you just a prisoner here!'

She handed the girls their heavy serge smocks. With a sob of despair, I took mine.

'Form line!' shouted the young guard – an order reinforced by the barks of his dog, growling fiercely as he strained at the leash. I gave a sob of despair as through the locked door came the sound of music and laughter. So near and yet so far!

'Hold out right arms!'

The manacles attached to the heavy chain were snapped onto each of our right wrists.

'Hold out left legs!'

The process was repeated with our left ankles. What would my charming dancing partner have thought, if he had seen me then?

'Hands on heads!'

I felt the heavy weight of the chain hanging from my wrist.

'Double march!'

The guard's whip cracked. Desperately each girl tried to raise her knees high under her heavy smock as awkwardly the line of frightened young women pranced out of the room – down back to the line of dungeons.

14

Shorn!

'So,' said the wardress, 'are you all looking forward to the same thrashing as you got yesterday? Or are some of you going to be more sensible?'

She ran her hands down my fine blonde hair and smiled at me encouragingly. 'Hair is such a simple thing to give up! And you know how much the young guard's long black whip can hurt.'

I shuddered. It was the morning after the party, the cruel Cinderella Party. As on the previous morning, still dressed in our heavy serge prison smocks, we girls were once again lined up in the bare punishment room. Once again we were chained one behind the other by two heavy chains that linked each of our wrists. Once again the young guard, stripped to the waist with his well oiled torso gleaming, like his whip, was striding up and down, cracking his whip menacingly.

But this time we girls were not blindfolded and gagged. On the contrary we were looking with dread and forebodement at the large wooden wheel, strapped to which we had all been given a daily thrashing for the amusement of the Countess's clients.

Silently watching in the gallery with the Countess and her other guests, the gangster, accompanied by his bodyguards and the black nanny, was staring at the exposed faces of the young women. Like those of the other spectators, his eyes were gleaming cruelly, partly at the looks of terror on the girls' faces and partly in anticipation of what was to follow. Evidently, this little scene in itself made worthwhile the very large sum he must have paid to the Countess for the invitation to stay at the castle.

Again I shuddered. How could I voluntarily give up my

lovely hair, my crowning glory? But equally, how could I stand yet another beating from the young guard?

The horrible wardress unfastened the wrists of the first young woman.

'Now, you must be nice and naked for the whip,' she said, taking off the trembling girl's thick serge prison smock.

Stark naked and shivering with fear, the girl let herself be led forward to the wheel. She looked terrified, her eyes fixed on the black whip held by the young guard who was now standing in front of the wheel, drawing the tip of the long black whip up and down on the floor.

Suddenly her resolve broke.

'No! No!' she screamed. 'Not that whip! No!'

'So you'd like to have your head shorn?' said the wardress with a knowing smile. 'So you want to have a nice smooth, bald little head?'

'No! Please! Please!'

'Then it'll have to be the whip, won't it?' said the wardress.

The young guard flicked his long whip, with a smile. The watching spectators held their breath.

'Won't it, little girl?'

'Yes! . . . No! . . . All right!' she sobbed. Then she raised her head pleading prettily. 'But please don't take it all off – just a little.'

'Oh, no, little girl, it's all or nothing,' called down the Countess. 'And you're going to have to beg to have it taken off – to be made into a lovely wig and sold for a large sum to one of our lady guests. A wig made of genuine soft European hair! And every time she wears it, she'll be thinking of the exciting sight of your bald little head – bald, just like that of a real prisoner!'

There were some excited gasps of delight from the spectators, and gasps of horror from the three watching girls. So that was why the Countess wanted us to agree to having our heads shaved. To make more money! Oh!

'Or you must have the whip again . . . Well, which is it to be? . . .'

There was a long pause. The terrified girl was still eyeing the whip.

'All right!' she sobbed. 'Take my hair!'

'No! Say it properly,' the wardress insisted. ' "I want to give up my hair and be bald, just like a real prisoner." '

'I want to give up my hair and be bald, just like a real prisoner,' the girl sobbed.

'No! Say it louder – so that the spectators can hear you . . . or it'll be the whip!'

There was a pause. The cruel young guard cracked his whip sharply. The girl gave another sob. Then she raised her head. 'I want to give up my hair and be bald, just like a real prisoner!' she cried.

'Good! And you soon shall be. Come over here.'

The wardress led the sobbing girl to a strange looking table and stool bolted to the floor. The table had a hole in the centre and was hinged so that it opened around the hole, like a sort of horizontal stocks. She motioned to the girl to sit down on the stool. Then she pulled back the top of the table and closed it around the girl's neck fastening the two parts together with a catch on the top of the highly polished table.

The girl's body was hidden from the spectators by the table top. Her head now appeared to rest on the table as if it had been cut off. But under the table the girl's little hands were scratching in vain to get at the catch.

Slowly and ponderously the male nurse now came over and laid out his implements on the table, alongside the girl's immobilised head. Horrified, the girl gave a scream of protest as he placed alongside her head an assortment of scissors, clippers, razors, a shaving brush and bowl and a pot of special ointment. But it was too late now!

He picked up some clippers. They were old fashioned hand worked ones. He gripped the girl's hair to hold her head still and then slowly and methodically began to clip off a narrow line of the girl's long blonde hair that ran from her forehead to the back of her neck, placing the strands of long blonde hair carefully on the table.

'No! No!' the girl was crying, her hands running helplessly

167

up and down under the table as she watched what was happening in a mirror on the wall in front of her. But the male nurse continued remorselessly. The other three girls watched, all of us spellbound with horror.

Soon another swathe of hair had been cut off, this time running over her head from one ear to the other, and crossing the first swathe at the top. The tresses of hair were carefully laid down on the table next to the first set – ready to be made into a beautiful wig of real long bonde European hair.

The girl now had a strange and bizarre look with two bald strips, each two inches wide, running at right angles to each other across her head. The male nurse turned the girl's head from side to side, and bent it forward, so that the spectators could see and enjoy and the strangely inhuman effect.

Then he picked up some scissors and slowly began to cut off the remaining long strands of hair, again laying them down carefully alongside the others. He now stood back and admired his handiwork, leaning forward to cut off the few long strands that he had missed.

He now turned to the table and began to mix a soapy solution in the bowl, stirring it with the shaving brush. Then he began to cover the girl's head with the lather. He picked up a razor and, holding her head still with one hand, began to shave the whole of her head, periodically dipping the razor in the bowl to wash it clean.

Slowly the girl's head re-emerged from the soapy foam – now completely hairless. She seemed even more inhuman than before – an effect that was heightened as he also carefully shaved off her eyebrows.

But he had not finished. He now began to rub the ointment from the pot into the girl's bald cranium. She cried out as she felt it burning off any remaining stubble, her hands again scratching at the under side of the table as she tried in vain to get at her head. It was an ointment that, rubbed in every day, would also hold back the re-growth of hair and so keep her cranium completely bald.

Still the male nurse had not finished. He now rubbed

white shoe polish into her hairless skin and with soft brush and a polishing cloth began to buff up the girl's cranium until it gleamed.

My God! I thought. I would go through almost anything to avoid that being done to me. I remembered how back in England, the Countess had stroked my soft hair admiringly and said that it would make a very pretty wig for her or her friends. I had not then taken her seriously. But, my God! I certainly did now.

I knew how the Countess would enjoy showing me off to her friends with a carefully polished bald head. She would enjoy the thought of me having to wear a cheap wig at home and in the office to hide the truth. Moreover, I realised, I would no longer want to see Henry or my other men friends, for fear that they discovered the ugly truth and turned away from me in disgust. But, I thought, that awful looking gangster, like the Countess and her women friends, would probably enjoy the erotic sight of a rather overgrown but bald headed young woman in his brothel! How awful!

No, I decided, I must be brave.

I would endure another ten strokes of the black whip.

It was a decision that the other two girls had also taken, and soon our cries of pain echoed through the punishment room – much to the delight of the spectators. It was also, evidently, much to the delight of the smiling Countess for, I suppose, she would not have wanted us to give in too quickly, or there would have been no daily beatings for her clients to watch and gloat over – or to bet on how long each of the remaining girls would hold out for.

One girl giving in every few days must have been ideal! It kept up both the tension and the spectacle, I reflected, wondering how much longer I could hold out for.

15

Inspected!

'Up!' ordered the wardress, emphasising her order with a sharp tap of her cane on Yellow and Green's buttocks. It was about another two days later.

Blushing with shame, but carefully keeping her hands clasped behind her neck, the naked girl stepped up onto the bench. Immediately in front of her was the chair in which the large black woman was sitting.

'Legs apart!' ordered the wardress to Yellow and Green. I could see the girl's blush spreading to the back of her neck.

'Bend your knees – and keep your hands behind your neck, and elbows back!' She ordered, raising her cane warningly.

My God! I thought, standing at attention just behind Yellow and Black, also naked and also with my hands clasped behind my neck. Would I, too, have to display myself so wantonly to this frightening looking woman? How awful!

I glanced across the room to where the Countess and the gangster himself were in eager conversation, periodically pointing to me and to Yellow and Green.

I could hear snatches of what the gangster was saying quietly in English with a strong accent that might have been Italian.

'Yes, it really is very profitable . . . to keep a group of sophisticated beautiful women in a secret "establishment" . . . being looked after and controlled by a strong minded woman who stands no nonsense . . . available to be made, against their will, to pleasure cruel men . . .'

I was straining to catch his words.

'. . . I have certainly found it delightful . . . the sensation

170

of knowing that she herself is horrified at what is happening to her . . . but is too scared of the whip not to try and please . . . the joy of lying back and receiving pleasure without having to bother about giving any in return . . . the feeling of power that comes from knowing that the girl is driven simply by fear of the whip . . . not only the whip held by me, but also the sure knowledge that the whip of my assistant will also be awaiting – unless she strives her utmost . . . Many men do not realise what they are missing by always having compliant women!'

'May be,' I heard the Countess reply, 'but certainly I and my women friends share many of your ideas when it comes to enjoying girls. We, too, also find it exciting to use a girl who is reluctant, but you must appreciate that such girls are rarely available for transfer to establishments such as yours. It's something we specialise in here.'

'That's why I delight in acquiring any women through you, Madam,' cut in the gangster. 'Especially as you can so cleverly arrange for the girls to disappear, so that no one comes looking for them in my establishments, or those of my colleagues. Yes, you've almost a monopoly in the supply of such girls.'

Horrified and still somewhat mystified by what I had heard, I remembered that the Countess had said that the black woman was in charge of the secret 'establishment' in which the sinister man, I had mentally dubbed the 'gangster', kept his women.

As such, she was treated as an important woman – not just by the gangster, but also by the Countess. Certainly she looked very stern. Clearly, she would not, I decided with a shudder, stand for any nonsense from the young women in her charge. But why was she here? And why was the Countess showing off her prisoners to her?

With an expressionless face, the black woman reached forward and began to run her hands in an experienced way over the girl's body. She weighed the girl's breasts, testing them for firmness, and then went on to knead her nipples, looking for a reaction. She smiled when they became erect and the girl gave a little moan. Then she dropped her hands to the girl's belly and hips, examining them closely as if judging the girl's ability to carry and deliver a child. Apparently satisfied, she called out something to the gangster, who in turn also smiled.

'An interesting specimen!' I heard him murmur to the Countess. 'A very interesting specimen!'

The scene was very similar to that described in the notes I had found hidden in my cell. A sophisticated woman was being examined prior to being bought or hired, for use by the buyer's clients. It was their reluctance that evidently attracted men like the gangster and his clients – and the fat man described in the notes that I had found. This, I now realised with a shudder, was one of the demands that the Countess specialised in meeting.

The gangster stood back and turned to the Countess. He looked very pleased.

'But now let's see the other girl.'

'All right, but I must warn you that she may not be available for long . . .' whispered the Countess, nodding to the wardress.

Seconds later, highly embarrassed, I replaced Yellow and Green, standing up on the examination bench in front of the seated big black woman.

'Legs wider apart! No, keep hands behind neck! Bend your knees more!' The orders were coming fast and furious, each marked with a sharp little tap of the wardress's cane across my bare little belly. 'Keep your head up – don't you dare look down! Eyes fixed straight ahead! Elbows back . . . That's better, now thrust out your breasts and belly for examination!'

Horrified, I felt the black hands carefully lifting up my breasts and then gently pulling out my nipples as if I was being milked. I could not help becoming excited.

The black woman nodded and called out something.

'Has she yet . . . nor been used for . . .?' I heard the gangster say. But I could not make out exactly what he was asking.

'Not yet!' she heard the Countess reply. 'But I agree that she has the makings of a very suitable one – just as your black lady says.'

Mystified as to what they were talking about, and not daring to look down, I now felt the gangster's hands on my belly, then on my mound. I bit my lips to stifle a scream of protest as I felt him part my beauty lips and then feel deeply inside me. I heard him give a grunt of satisfaction and then I felt his finger on my precious beauty bud. I heard the black woman make a remark in a disparaging tone. It was a tone that was repeated when the gangster then murmured something to the Countess.

'No,' I heard the Countess reply, 'but, if you are really interested in her, I might be able to hire her to you for a week or two, at a price, in a month's time.'

'A whole month!' cried the gangster.

'Well . . . I suppose I could let you take them both away with you in a few day's time. But I'd have to have her back, this time, in a week – of course, we can then make plans for her to pay another and rather longer visit to your island!'

'Yes,' replied the gangster with his usual unsmiling expression. 'That will suit me very well.'

'And I don't suppose she'll be able to hold out for much longer without having her head shaved. I expect you'd rather have her bald with a long wig of long plaited pigtails?'

'Indeed!'

'Look!' said the Countess earnestly. 'Why don't you watch them both being put through it tonight. See how she performs! And then if you like what you see I can have her sent to your room so that you can try her out.'

My God! I thought. My God!

16

The performance

An hour later, I was kneeling on the bottom edge of a huge bed in a large upstairs room of the castle.

Yellow and Green and I, had both been groomed and scented by the wardress, and then humiliatingly washed out by the male nurse, before being brought up to this room.

Now, blindfolded, we were kneeling alongside each other on all fours. We were naked except for an identifying coloured sash round our waists which was tied in a pretty bow in the small of our backs. My sash, of course, was red and blue, and the other girl's was yellow and green.

Our wrists were fastened half way up the bed poles so that our arms were stretched out.

A bit had been forced into each of our mouths, and was held there by a strap fastened at the back of our necks. Two big bit rings at the corners of our mouths linked the bits and the straps. Also attached to the rings were braided leather reins that led back to the small of our back.

Hidden in each of our mouths was a flat flange of thick rubber that was fastened to the centre of the bits. Normally this lay on the top of our tongues, ensuring our silence. But if the reins were pulled, or tugged, then the stiff rubber flanges would be pushed up against the roofs of our mouths. Ingeniously, this would, in turn, make us raise the back of our heads, pull back our shoulders, dip our waists and push back and raise our buttocks.

Another pole, almost on the edge of the bed, had been fastened behind our knees, holding them quite still and keeping our buttocks raised over the edge of the bed and available to any one standing at the foot of the bed.

As I was on the right, the male nurse had tied my left

ankle to the right ankle of Yellow and Green. My right ankle and the other girl's left one were tied to a strap at the end of the pole that ran behind our knees. Our buttocks were thus forcedly held apart.

Unable to move, unable to see and unable to speak a word, I and my companion knelt on the bed. Horrified, we felt the male nurse grease our well exposed little rear orifices.

Suddenly I heard footsteps and voices. I heard the voice of the Countess apparently ushering her guests into the room. Horrified I thought of their view of my intimacies.

Then I heard the scraping of chairs as they sat down around the bed and made themselves comfortable. I heard the sound of champagne corks being pulled and of glasses being handed round. My God! They had come to see what was going to happen to us! They knew what was going to happen, but we didn't.

'Ladies and Gentlemen!' came the voice of the Countess. 'We're now going to re-enact what was, as you can imagine, something that played an important part in the life of the young women who were imprisoned here. It was, indeed, a very important part – not only in keeping the guards satisfied but also in ensuring that the young women played their role in increasing the national birthrate! Indeed it was firm policy not to release any woman until she had done her duty. I'm sure you will appreciate that for the guards much of the enjoyment came from knowing that many of the young women were married or engaged, and that their husbands or boyfriends did not know what was happening to them.'

The audience gave a little laugh.

'Well, the girl on the right, Red and Blue, is a married woman and her husband does not know that she is a prisoner here. He would be appalled if he knew what is happening to his precious young wife! But neither of these girls will be made to conceive tonight – though, may I remind you that one of our services is to provide a choice of surrogate mothers for clients who want to adopt a child. Clients can be sure that there will be no trouble as the girl

175

will be kept locked up here until after the happy event, and that even if she is then released she will then have no idea of the identity of the adopting couple.'

Horrified, I gave a little gasp behind my bit and twitched my buttocks in protest – something that produced another laugh from the audience. How awful, I thought. Surely the Countess wasn't thinking of . . .?

'Often,' went on the Countess cutting into my thoughts, 'there would be a competition with the girls forced to compete against each other to give the guard the greatest pleasure – and the girls knew that the loser would get a thrashing!'

There was an intake of breath from the audience.

'Oh, incidentally, I forgot to mention,' the Countess laughed, 'the girl on the left, Yellow and Green, had the temerity of loving a young man behind her Mistress's back – something for which she has been punished by being sent here, with the first task of satisfying the lust of our randy young guard! So let's start.'

Suddenly our blindfolds were removed. I blinked in the bright sudden light, and saw that a spot light had been trained on me and Yellow and Green. The spectators were half in darkness, but I saw that they included the dreaded gangster and his horrible assistant.

There was a sudden angry barking of a dog. A door in front of us, by the side of the bed, burst open. I screamed behind my bit, as I saw the young guard standing there with his dog pulling on his lead as if desperate to get at us.

That wasn't the only thing that had made me scream. Apart from his high peaked cap, all that the virile looking young guard was wearing was a pair of black leather chaps that covered his legs and belly, leaving his muscular buttocks bare. Over his manhood was a hugely bulging leather cod piece buttoned onto the chaps. The muscles of his powerful torso and back had been well oiled and gleamed in the spot light.

He bowed to the audience and then came behind us. I gave another scream as I heard the dog growling just behind me and I felt his eager hot breath on my exposed body. My God!

Then I sighed with relief as I saw the guard lead the angry dog aside and fasten his lead to the side of the bed, from where he was to watch the performance with interest.

Then the young guard came and stood behind me. With his left hand he picked up the reins and pulled back my head, making me raise and offer my buttocks to his right hand. I felt this hand begin to play with my intimacies.

I was determined not to respond, and shook my head violently from side to side, and backwards and forwards, bucking like a horse in my efforts to avoid having to present my buttocks to him. But he cleverly used the reins to force the rubber flange up against the roof of my mouth, making me raise my head and arch my back downwards – and thus again raise my buttocks towards him. Again and again I shook my head and bucked, seeking to pull the reins out of his hands, and again and again he mastered me and made me push back with my buttocks.

Finally exhausted and feeling utterly mastered, I quietened down and, obeying the bit, presented my buttocks. There was laughter and applause for the young man from the audience.

His hand was still on my beauty bud, and soon I could feel my juices beginning to run into his hand. I felt so ashamed and so helpless. I was being completely controlled by this awful but strong young man.

Then with a grunt of satisfaction I felt him move to behind Yellow and Green, whilst still keeping my reins still taut in his hand. I saw her reins tighten. I realised that he must now be holding both our reins in one hand whilst with the other he now began to play with Yellow and Green.

Soon she, too, was bucking and shaking her head in a vain attempt to avoid the bit. Then she suddenly stopped, and panting, like me, arched her back obedient to the bit, and presented her buttocks. Again there was a round of applause.

The muscular young guard then put down the reins, and came round to stand in front of us. I could not take my eyes off his straining cod piece.

Then there was silence, followed by a gasp from the audience, as he slowly put his hands to the cod piece, undid the buttons and flicked it off, revealing a large and already half erect manhood. Gloating over the sight of our naked and helplessly chained bodies, he massaged himself. Very soon his manhood was in full erection.

My eyes were on stalks as I watched him, like a rabbit hypnotised by the stoat who is about to kill him. I saw him now pick up a short riding whip with a pretty little red leash on its end, like a small dressage whip.

I sobbed as I realised that I was going to be violated — violated as a little entertainment for the Countess's guests.

The muscular young guard came behind us. I felt him stand between my bent and outstretched legs. My bit gave a jerk as he picked up my reins. I felt a sharp tap from his whip on my buttocks, as if to remind me that he would stand no nonsense.

But I could not help giving a furious buck as I felt something firm and hard press against my rear entrance. Could it be his manhood?

'No! No, not there!' I tried to scream. But the harsh bit in my mouth reduced my cries to little unintelligible whimpers.

Terrified and trying to scream in protest from behind my bit, I jerked forward to get away from the growing pressure. But only for an instant, for the reins quickly tightened, forcing me to push back with my buttocks to ease the pain in my mouth.

I was now bucking and fighting the bit furiously, but I heard the guard laugh as again and again he pulled my head back with the reins, and beat me into submission with his whip.

Finally, exhausted, I surrendered, and guided by the reins and bit, thrust back with my buttocks, and again arched my back downwards.

'That's a better position!' I heard the Countess explain. 'See how my young guard has used the reins to get her backside now nicely curved upwards — ready to receive his upwardly curving manhood.'

I was now held quite still by the reins. Momentarily forgetting the threat of the whip, I desperately tried to squeeze my buttocks together. But my ankles, tied well apart, made me keep myself wide open. Hugely embarrassed I heard the gangster laugh.

The pressure was growing and growing. It was terrible. Awful!

Seconds later, my mouth held wide open by the bit, I gave a muffled scream as, holding the reins and his whip in one hand, and his manhood in the other, he thrust forward. With a grunt of satisfaction he penetrated deep inside me. Oh, how subservient it made me feel as my flesh was stretched by this cruel and virile young man.

It really was the most awful and humiliating experience.

So this was why the male nurse had washed me out behind! It had all been planned this way. Was my usual entrance being reserved for someone else? I remembered with a shock what the Countess had said to the gangster about making me available to him after my performance. My God!

The young guard was now riding me in and out, in and out, pulling back on my reins in time with his movements, and tapping me across the shoulders with his whip as he did so, forcing me to give him more pleasure by moving my buttocks to meet his further thrusts.

But suddenly he withdrew and let go of my reins. I couldn't help but give a little sigh of relief. But then a frightening thought struck me. Had he withdrawn because he was dissatisfied? Oh my God! I thought, remembering the Countess's opening remarks. Did that mean that I would get a thrashing?

'Oh, please give me another chance!' I tried to cry out, utterly humbled. 'Oh, please take me again. I promise I'll be good and will really please you! I will! I will!'

The young guard now stood behind Yellow and Green. 'Let's see if she feels any better than the other girl!' he cried out. The audience laughed.

He now repeated the whole process with Yellow and Green. Kneeling alongside her, I could feel her bucking and fighting just as I had done. Then she too surrendered. She too gave a cry as she was penetrated deeply. I almost felt jealous as she, too, was made to move in time with his movements.

I heard her, too, give a little cry of sad protest as he withdrew from her. Then, accompanied by a little cheer from the audience, he tightened my reins and started to ride me again.

This time he reached forward with one hand. I felt his finger on my beauty bud. Again I bucked but the bit held me back, forcing me to accept his caresses. Against my will, I was soon highly aroused and, like a well schooled horse, was moving only too willingly in time with him.

I was becoming more and more excited and carried away, when with a cruel laugh he suddenly withdrew again. He let go of my reins.

'No! Don't stop!' I heard myself cry out. The audience laughed and applauded the young man for mastering me. I felt so ashamed.

I heard him again penetrate the other girl. Was she giving him more pleasure now? I remembered what the Countess had said about a competition and the loser getting a thrashing.

Fearful of the threatened beating, I had to kneel there in silence, listening to every little encouraging noise that the other girl made. The thought of the thrashing produced in me a strange mixture of savage jealousy and utter fear. What could I do?

Suddenly I was mounted again. Desperately I gripped and relaxed – all thought of my own pleasure utterly banished from my mind.

Then again he withdrew – anxious to spin out his pleasure.

I forget how many times he alternated between us, cheered on by the audience. It was so degrading and yet so frustrating as he occasionally played with my beauty bud to keep me aroused.

Finally, it was when he was in me that he gave a raucous cry, and I felt his seed jetting up inside me. At that moment

I desperately wanted his finger on my beauty bud, but to the amusement of the audience was left crying out with frustration.

Moments later the young guard stood up, buttoned up his leather cod piece, bowed to the audience and to another round of applause left the room.

Then, shocked and horrified, I heard the Countess make another announcement.

'Well, ladies and gentlemen, that concludes that little performance but there will be more! Red and Blue has been promised to one of our guests later tonight,' I saw her give a little bow of acknowledgement to the unsmiling gangster, 'and so must now be taken away to be prepared. However, the other girl, Yellow and Green, will remain tied to this bed for the evening and you are all invited to make use of her! Ladies, you will find a choice of suitable dildos on the dressing table ready for you to strap on before enjoying this young lady! Now dinner is served, but please feel free to come back here between courses to assuage your desires!'

17

Tried out – and escape

It was two hours later.

I had been taken back to my dungeon to rest. Then I had been washed and made up, and dressed – this time like a little girl in a party frock with a blue ribbon in my hair. Then, helpless in handcuffs, I had been brought to the gangster's upstairs suite and handed over to the tender mercies of the big black woman, dressed like a nanny.

'Yes,' the woman said in a strong African accent, stroking my hair, 'now Master want to try you out – behaving all the time like little girl. You run about like little girl; you sit on the Master's knee and look up at him, or whisper into his ear, like little girl; you lisp like little girl and you talk like little girl.'

'What!' I cried. Just what sort of a nut case was this gangster, I wondered. 'But why?'

'Because Master considering hiring you for a few weeks to take back to his private island, to be a little girl, just like all women in his secret nursery on his island.

'Oh, no!'

'Oh yes, I think you soon be one of them! The Countess happy as she will be well paid. And you? On island you live in nursery like happy little girl, you dress like little girl, you eat like little girl, you play with ball and skipping rope like little girl, you even have lovely doll to dress and play with. Soon you think like little girl, and I watch over you to make sure that you remain pure like little girl.'

'Pure?' I repeated astonished, becoming more and more alarmed. 'But why?'

'Because Master's clients want pure little girls!'

'Clients!' I again repeated.

'Yes, many rich men visit island to watch and enjoy our

little girls, rich Arab sheiks, rich African politicians, rich European businessmen. They pay well to see and be pleasured by grown up women, dressed and running around like little girls. You earn Master plenty money – and me . . . And you not think you can escape. No escape from nursery, for nursery garden has high electrified fence, and no escape from island as all the boats kept locked up. No woman has ever escaped from nursery.'

So this particular man's 'establishment' was a sort of nursery for grown-up women! A nursery where rich men indulged their fantasies. I was wondering how they made the women comply when I saw that the terrifying woman had produced a long whippy cane. I jumped with fear as she brought it down hard on a cushion.

'And all the women know they get twelve strokes of black kourbash, made from rhinoceros hide if they ever dare not to behave in anyway like a little girl. They all know what kourbash feels like! Not like this little cane. It really hurts! They all terrified of kourbash. It hangs on wall of nursery. They can't take eyes off it. They all know Master has given me authority to use it to make sure they always behave like pretty little girls. They all know that I not mess about. They all know, when I beat a girl, I really beat her – and I really enjoy beating spoilt women . . .'

I was listening with my heart in my mouth.

'And how they know all this? Because, when they first arrive, they all get initial beating, twelve hard strokes, from kourbash. So they know what awaits them if they ever the least bit disobedient, or just grown up. They never forget initial beating. They will do anything – yes anything – not to have it repeated. And to hammer lesson home, each new arrival gets her initial beating in front of the other little girls. Yes, all beatings are carried out in front of all frightened little girls – but many beatings not needed after good hard initial beating. All women too frightened of kourbash!'

She paused, smiling to herself and tapping the cane against the palm of her hand.

'Yes, all little girls in my charge are haunted all day long by the fear of another twelve strokes from kourbash. And when they in client's bed, or merely just playing in his presence, they terrified he might not be pleased with them. Each girl knows, unless client fully satisfied with her performance as a little girl, then he tell me and I then give her twelve strokes of kourbash. So even in client's bed, fear of twelve strokes of kourbash is all that one of my little girls can think about!'

She paused again. I was trembling with fright.

'And fear of twelve strokes of cane now going to be uppermost in your mind tonight, too! You lucky I not have kourbash here. You also lucky not now time for you recover from a twelve strokes of cane. You get full initial beating from kourbash when I have you in nursery on the island! So now I just give you three strokes of cane to make you remember that slightest complaint from Master tonight and you get twelve from me tomorrow morning!'

'But you've no right,' I cried. 'The Countess . . .!'

'The Countess!' the black woman laughed. 'She quite happy you get cane. She going to make a lot of money out of hiring you to Master. Provided, of course, Master pleased with you tonight! So you now bend over . . . tightly . . . more!'

Horrified and helpless, with my wrists in handcuffs in front of my body I obeyed. I felt my little girl's party dress being lifted up.

'So, I give you three stokes of cane now,' I heard the black woman say. 'Just you remember, if you not lisp and behave like little girl, you get twelve from me afterwards.'

Suddenly there was swishing noise and my buttocks felt as though they were on fire. The pain was awful but, with my wrists handcuffed in front of me, there was nothing I could do to ease the pain, except to hop up and down. The humiliation of it – me, a grown-up woman, being beaten like a child by a nanny, the servant of the sinister gangster – was quite awful.

'You now get second stroke – just to make you think all the time when with the Master of how you must give him great pleasure, and behave like little girl – or else you get twelve strokes from me!'

Down came the second stroke. It was even harder than the first.

'Now third stroke. This hurt a lot! Very painful! But it also make sure you just thinking all the time of my twelve strokes, waiting for you if Master not fully satisfied!'

As she brought the cane down again, she was shouting, 'Think! Twelve strokes! You will now do anything to please Master and not get twelve strokes! Anything!'

'Yes,' I screamed. 'Yes, I'll do anything, but please don't beat me any more.'

The woman put the cane down with a satisfied smile.

A quarter of an hour later the gangster appeared.

I had been kneeling awaiting his arrival and was trembling with fear. 'Remember the twelve strokes!' the black woman had kept repeating.

Suddenly he was there dressed in a long silk dressing gown. He sat down in an arm chair. He beckoned to me silently.

'Go and sit on his knee, like a little girl,' whispered the black woman as she turned to go, leaving me alone with this frightening man.

Remembering the woman's threats, and how Ursula had taught me to run like a little girl, with my arms straight, I rushed over to him.

'Can I come and sit on your knee?' I lisped.

He grunted. I climbed up onto him, like a little girl might, and forced myself to put my arms round his neck. He was horrible. But twelve strokes, I kept thinking, and each even harder than the three from which I was still smarting. I kissed him on the cheek. Was he pleased, I wondered desperately?

Suddenly without saying a word, he snapped his fingers and pointed to the floor at his feet. Obediently I dropped to my knees.

Again he snapped his fingers and without saying a word pointed down at himself. It would have been so easy to have pretended that I did not know what he meant me to do. But the memory of the threatened twelve strokes quickly put that idea out of my mind.

Reaching up, I parted his dressing gown. I was just about to lower my head when, astonished, I saw a manhood that was nearer to the size of a small boy's than that of a large gangster!

My mind was reeling.

Was this the reason he liked his women to pretend that they were little girls? Was this the reason he kept them locked up in a nursery under the supervision of a sadistic nanny? So that they would be too terrified to laugh at him? Was this why his assistant had beaten me and then threatened me with another twelve strokes if he was not pleased with me?

Was I now too frightened to laugh at him? Yes, indeed, I quickly decided, as I humbly lowered my head and took his little manhood in my mouth. I felt him grip my hair, holding me down. Anything, I reflected as my head went up and down, rather than twelve strokes from that cruel black creature.

My neck muscles were getting exhausted when I heard him ring a little bell. I heard the nanny respond to his call. Then he pushed me aside, got up and left for the bathroom, leaving her to prepare me for the next round of her Master's pleasure.

I was led to the bed, pushed down onto my back and my neck was strapped down with a collar and short chain. Then I was blindfolded.

'You use tongue very well now. Or you get twelve!' was her last remark after she had tied me down, before leaving me to the tender mercies of her Master.

Tongue? I thought, as I heard the gangster clambering up onto the bed. Tongue?

I heard the high pitched voice of the fearsome woman. Then I heard her again leave the room. I heard the rustling of silk. Was the gangster baring his body? I heard him pick something up. It sounded long and flexible.

Suddenly there was the crack of a whip – just over my body. The gangster laughed but did not say a word. I gave a little shiver of fear. I felt utterly helpless. I could not get the threat of twelve strokes from the nanny out of my mind.

Suddenly the gangster was kneeling over me. I could see nothing, but I could smell his arousal.

'Tongue!' I heard him order. 'Tongue!'

With the assistant's warning still ringing in my ears, I reached up with my tongue. It touched flesh. Oh no! No, not that! No!

I felt him lift himself up slightly and lowered himself down so that another part of his body would be caressed by my tongue. Oh no! Not there! I tried to turn my head away. Then the awful result of my recalcitrance suddenly hit me. Twelve strokes! Oh, no! I raised my head and submissively reached out with my tongue again. It was disgusting – but anything was better than twelve strokes.

Five minutes later I received the gangster's accolade – on my belly.

Then, still without a word, he fell asleep using my breasts as a pillow, whilst I remained chained down.

When he awoke at dawn, it was to resume where he had left off, and this time it was my breasts that received his morning offering.

Apparently satisfied he told the black woman not to thrash me, but to return me to my dungeons to rest before he took me and Yellow and Green off to his island.

The door of dungeon was opened. The wardress entered. Far too horrified at my forthcoming fate to sleep, I hastily sprung out of bed and stood to attention.

'Red and Blue! The Countess has just had a telegram saying that your sister Teresa is seriously ill and that you must return to Ireland immediately.'

My sister, Teresa? I could scarcely keep a straight face. I had no sister Teresa! But Henry and I had often invented her and used her name in our games and as cover for arranging our meetings.

'Could you ask Teresa if she will meet me next Wednesday at the Ritz at six,' Henry would leave on my answer machine, knowing that my husband John, or someone else might hear it. 'Teresa says that she can meet you as arranged,' Henry would later find on his own answer machine.

Now clearly worried by my silence since arriving in Romania, he had resurrected Teresa as a way of getting me out. Clever old Henry!

'The Countess is very disappointed indeed that you must leave just when your visit was showing such promise, but has booked you on the flight to London tomorrow morning. However she has also booked you back here again in two week's time when she will have a very special treat laid on for you.'

'Oh, how very kind of her, I can't wait to come back to her,' I lied.

A special treat indeed! She had by now got a good idea what that might be! The Countess would have to be very persuasive to get me to return to Romania!

Anyway thank God for Henry!

AN INTERREGNUM

I woke at about five – perhaps because I got used to waking up early in the terrifying dungeons of the Countess's castle, even though I've been back now for over two weeks.

Perhaps it's because I've been so unsettled by all the beguiling telephone calls and letters from the Countess begging me to return – and saying that I was just imagining that she had any sinister plans for me and that, of course, she would not take me back to the castle. She says there is so much to see in Romania. Certainly I saw nothing of it last time, just nothing – except the airport and the dreadful castle. But can I trust her? Might I not end up with poor Yellow and Green in the gangster's so-called nursery – and with my head shaved into the bargain?

Anyway, this morning I was carried away on a wave of excitement with my head full of thoughts of younger girls. Having been humiliatingly treated like one in the castle, perhaps I am now longing to have my own coterie of young women. So I went to my little studio in our new country house which I am gradually getting nice and in order.

I definitely will call it 'The Girls' Room'. Yes, I like the sound of that. It was all Mark's idea. I must tell him how clever he was!

Next day

Yesterday I could have written hundreds of pages about all that went on in the castle – and, of course, Henry will want to know all the most intimate details. But do I really want to share it all with him now? I wonder?

At times I feel closer to him than I have ever felt towards anybody in my whole life. I find it exciting just thinking of him. I am now his only slave girl. There are other women, of course, but I am his only slave. Perhaps, if he got another slave, I could be promoted to Head Slave with extra little rewards – I could, maybe, help to train his other slaves!

Next day

John has gone off to his office so I'm in my new little girls' room thinking up some lovely fantasies! One side of the room is all mirrors and as I look at myself I can't help wishing that the Countess was astride me once again – despite the dreadful way she treated me in the castle, and what she may have been planning for the future. If only she was beating me now!

Oh, if only Henry was free. I feel so frustrated . . .

I've just rung him. Blast! He can't talk. He's with the nice woman he hopes to marry. God, this makes me so frustrated. I'm in a fever . . .

I've been playing with myself for half an hour – watching myself in the mirrors. It's so exciting! I imagine Henry is watching me. I know he'll be very cross. But I don't care – serves him right for never being available on the telephone when I most need him.

I wonder what the Countess is up to? What's she doing now in that fantastic castle of hers? Oh, I do wish it wasn't all so far away! Or her! Despite everything I do miss her!'

Several days later

I stopped writing up this journal as I was so worried about: –
1. The Countess wanting me back.
2. Mark's new infatuation with me.
3. Henry's possible marriage.

Stop being stupid I keep telling myself.

Henry has been warning me against the Countess. He's usually right. But, in a way, I want to defy him. I know that sounds nasty but he's somehow so smug with his well organised life. I suppose it's not really him being smug – it's just me being jealous. But deep down I know he has no alternative. He has found a perfect person in Henrietta and I couldn't really be jealous of her. I suppose my problem is that I have felt excluded.

Anyway, I must concentrate on my business, make lots of telephone calls, fill up my business diary. The Land Banks were a success and so was CCT; two successes this month already!

Mark is coming to stay for the weekend. I think he's back with Isabella again in Paris – anyway they're friends again. He talks about us all meeting up again next month! Would I like that? Would I!

It's amazing the change in Mark. He's now so good humoured and always showering me with invitations. It's as if I had brought him and Isabella back together again, and now he's so grateful and wants me around all the time as if I were his lucky charm!

I suppose I could argue that Henry is equally much nicer and easier to get on with since he has had Henrietta. Yet he seems to give me 'prime time' when we are together. So why am I worried? It's just the nagging feeling that it's all just too good . . .

Two days later

Mark has been very nice to John and brought whisky and a marvellous cheese.

We had a dinner party for twelve. I merely had to put things in the oven and boil the vegetables as a friend had done all the catering.

Mark had asked me to wear my black dress as it reminds him of Isabella. However, to my amazement and horror, when I was in the kitchen after the first course, he came in, shut the door and pulled the dress up to reveal my bare bottom! This excited him so much that he immediately told me to bend over the kitchen table and in two seconds he had taken me from behind. With all the guests chatting away just the other side of the door, I couldn't scream or do anything. I was terrified. John might come into the kitchen and find a locked door! But it was also unbelievably exciting – there is something very exciting about doing something when you might be caught!

It was all over in seconds. I was flushed and exhausted, and longed to go and lie down. But I only had time to pull my dress down quickly, and push Mark out of the door, before I heard John calling, 'Need any help, darling?'

All through dinner I could feel myself getting very excited thinking of Mark's little seduction act. I had hated it at the time, but somehow now just thinking of it was very exciting.

What would Henry say?

He would not be pleased!

Later

I think of Henry a lot. That wonderful evening on the water's edge at Windsor – our own wonderful Venice. He's now my one and only dominant Master.

I must keep things in perspective. I am a contented little slave – an animal, a dog.

Mark keeps saying that I have a new glow. What can it be? I do feel wonderful with Henry, and yet I shouldn't be, for he's courting someone else. It's all very strange.

At night I don't now think of the Countess or Mark. I think of my big Master, Henry. When I am in my little studio, the girls' room, I lie on my chaise longue, legs apart, first playing with my breasts and then gradually lowering my hands, thinking of my big Master and the walloping he will give me when he makes me confess what I am now doing.

I do sometimes fantasise that the Countess is with me

and that Henry is watching us in the mirrors. Oh, if only the Countess was content just to be my girl friend. She's adorable to be with for a day or two, but then she's grotesque with her dominating ways and her dungeons.

Should I go back just once and see if we could have a normal relationship. But what's normal with her? I'm frightened that I'd end up back in the dungeons, or on the gangster's island, or even worse.

Newmarket

Mark has joined us for the racing. He's very attentive – it's nice.

He had telephoned Isabella in Paris from our house. The call only lasted about two minutes, but he was beaming all the weekend. I long to know where and when they are going to meet. Having encouraged him so much, I now feel suddenly shut out again.

Yet to give Mark his due he's at pains to be nice to me. It's as if he can't move without his 'lucky charm'. I even asked him about taking his lucky charm with him everywhere – meaning next time that he meets Isabella. Oh, Isabella! My Isabella! But Mark just roared with laughter and didn't get my point at all. All he said was how clever and that from now on he would simply call me Lucky.

Lucky indeed!

So Newmarket was spoilt. I went into a sulk, and Mark was too stupid to know why! Oh the pain and anger. I am furious.

Henry, meantime, is equally pleased with himself. Why do I bother praising all his girlfriends and then having to listen to how wonderful they are indeed. Why can't I just be a bitch and say 'Shut up!'

But both their women are wonderful and they make Mark and Henry so happy. So why don't I just console myself with the thought that it's far better being the mistress of a happy man than a boring and unhappy one.

In fact for them it's all working out so marvellously. I've

encouraged Mark and Henry to get involved more with their girlfriends, and they are delighted.

So that's all right – bully for them! Now I'm going to ring the Countess!

I think I'm strong enough not to get too involved again. But it would be lovely to walk down the street with her holding hands . . . going to restaurants together . . . dancing together . . . like we used to do.

After the call

She was adorable. Yes, we shall dance and we shall make love. No dungeons. No awful male nurses or young guards. No gangsters with strange desires. Just come! A quick weekend together. Come!

I am elated!

A weekend with Henry

Another weekend is approaching, and the excitement is building up. It will be the first time I have seen Henry for weeks, since before going to Romania. But we have spoken a lot on the telephone, and I feel that I am more and more becoming Henry's slave, and the great thing is that he welcomes the idea.

This weekend I am determined we shall come to some secret agreement. In particular he must become more in control, more dominant, and I for my part must be more of a willing slave.

I also have to learn to separate his private life from our own relationship. What we have is something completely different. It will not interfere with his future life, it should only enhance it – I must explain this better to him. As far I am concerned he will probably have a wife and a perfect family life – just as I have. We can both take a mild interest in our respective family lives, but this secret will be something special, just between the two of us. It will be a ripple, a constant electric current which runs in both our houses. The odd letter or telephone call will jolt us into our roles. If the slave is not reporting, she will get a nasty letter from her Master demanding full details, and of course he will be telling her what punishments she will be given if she does not do as he tells her.

This black diary has been the start. It sits in a drawer in my girls' room. This is where I can be quiet and undisturbed as I think of my Master, and fantasise about him. It's also the room into which, hopefully, I can invite girlfriends without risk of being disturbed – but that will be for later . . .

Saturday

I drive off early. I am determined I shall see my Master passing in his car as he drives off to go hunting with a neighbouring pack. Although he doesn't know it, I shall take the same route but in the other direction and hope to see him. I should be in plenty of time as he rang my car phone at noon to say he was then leaving, and I was then well on my way.

The seat of my car was becoming hot and sticky as I had not any pants on, and as I was getting very excited at the thought of seeing my Master flash past in his hunting clothes. Would he then stop his car and come and check up on his little slave? He would find her very wet!

Before I left, the Countess rang. She was very nice and friendly. You could say she was almost motherly – I loved the feeling, it was almost like sucking at one's mother's breasts. She has asked me to go back next weekend. I know it's mad but I can't resist the idea of being friends with her again. But I wonder is there anything sinister in her so wanting me to go back . . . gosh! What terrifying plans does she have for me there? Would I ever get back again?

I passed first one town and then another on Henry's route, but to my enormous disappointment there was no sign of my Master's car. He must have gone another way.

I so desperately wanted to be touched, and perhaps for him to put me into a chastity belt – for I know that when I get to his house I shall misbehave with myself, and he will be cross.

So when I arrived at the cottage it was deserted! But oh the joy of being here – the garden, his late wife's room, the horses, the smells. The feeling of my Master is all around: his hunting boots, the leather crops, the masterly air – I just love it. I feel an overwhelming closeness to Henry which is very strange as I am not really part of his life.

Oh the joy of being alone here.

I imagine my Master on his horse, galloping very fast. He has his slave, naked from the waist up, on another horse nearby. She is embarrassed but he loves the sight. She has very tight trousers with nothing on underneath. He makes her ride very fast like that, whipping her across her breasts if she protests . . . But, alas, my Master is not here. He is away hunting.

I find his games bag with all the little toys he uses on me. I find the little balls containing heavy weights, which he has forgotten all about. I push them up inside me – and feel thrills of excitement as I move about. Then I start to look at some of his books, particularly at the illustrated ones of slaves like me.

Suddenly I hear the housekeeper. Bother! I pull down my skirt and hope I do not look too flushed – but inside I am like a bitch on heat. I go downstairs.

'Oh hello!' I say. 'Do have tea with me.'

She hasn't noticed anything, so we have tea and talk . . .

I wish she would go away, as I long to get back to the naughty books – and to use the dildo. I wonder if I should try and ring my Master and tell him down the telephone what I am up to. But I remember our house rules. We do not go on each other's territory.

I would love to ring Mark but he has gone to Paris to see Isabella . . . I should be very jealous. How I'd love to be with her. But I now realise, or at least I think I do, that in a really good realtionship, you are not jealous. In fact you want the best for the other person. Jealousy seems to warp the personality – and there are already too many warped people about. Anyway, I am going to visit the Countess again!

Mark had tried to pass it all off as only seeing Isabella on my behalf. But that's rubbish! He is desperate for her, and if she is rude to him he will be back crying for me. But I think I'll just disappear for a bit. Yes, I think I will go back to Romania next weekend, and damn the consequences, for my Master is also booked up then. Mark had wanted me to go to Paris too, but I told him that the lucky charm was wanted elsewhere. Oh I do hope it'll work for Henry too. I do want him to be happy.

Later

Two hour's sleep! My God! My Master has just telephoned to say he will arrive in half an hour. Panic! Bathe, and get ready.

My legs are weak with excited anticipation. I bend them and stand in the corner, facing the wall. But then I remember that my Master hates to see anything when he first arrives. But I hear a thud at the door and a heavy step. It's too late to change my plans now. My Master has returned from the hunting field – or is it from the bed of his girlfriend? I fear he will be too tired – but it turns out to be quite the reverse.

I hear him grunt behind me. I am terrified. He inspects his little slave. Initially he is not pleased. He pulls her hair vary hard as he holds her, and then down comes his cane.

'I'm going to beat you, you little slut. Now bend over!'

His whip was scorching. I wanted to cry. It was extremely painful and he used it a lot. But I knew it was my deserved punishment – and I climaxed several times, like a good little puppy.

It's always different the third time. I felt I was somewhere else – as if I were high on a drug. Is sex a narcotic? I think there must be some sort of drug involved. Is it an addiction? Who cares! But I think I must be addicted.

He makes me lick him behind, lick him clean – and then lick his feet. I turn myself into a completely helpless slave. Oh the Heaven of being a properly trained, humble, slave without a care in the world! A dirty little slave girl must attend to all her Master's demands, no matter how awful they are. Slave girls are not allowed to have feelings, they just do what they are told.

He takes his slave girl from behind. His manhood is strong and hard. It glides in with ease. He keeps it there and then goes in and out, holding it occasionally and making her arch her back so that her little body can accommodate his large size. He is pleased and turns her over to lash her breasts with his whip.

'Now little slave, I want to know everything you've been up to.'

Sunday

The following morning her Master is even more masterful. He gives her ten strokes of the cane and drinks her juices. The little slave climaxes three times, the first time just from thinking about her artful Master.

It all goes too quickly. She is now completely in his power. She feels as if she is being hypnotised by him. If he says 'Crawl', she crawls. If he says 'Stop eating', she stops. She is putty in his hands. Normally this self-possessed woman prides herself on her independence and strength but here she is now a mere little humble slave, begging to be violated and mauled by her Master. She knows that she is just his plaything and, worse, she knows that this is what she wants more than anything.

I tell him about my plans to go back to see the Countess again. He is furious. I must make a promise to write to him next weekend from my home, to show that I really did not go away. Masters do not like deceitful behaviour!

'You will get twenty strokes of my cane, you little tart,' he says, 'if you even dare think of the Countess.'

Should I now tell him about the castle, about the terrifying young guard, about the gangster and the black woman, and about the Countess's mysterious plans for her?

When I did, he firmly said, quite correctly, not to go back there. I know he's right. So I left a message on her answerphone.

Yes, I am a coward, avoiding speaking to her in person. But who cares? I'm just so happy. I wonder how Mark's weekend went?

Part IV

URSULA RETURNS

1

Entrapped again

Idly I picked up the envelope.

It felt stiff – obviously an invitation. Posted in London! Well! But I did not recognise the writing.

Might this lead to some new relationship, some new friendship? Oh how I needed one! Isabella was, it seemed, no longer interested in me and, anyway, she was away in Paris. The Countess was still trying to contact me. A fax had come in from her to my office only that morning, pleading with me yet again to come back to Romania, and saying that I had nothing to fear. Nothing to fear! I didn't trust her, and Henry had told me that I would be mad to risk going out there again.

Henry! Oh how many times had I longed to be able to pick up the phone and hear his cheerful voice. But he was always so busy trying to get married. His intended bride was now living with him and I had been told not to ring lest she pick up the phone and recognise my voice. It was all so frustrating, so unsatisfying.

I slit open the envelope.

Then my heart beat wildly. I felt that fate was knocking on the door.

Although it was an apparently innocuous invitation to an exhibition in a London gallery of pictures by a modern artist, there written across the corner in Ursula's distinctive writing was the message: 'Do come – it would be fun to see you again.'

If the envelope had been written in Ursula's handwriting, I would have torn it up unread. But it hadn't been and now here was the invitation in my hand. Could I resist accepting?

It was now eighteen months since I had finally broken

with Ursula. Her demands, and indeed her power over me, had reached such a pitch that finally I had realised that either I must give up my husband – and the friends, relations and very pleasant lifestyle that went with my marriage – and go and live with Ursula as one of her girls; or else I must give her up.

Ursula had been like a drug. I knew that it was wrong, and that Ursula was a self interested bitch; interested only in her power over other women. But I had been obsessed by her.

I had been thrilled, even when we were apart, by the way that Ursula had established a continuous, twenty four hours a day, seven days a week, strict control over me; over my thoughts, my movements, over who I saw, over what I did, and even over my natural functions.

Only Henry knew of all this, but by comparison, my relationship with him, dominant though he was, had been mild, intermittent, and often rather unsatisfying. It was fine when we met, but he did not seem to understand my need to be constantly dominated, even when we were apart, and to be forced into continuous submission.

But Ursula had understood all right. She was a woman! The control she enforced was continuous and unrelenting in a way that no man could be bothered with. And it had been the control that I had found deliciously exciting.

I had often compared it all to my experiences in the harem of the very dominating Caid. But even he had left the day to day control of his women to his eunuchs. And the continuous twenty four hours a day control that they had enforced with their canes was not dissimilar to that established by Ursula with hers.

Just like Ursula, the eunuchs had kept me in a state of almost continual arousal and frustration by not allowing me any contact with any other man except the Caid himself, and by making sure that I had no opportunity for self pleasure or pleasure with his other girls unless ordered to do so as a special performance. In their case they achieved this by constant supervision. Ursula, like the Countess, had achieved it by the use of one of those awful chastity belts.

Again, just like Ursula, the eunuchs had brain washed me into being utterly infatuated by my Master. Moreover, and this was, I realised, a strange and yet significant similarity, just like Ursula, they too had enjoyed exercising a strict and humiliating control over my natural functions, as a way of making me realise that I was now no longer mistress of my own body.

Finally, fearful for my own mental stability, I had broken with Ursula – much to Henry's relief.

It had been a painful period of readjustment – made tolerable only by my new infatuation with Isabella and then with the Countess. But all the time, whilst firmly sending back unopened Ursula's many letters, and putting down the phone the moment I heard her dulcet voice, I had been hankering after her. I kept thinking I saw her in the street when I went to London. I kept wondering whether I would see her when I was taken to one of our old haunts. I kept wondering what I would do if I did. I had missed the exciting lesbian parties that formed part of Wimbledon, and wondered what Ursula and all her coterie were doing there.

Once again only Henry had known of all this pain. My husband, John, and even my women friends, had no idea what it was that was so often making me bad tempered and difficult.

I knew that Henry was right in saying that Ursula was an evil influence over me, but, goodness, it was difficult to keep away – especially now that I had also broken with Isabella and the Countess, and now that Henry was so busy elsewhere trying to get married . . .

Idly I turned the invitation over in my hands. Yes, I decided, I would go. But I would not tell Ursula that I was going. I would go there with a man. That would put Ursula in her place! I had many innocent admirers to choose from, none of whom would have any inkling of the secret undercurrents that might be flowing. I would then just take a look at Ursula and see if the old chemistry was still working . . .

I held my breath as I saw Ursula coming up to us, smiling. But, rightly or wrongly, I felt completely in control of myself. I could handle Ursula now!

We made polite conversation. Ursula soon established that my male companion meant nothing to me. But, clever woman that she was, she did not push matters at that stage. Instead, I left the gallery wondering what on earth all the fuss had been about eighteen months ago. Ursula was just a highly intelligent and fascinating woman, much involved in the world of art; a woman with whom I could relate in a perfectly sensible and unemotional way.

So it was that, since Wimbledon was fast approaching again, I was not surprised a week later to receive another invitation card, this time to a big very private party at a house that I remembered that one of Ursula's friends, the hostess, used to take especially for Wimbledon. Doubtless several of the women players would be asked too.

'It was lovely to see you again, looking so pretty,' Ursula had written on the back of the card. 'Why don't you come and stay for this party? It'll be such fun and I can give you a bed. Come the day before, so that it will be more relaxing and then we'll go to the party together.'

It was all so beguiling, so innocent sounding. Had Ursula changed? Could a leopard change its spots? Apparently, it seemed.

Hastily, before I could change my mind, I rang Ursula to accept. What would Henry think, I wondered. I had promised him I would not see Ursula again, and here I was accepting a second invitation from her in two weeks. Normally it was great fun confiding in Henry, but in this case it would be best, I decided, not to say a word to him.

I'm sure that Ursula would have smiled to herself upon hearing my eager little voice on the phone. The prey had taken the bait! But, again cleverly, Ursula did not rush things. Instead, she remained a little distant, simply saying that she so much looked forward to seeing me again and that there would be many amusing people at the party.

'But what should I bring to wear?' I asked, anxiously.

'Oh, don't worry, I'm sure I can fix you up so that you'll be a great success,' Ursula replied with a kindly and reassuring laugh.

Yes, thought I as I put down the phone after a very friendly conversation, I can handle Ursula now. I'm no longer obsessed by her, no longer in her power. I can just enjoy her now as an amusing friend. It will be fun to go and stay with her, and to spend a day getting ready for the party.

I felt strangely excited as I stood in front of Ursula's house and rang the bell. How many times in the past had I done this, fearful of a beating and yet thrilled to be Ursula's slave. But those days were all over now. Now I would just have a pleasant relationship with a highly intelligent woman.

So I was taken aback when the door was opened by Rafaela, Ursula's housekeeper, a sour faced woman who had witnessed so many of my humiliating experiences in this house.

'Ah, Miss Emma!' she said with an unexpected but reassuring smile, 'Madam will be pleased to see you. I'll take your case, and you go up to join Madam in the drawing room for tea.'

It was all so strange being treated as a guest in the house where usually I had been used as a mere servant, or worse.

2

The spider and the fly

Ursula was all charm as we sat toying with cucumber sandwiches and sipping China tea. Deliberately I sensed, she did not at this stage want to question me about what I had been doing for the last eighteen months. Instead she talked about herself, about her paintings, about her exhibitions, about the art world, about her travels, about the theatre and ballet.

I sat there spellbound, my eyes lowered. What a wonderful woman Ursula was! Had she really done all those awful things to me? I had been terrified lest Ursula questioned me about Henry, or dragged out of me my involvement with Isabella and the Countess. But instead we were like old friends, picking up the threads again as if nothing had happened in the interim. Reassured, I raised my eyes and smiled.

I hardly seemed to have changed, Ursula said. I was still a pretty, well dressed and vivacious young woman. However, she thought, perhaps I would have to lose a little weight to get down to the almost waif-like figure that she preferred in a girl. It had been amusing, she must have been thinking, for her to have a young married woman as one of her slaves. Now it would so be again! It was time, she must have decided, to start gently asserting her authority and bringing out my inbuilt desire to be submissive.

'Pour me another cup of tea!' she said, quietly.

My heart raced. Was this an order? Was my former Mistress giving me an order? Or was it just a casual request? Either way, I found myself pouring the tea carefully and offering it respectfully to her. ˙

I saw Ursula looking at me enquiringly. Was I accepting my old role as a slave? She saw me lower my eyes in embarrassment. Ursula smiled with pleasure – she was winning!

'You always used to offer me tea on your knees,' she murmured.

I gasped. For a moment I hesitated. I did not dare look up.

'Yes, on your knees,' came the soft hypnotic voice.

I dropped to my knees. I held up the cup, my eyes still humbly lowered. I could feel myself becoming moist with arousal. It was fantastic the effect that Ursula always had on me.

Ursula took the proffered cup and put it down. Then she stroked my hair.

'Little girl,' she whispered gently, 'my little girl.'

I gave another gasp. I felt Ursula gently pushing my head down onto her lap.

'My pretty little girl! Back with her Mistress again.'

'Yes!' cried I with a sob, 'Oh, yes.'

'My little girl! My pretty little girl', Ursula murmured over and over again. I was too intelligent to say anything more. She continued to stroke my hair as I continued to sob with pleasure on her lap.

'Would my little girl like to serve her Mistress at dinner tonight?' she whispered. 'She doesn't have to if she doesn't want to.'

'Oh yes!' I cried. I adored dressing up as a maid. I would love being my Mistress's maid again.

'Well, off you go and report to Rafaela. She'll give you your uniform and show you what to do. You can have the maid's bedroom. Then have a bath and get yourself ready. I shall expect to see a very well groomed and pretty young maid waiting to serve me dinner in the dining room at eight o'clock sharp. Now off you run, little girl!'

I saw Ursula smiling to herself at the sight of me running across the room and out of the door. It had all been so easy, she must have been thinking. I was sure that she was toying with the idea of asking one or two of her women friends in to supper, partly to show off her success in getting me back again, and partly to make me feel more of a servant girl again. But she must have decided not to do so. Perhaps she felt that it was still a little early to present me in public. That had better wait until tomorrow by which time she would have really reasserted her authority over me.

Ursula opened the door of the dining room. She was dressed in a long and striking black robe-like dress. She smiled as she saw the lit candles and the shining silver. She smiled even more as she saw the pretty young maid standing respectfully up against the wall.

I was dressed, or perhaps undressed, in a frilly little black skirt that barely covered my intimacies, a white lace blouse through which my red painted nipples could be seen, a black silk choker collar round my neck, a white little maid's cap on my head, black stockings on my legs, white gloves on my hands and black high-heeled shoes on my feet. My right hand was straight down to my side. My left hand was held across my tummy and from it hung a white napkin. I was looking straight ahead.

Ursula walked slowly over to her maid servant. She looked me up and down whilst I kept my eyes fixed on the wall in front of her. I had not forgotten my training!

Idly she flicked up the front of my short little skirt. Yes, I was naked under it, and my body lips were shorn and painted red, outlined in black kohl in the way that she liked her girls' intimacies to be made up. Yes, indeed, I had certainly not forgotten my training.

'Very good!' she said, and turned towards the table.

Instantly I rushed forward, and held her chair for her.

Then I served Ursula, poured the wine, and stood back against the wall again. I watched as my mistress ate, and drank her first course, whilst looking at some papers she had brought in with her and occasionally writing notes.

Once she dropped the pencil as a test. She smiled to herself as I rushed to pick it up. It really was all going very well, she must have been thinking. Perhaps she would use me as her ladies' maid when she undressed and went to bed. And then, perhaps . . . She would have an early night.

Perhaps she could hardly wait to get her hands again onto such a delicious and pliable young woman!

Silently I hung the robe up in the cupboard. I had not spoken a word since tea time except the occasional, 'Yes, Mistress'. I had just listened to Ursula. It was all, I felt, an emotional moment. It was like coming home. All thoughts of Henry, of Isabella or of the Countess were banished from my mind. What were they compared to Ursula?

I wrapped a long silk peignoir round my Mistress's gloriously tall slim body, and pulled back the fine linen sheet so that she could get into her huge bed.

'Now, girl!' Ursula's voice was becoming increasingly firm as I accepted my authority. 'I don't want you spoiling your uniform, so take it off and fold it up carefully. But keep your stockings and gloves on – and your little cap and black choker.'

Embarrassed, I did what I was told. Ursula's voice was so hypnotic!

'Now come and stand by the side of my bed. Head up! Eyes straight ahead – and don't look down. Pull your tummy in and clasp your hands behind your neck.'

As I strained to hold my position, I felt the tip of Ursula's nails running down my now totally exposed body. It was madly exciting. I gave a gasp as I felt her gently squeeze my nipples.

'Now open your legs and bend your knees,' murmured Ursula gently, 'and let's see what our little maid has to offer her Mistress ... Yes, very nice and soft ... Oh! But aren't you a naughty girl ... So wet and excited! I wonder what you've been thinking about?'

Ursula smiled as she heard me repeatedly catch my breath. It would pay to keep me well frustrated! She lay back and opened her peignoir. This would be the moment of truth. She evidently felt confident that I was now ready to obey.

'Now little girl,' she said, 'maids don't come into their Mistress's beds, but you can always kneel down by the side of Madam's bed and offer to please her. Can't you, little girl? And you know you'd love to do just that, don't you? Well? Come on, child!'

Ursula watched closely as, now highly aroused, I gasped, hesitated for a moment and then knelt down. She smiled again, as after another little hesitation, I submissively lowered my head and reached forward with my gloved hands. This really was going to be delicious for her!

She gripped my lovely long blonde hair, and held it, moving it to guide my mouth and tongue to give herself a succession of exquisite pleasures. I moved my head up and down, and from side to side, to excite her body all the more. I raised it frequently to spin out the pleasure, and then lowered it to start again. I moved my gloved fingers from her nipples to her beauty bud, to join my tongue. Then I moved them back again. Not for nothing had Ursula had me trained at that school in Paris for the slave girls of demanding lesbian women!

What a sense of power she must have been feeling! Of power over a beautiful young creature. She could hold out no longer.

'Drink, little girl, drink!' she cried, and then lay back exhausted . . .

'Now as a special reward,' she told me as I still knelt by her bedside, 'you can come and sleep across the foot of my bed . . . Yes under the bedclothes . . . But don't you dare try and creep up the bed. I just want to feel your warm little body keeping my feet nice and warm all night!'

I was thrilled. I accepted the fact that I had not been allowed any pleasure myself – yet. Surely that would come. But meanwhile it had all been so exciting, and so very excitingly frustrating!

3

The party

The next day Ursula was all charm and smiles. She treated me more like a close friend than as a woman she had used as a maid servant only the evening before. But she was evasive whenever I asked about the party that evening – especially when I reminded her that I hadn't really anything suitable to wear.

'Stop fussing, little girl,' was all that I could get out of her. 'I've already told you to leave everything to me.'

That afternoon she took me off to her beauty salon. But whereas in the past she would stand over me as I was depilated, pointing out the slightest sign of a hair, this time she left it all to the beautician.

'You know what I want,' she said, rather mysteriously to the girl, 'so just do it, and, if you want a tip, don't let my little friend here have any say in what you do.'

I was about to bridle with anger, but Ursula turned to me with a laugh.

'It's all right, darling, just leave it all to me – it's a rather special party. Meanwhile just keep quiet and accept everything.'

When I was finally able to look in the mirror, I saw that, as well as my hair being prettily swept back in a distinctive way, my bare smooth mound had been decorated with pretty designs painted in henna, with more on my belly and the tops of my breasts. And on my left upper arm was painted, like a tattoo, a large 'U de V', Ursula's initials. My eyes had been made up like those of a Middle Eastern dancer and on my forehead was painted a red spot, like that worn by a Hindu woman.

Goodness, I thought, it must be a fancy dress party. How exciting!

I was not therefore all that surprised when, whilst dressing at the beauty salon, I saw Ursula laughing with a pretty young girl whose equally pretty blonde hair had been done just like mine and whose face had also been made up just like mine. Obviously she was another girl going to the same party, also as an Eastern houri. But why, I wondered, had Ursula not been made up in the same way.

That evening I was surprised to see Ursula dressed in a smart cocktail party dress. But I had to admit that she looked very distinguished with her thin face, high cheekbones and short mannishly cut hair.

'Now, Emma,' she said when I joined her, having just bathed and wearing only a towel. 'I want it all to be a big surprise for you. So I'm to blindfold you while I dress you. Now remember what I said about keeping quiet and accepting everything ... You're going to look very beautiful – one of the belles of the ball!' she added with a strange little laugh.

I found it all rather exciting as the towel was removed and I felt something thin and silky being draped over my body. I began to get worried as I felt my wrists being bound behind my back, but remembering what Ursula had said I didn't say anything.

Then suddenly something was thrust into my mouth. I felt my mouth being held open. I tried to spit it out, but Ursula had quickly fastened it with a strap behind my neck. I had been gagged! I tried to cry out, but all that came out were little croaking sounds.

Then I felt something metal being fastened round my neck.

Immediately I heard footsteps. Someone else had come into the room! How embarrassing!

I heard Ursula say something in what sounded like German. I heard a girlish voice reply laughingly – also in German. I felt a pull on the metal collar round my neck and the click of a padlock. My neck now seemed to be attached to something.

There was a pause and then Ursula said with a laugh:
'Now in a moment I'm going to take off your blindfold and

you're going to look in the mirror. Then you'll see how pretty the two of you look!'

Two? What could Ursula mean, thought I, suddenly worried.

'But just remember that you're still gagged and your hands are still bound, so don't think you can start trying to make a fuss! Now let's see how you like yourself.'

The blindfold was removed. I blinked in the sudden light, anxious to know what had been done to me. Behind my gag I gasped in horror.

Right in front of me was a large full length mirror, and there staring back at me was indeed an Eastern houri, dressed in a bright blue silk, but totally transparent, sari. It was gathered at the waist and thrown back over my right shoulder. Through the material I could see my painted beauty lips and nipples, and the henna decoration on my mound, belly and breasts. The imitation tattoo on my left arm was exposed. My eyes were still made up in an Eastern way, but my brightly painted lips were curled over a white ball-like gag that was held in my mouth by a black leather strap – the one I had felt being fastened behind my neck. And round my neck was locked a pretty metal collar, fastened by a large padlock that hung down prominently on my chest.

But it was not the sight of any of this that had caused my attempt to cry out in horror. No, it was the sight of an identically dressed, and equally blonde, but much younger girl who was standing next to me. The two of us were rigidly joined together by a metal rod about three feet long that was fastened at either end of the collars round our necks.

'This is Bridgit, my Head Girl and the favourite,' I was horrified to hear Ursula say. 'As she's my Head Girl, she's superior to you, Emma, and you must do what she says. That's why she's not gagged and her hands are free.'

Ursula fastened a chain dog lead to a ring in the middle of the rod joining our two necks. She held it in one hand and laughed.

'But where she goes, you go, and where I go, you both go.'

Appalled at what Ursula, my beloved Ursula, was saying, I turned and looked angrily at my companion. I had seen her before. Yes! It was the girl at the Beauty Salon!

Feeling furious and with a sudden wave of jealousy, I realised Ursula must have kept her downstairs, out of sight, the day before whilst she seduced me back into her service. She must have sent her separately to the Salon. And this chit of a girl was superior to me! Oh no!

I almost choked behind my gag in my effort to scream out my rage and fury. I tried to get at the girl to tear her eyes out. But my hands were held bound behind my back. I could do nothing.

My eyes blazed as I realised how I had been tricked, tricked by Ursula just as I was thinking how nice she really was.

'Yes, Emma, I'm taking you both, dressed as you are and fastened together, to the party as my slaves.'

She paused.

'Yes I shall lead you both around the party, silently following me everywhere I go like obedient little dogs. Thanks to you both, I shall have a great success. I expect several of my friends will recognise you, Emma, and congratulate me on getting you back into my clutches! But you're going to remain gagged and bound, just to make sure you don't spoil anything. Bridgit, of course, doesn't need to be gagged or have her wrists bound, she's just very happy to be my head slave girl.'

I gave a little grunt of protest.

'Shut up! You ugly old woman!' said Bridgit in a strong foreign accent, giving the helpless me a nasty pinch.

'Old woman! How dare you! You young chit of a girl!' I tried to scream. But, of course, the gag smothered my words.

Ursula went to a sideboard and picked up a thick marker pen.

'This is to help people identify you both, and to make clear which is my favourite,' she said, writing the figure '1' prominently on the forehead of the proudly smiling Bridgit. Then, holding me still by my hair, she wrote the figure '2' equally prominently on my forehead.

'That's better,' she said standing back to admire her two slaves. Then she reached forward to adjust the two saris.

'I want the slit in the sari to be exactly over your beauty lips,' she said, 'and to be tight over your bellies and breasts so that they and your expensive decorations can be seen through the material. You're going to be the sensation of the party and the envy of every woman there – and the men. Oh, this is going to be so exciting. You girls can't imagine what a feeling of power leading you both around will give me.'

Ursula fetched two cloaks and put them on us.

'Now I'm going to drive you both to the party. You'll sit side by side in the back and keep quiet whilst I drive. And don't try and do anything silly, Emma! Just remember that you're locked to Bridgit by the neck. You can't run away to go back to your husband or to your boyfriends, no matter how much you may now want to.'

With a sob, I realised that it was true. And indeed I had been thinking of John, and of Mark and Henry, and of trying to run away. But obviously, no matter how humiliating the situation was, it was quite impossible to get away now.

Anyway, except for feeling bitterly jealous of Bridgit, I was beginning to wonder if it might not all be rather exciting – being displayed to a lot of strangers, half naked, gagged and bound!

Ursula's entrance at the party was indeed a sensation. There was a sudden hush as everyone turned to admire the haughty looking Ursula and her two beautiful, and apparently docile, followers. The fact that one of them was gagged and had her wrists tied behind her, and kept looking jealously at the other, only served to increase the curiosity of the spectators.

The women, and the handful of men who were there, all crowded round Ursula, asking her where and when she had acquired such beautiful girls. Some even parted the front of my sari to get a better look at my painted beauty lips and mound, or admiringly pointed to Ursula's initials on our left arms or to the numbers on our foreheads.

219

'Except for their ages, how alike they look with their identical hair styles and saris,' people kept saying. 'Are they a young mother and her teenage daughter? What a delicious idea! I'd love that! How clever you are Ursula!'

I felt madly jealous when some people, whom I remembered from the old days and who now recognised me again, kept saying: 'Of course, Ursula, it must be very nice having Emma back, but you are quite right to make the younger girl the favourite. That'll make Emma all the more anxious to please you.'

That night, no longer besotted, but still very jealous, I was allowed into Ursula's bed, lying on my Mistress's left, whilst Bridgit, as the favourite, lay on her right.

A cane lay on Ursula's dressing table. I could hardly take my eyes off it. It lay there, a terrifying and yet exciting sight.

'Now, you girls, the one who gives the least pleasure during the night is going to get the cane in the morning,' said Ursula lying back on the pillows, putting her hands behind her neck and spreading her legs.

She laughed as she watched me desperately starting to compete against the younger girl in giving her pleasure. I would, she knew, be thinking fearfully of the cane all night. What a wonderful instrument it was for controlling a young woman – not only controlling her actions, but her thoughts too.

She laughed again as she felt my soft little tongue trying to thrust aside Bridgit's harder one. How easy, she must have been thinking, it had been to get me back – back in her power, back as an eager and submissive slave again.

4

Birched!

I stood facing the wall in the anti-chamber of Ursula's main drawing room.

Indeed, by order of Ursula, my nose was actually touching the wall – just another exciting little act of submission, I thought.

Standing there, forbidden to turn my head round to see what was going on, I thought wistfully of the previous night when Ursula had been treated like a show business celebrity.

What fun it had been going back stage, as Ursula's guest, to meet all the dancers from the visiting Russian ballet company. How impressed everyone had been when I was introduced as a guest of the famous Ursula. For once, when in Ursula's sophisticated international set, it didn't matter that I couldn't speak any languages: because I was in Ursula's party everybody bowed and scraped.

It had been a heady night. I would certainly be able to boast about my night with the stars. I was photographed by several tabloids. How amusing it would be to cut them out and sent them to Henry!

Oh how thrilling being back with Ursula had been! But now look at me, I wailed to myself.

I was very conscious of how exposed I was: the bareness of my thighs, the lightness of the very thin panties I had been made to wear, and above all the little split that would show off my naked hairless mound if I turned away from the wall.

Why had Ursula told me to stand there? What had I done wrong? What was going to happen to me? Trying to be brave, I strove to keep my spirits up, hardening my heart with all my old hatred for Ursula and her evil friends.

In the distance I could hear the girlish laughs of the two chosen ballet dancers – Ursula called them her little Rose Buds. I longed to press my ear to the door, or even to just move from my present horrid position. But I didn't dare do so – for earlier I had caught sight of a young Indian girl, also standing in a corner in the anti-room, and also half naked. But the girl had been crying silently and I had seen the horrible red marks on her back. They had certainly not been caused by Ursula's little cane. Terrified, I had realised that they were the marks of the birch!

I heard footsteps approaching. I was so frightened that I hardly dared to breathe. The birch! My God! But why?

I could hear from the adjoining room the hum of conversation, the occasional burst of laughter, and the clink and clatter of plates and tea cups.

Soon the chatter died away. I strained my ears. I could now hear Ursula talking to the young Asian girl. It was her horrible harsh voice – not the amusing one she had been using earlier when talking to her Rose Buds.

'I will not tolerate it . . . let that be a good lesson for you.'

There followed the sound of little sobs. I longed to rush over and comfort the girl. I wondered who she was . . . what she was doing here? There was so much about Ursula that I did not know and did not dare ask.

The footsteps came closer. The stern voice was talking now to me.

'You are going to get the birch as well, Emma! Bridgit, how many strokes are we going to give Emma?'

I was trembling with fear. The fact that Ursula had that very pretty young Bridgit with her made it worse. How I hated that stuck up young girl with her superior air and the way she kept comparing to Ursula her own fresh young body to my rather older one. And to make it worse, Ursula continued to make it clear that Bridgit, and not me, was her favourite. I knew that Bridgit would be smirking as she enjoyed the sight of Ursula humiliating me, her hated rival for Ursula's attentions.

I heard Bridgit say something in German, and Ursula

reply. I longed to know how many strokes I was going to get, but I could not understand what they were saying. Anyway, what was I going to be beaten for? What had I done to deserve the birch?

'Now, Miss Emma, I'm going to teach you not to have airs and graces when I deign to take you out with me. Your role is to stand behind me in silence, just looking decorative, and to follow me about like a little pet poodle. Instead of which, last night, without asking my permission, you went dashing off speaking to people of your own accord – although you were not of the slightest interest to them. And don't think I didn't see you flirting with Sverge last night! I saw you give him your telephone number when you thought my back was turned – you little bitch.'

It was true, I knew. I had got carried away at the ballet. Yes, I had been enormously flattered that the young handsome dancer should have even bothered to look at me. Perhaps he enjoyed slightly older women, I had wondered. But whatever the reason, it had been a wonderful sensation being singled out and made a fuss of. And, of course, I had been delighted that Ursula had seen with her own eyes that I wasn't just a nobody and that I could attract handsome young men.

How cool it had been of Ursula to pretend at the time that she was not annoyed. In fact it had looked as though she was actually encouraging me. But now she was going to take her revenge! I shivered with fear, for I knew only too well how effectively Ursula could do that.

'This other little slave of mine also thought that she'd be clever and pick up a man at a different party. She also forgot her place as one of my slaves. And so she got the birch. And now she's learnt her lesson.'

Ursula turned to the Asian girl. 'Haven't you?'

'Yes, Madam,' sobbed the girl.

Ursula turned back to me.

'And now you're going to learn your lesson too. You're going to get the birch too. You deserve it, don't you, Emma? Don't you?'

'Yes, Mistress,' I sobbed. What a fool to have thought I

223

could get away with flirting with Sverge in front of Ursula. But, even so, the birch . . .!

'Yes, I don't think either of you will go chasing after men again for a little time,' said Ursula grimly. 'Nor forget that being one of my slaves means just that. As a slave you have lost your freedom.'

Lost my freedom, I thought. Yes it was that that made being with Ursula so exciting. But the birch! My God!

'Right! Now watch this, Bridgit,' Ursula went on harshly, in English. 'Emma, of course, is one of my older slaves, and I tire of her quite quickly. But she knows that giving her a good thrashing always restores my interest in her. It also gets her aroused. She knows all that and so longs to be beaten. Don't you, Emma? Even if you're terrified by the idea! You little slut!'

I felt disgusted. That was supposed to be a secret between me and Ursula. How could Ursula talk about me like that in front of that chit of a girl, Bridgit – and in such an insulting tone.

'Even the threat of a thrashing is enough to get her excited. She can't help it. So let's just see . . . Keep quite still, Emma! Bridgit, put your hand down and feel her. Is she wet already?'

Horrified, with my nose still pressed against the wall, I felt Bridgit's hand on my buttocks.

'Open your legs, girl!' ordered Bridgit. I hated being given orders by my younger rival – by Ursula's favourite. It was so humiliating. I resolved to ignore her. I stood there pouting.

'I've warned you, Emma, that Bridgit is my Head Girl, my favourite. She is superior to you and you'll damn well do what she says!'

With a sob of shame, I parted my legs. But Bridgit had not yet finished shaming me.

'Get those legs wider apart, girl,' she ordered hashly in her foreign accent. 'And now bend your knes.'

Shamefaced, I felt the girl's probing hands. It was, I knew, only too true that even talk of a beating never failed to make me aroused. Bridgit would already be feeling it.

Indeed I heard her say something to Ursula with a laugh as she took her hand away.

'Now stand up straight again, Emma!' ordered Ursula. 'Clasp your hands behind your neck and keep them there. And keep your nose pressed against the wall!'

Out of the corner of my eye I saw Ursula's eyes flash. She looked half crazed as, with easy rhythmic movements, she swung a birch to and fro in a series of practice strokes. The strokes might not have seemed to have great force, but I knew only too well that Ursula had excellent timing when it came to using a cane or a birch, thanks to her tennis and golf. I knew that it was the last second flick of the wrist that would give the birch the speed and impact that would in turn make me scream nicely without being really hurt. And Ursula would certainly make sure that I screamed!

I was trembling with fear as I heard Ursula swishing the birch.

Suddenly there was a definite whistling sound, followed by a crack and a desperate cry from me. I could not help doubling up with the pain as I desperately tried to reach down over my shoulders to ease the stinging in my back.

Ursula smiled cruelly. She let me go on rubbing my back for a minute as I sobbed. She enjoyed drawing out a punishment.

'Don't think that I've finished with you yet, Emma,' Ursula suddenly shouted. 'Now head up! Clasp your hands again behind your neck! And don't you dare move this time!'

There was another whistling sound, another crack and another cry from me, followed a minute later by a further crack.

The birching was over. Just three strokes, but they were enough. I was now sobbing hard as I tried desperately to ease the pain in my back. Never, never, I resolved would I ever even look at a man again. I was Ursula's property now. I belonged to her now, utterly to her.

Ursula smiled as she watched me crying. Doubtless, the same thoughts were going through her mind, and she would be feeling a tremendous surge of power at the realisation that I was again her property, her slave, hers to do with as she liked.

Then she must have decided that it would be amusing to frighten me even more.

'Well, Emma, would you like to see how your precious Sverge treats his girlfriends? One of them is here this afternoon and has been telling us all about what happened to her when Sverge discovered that she had made a date to go out with another man. Natasha!' Ursula called out. 'Come over here.'

With my nose still pressed against the wall, I heard running footsteps.

'Lift up your dress, Natasha,' I heard Ursula say, followed by: 'Now turn round, Emma, and look!'

I turned round. There standing in front of her were Ursula and the hated young Bridgit. But standing alongside them was a very pretty girl, apparently one of the ballet girls but a little older then the young Rose Buds. She was nervously holding up her dress, under which she was naked.

I gave a gasp as I looked at the girl's exposed body lips. They seemed quite hairless – just like my own, but were covered by a little slightly rounded, and curved, triangular shiny silver plate with a narrow little slit down the middle. Round the edges of the plate was a strip of soft leather, sewn onto a line of little holes in the plate to prevent the metal from rubbing the skin.

The plate was kept in place by a single chain between her legs and by two chains that ran up from the top corners of the plate and round the girl's hips. These chains met in a tiny padlock just above the girl's buttocks. The chain running up between her buttocks was also attached there.

'Yes, Emma, your precious Sverge has had his girlfriend locked into an old Russian form of chastity belt as a punishment. It's quite loose fitting and comfortable to wear, but it's also very effective – both physically to keep a girl chaste, and mentally to make her feel that she is no longer in control of her own body . . . And that's what is going to happen to you the next time I catch you trying to two-time me, you little slut.'

'Oh, no!' I cried in genuine alarm, for I could see that the belt was so simple that a girl could be made to wear it indefinitely.

'Yes, Emma! And so just you remember!'

The girl smiled at me, almost as if she was proud of having to wear the strange little plate. I could see that it might be rather exciting!

Ursula turned to the pretty girl. 'Thank you, Natasha. You can go back and join the others now.'

The girl dropped her dress and ran off. Ursula turned back to me.

'And as a further punishment, Emma, you're going to spend the night in the cage!'

5

The cage, the ballet girls and the wheel

'In the cage?' I stuttered.

'Yes, my girl, in the cage!'

I was still reeling from the pain of the birch. 'Oh no! Please, no!'

'Yes Emma – the cage!'

Ursula attached a collar and lead to my neck.

'Now crawl!' Ursula ordered, giving the lead a sharp tug.

'Ouch!' I cried.

'Crawl, I said – on all fours ... Get down. And crawl faster. Faster!'

I knew my destination. Once before I had experienced the bitter and incredible humiliation of being caged. I pleaded with Ursula, my head lowered to the floor.

'No! No! Please, Ursula, don't. Please let me go home. Please ... please ...'

'Shut up, you half wit!' Ursula kicked me with a stiletto heel. She pinned my little neck down with her shoe. Then she kicked me again and pushed me into the tiny cage.

It was so small that I could not even kneel up. I lay all hunched up – a sorry sight. The next minute a thin black silk shroud was placed over the cage, the bedroom light was switched off and I was left.

Alone with my thoughts in the darkness, I could not help remembering the old saying 'pride comes before a fall'. Well, how I certainly had fallen. Who would have believed that the clever and attractive Emma, who only the night before was a star, was now a hidden object locked up in a shrouded cage?

Some hours must have passed. I was in pain – partly from my thrashing and partly from my cramped position. Suddenly I was no longer in darkness. The lights in the room had been switched on. Through the thin silk I could just about make out Ursula coming into the bedroom followed by the two gorgeous Rose Buds.

They were dancing along behind her. One was carrying Ursula's handbag, and the other was gently fanning her. Ursula was at her most majestic – wearing a long golden caftan with wonderful jewellery. She looked like Jean Harlow.

I was suddenly hit by cramp. I was about to cry out with the pain when I was transfixed with what I saw next; two beautiful Rose Buds gradually undressing themselves to expose the most exquisite little-girl figures. There was not a trace of hair on their bodies. Their breasts were tiny, with little nipples that seemed like ripe cherries.

I could not help panting with excitement. Being attracted to young flesh was a new experience for me, something I had barely allowed myself even to dream about. Hitherto, I had always been the slave of an older woman, but now I knew that there was no such thing as a totally submissive or dominant woman – given the right circumstances even I could be dominant.

It was therefore all the more cruel that I had to watch these two beautiful little Rose Buds being taken by the harsh Ursula.

I saw them climb into Ursula's big bed, never suspecting, the little darlings, that they were being watched. I saw Ursula tease them with her vibrator. They seemed very inexperienced and it was easy for Ursula to get them excited as she made them play with one another.

I could see their little pink faces becoming flushed, and their little pert nipples getting big. I watched as Ursula made them suck each other's nipples – and then just when they were coming to the height of their little passions, she stopped them and made them give her pleasure.

She started to train them. Simultaneously they had to lick her beauty lips and suck her breasts. Obviously they had never used a vibrator before, but Ursula in her cunning way soon had them working it perfectly.

In and out. In and out. The two young girls were fascinated by the way Ursula's big body was moving in time to their ministrations. They could feel her rising excitement.

'Lick!' Ursula screamed.

Poor me! I just couldn't stand it any longer. In my frustration I let out a scream.

'Help!' I cried.

The little Rose Buds got a terrible fright. They rushed over to where the cry had come from. They uncovered the silken shroud.

But Ursula had been about to climax. Her beauty bud was prominent. She had been about to have the most wonderful orgasm of her life – when that stupid slut had spoilt everything.

Furious, she clenched her teeth. 'That damned impertinent bitch, Emma! I'll soon teach her not to interrupt her Mistress's fun,' seethed Ursula. 'Bridgit!' she called out. 'Get the wheel ready.'

A few minutes later I was dragged, cringing, out of the cage and down into a brilliantly lit large basement punishment room.

'Strip her and put her on the wheel,' ordered Ursula in a quiet menacing tone that I found almost more frightening than being shouted at.

Bridgit pushed my naked back up against a large wooden wheel in the centre of the room. It looked rather like the wheel of a cart. It was held in a frame and could be turned on its well greased axis by a handle at the side. I had seen pictures of such a wheel in a medieval torture chamber. I remembered the rather similar one in the castle in Romania. Now Ursula had one too!

Bridgit now pushed me further back and fastened my wrists to a hook on the top of the wheel, well above my head. Then slightly turning the wheel by the handle, she pulled my ankles down taut and strapped them to the wheel as well.

I was now held, staring up at the ceiling with my body

curved back below me along the outside rim of the wheel. I gave a scream of fright. This was as bad as the Countess's wheel!

'You can scream away, all you like, Emma,' laughed Ursula unpleasantly. She pointed to the padded walls and then to the video camera that was pointed at the wheel. No one outside will hear, and your screams will make my video film all the more exciting to play to my friends.'

I gave a little groan. Oh what a fool I had been to have jealously interrupted and spoilt Ursula's acute pleasure with the Rose Buds. Would I never learn! Ursula was a cruel and vindictive woman when she was crossed. And she insisted on complete obedience to her every whim.

But could I really have gone on watching my Mistress enjoying herself with other girls? It was so humiliating, especially as I was being kept frustrated myself. Deep in my heart I knew that the answer was yes. Other girls of Ursula's had apparently been made to do so. So what was so different about me? Why had I baulked at being pleased that my wonderful Mistress was having fun with some other delightful little creatures? After all, I remembered, I had also found them strangely attractive.

Indeed, what a fool I had been. And now I was going to be punished for my insolence. I knew that I deserved every stroke that I was going to get. But this wheel was really terrifying!

Bridgit turned the wheel a half circle. I screamed again, but it was more from fright than from pain or real discomfort.

Ursula now came round to the other side of the wheel, to where I was held helpless, curved back on the wheel, my body exposed and my hair hanging down to the floor. Idly Ursula started to play with my beauty lips which were now level with her own eyes. Ashamed, I could feel my body beginning to respond.

Then, as if she knew the very thoughts going through my mind, she said, 'You know you deserve to be punished, don't you, Emma?' She squeezed my exposed beauty bud. 'Don't you?'

231

'Yes, Madam!' I cried awkwardly as I was held upside down. 'But please, please, not too hard – and not like this ... It's awful being upside down ... Anyway, I'm very sorry. I really am!'

'It's too late to be sorry now,' said Ursula bitterly. 'The little Rose Buds have had to go now. But, I'm going to use my new wheel and give you a thrashing that you'll never forget for the rest of your life.'

Ursula turned the wheel. I began to spin round to the other side. There was a sudden crack of a whip. Terrified, as I hung upside down, I saw that Bridgit now had a long black cattle whip in her hand. It had a short handle and a well oiled tapering lash of about six foot long with a little red leash at the end. I gave a cry of genuine terror. I may have deserved to be punished – but not like this.

'No, please madam, not with that whip!' I screamed. 'I promise I'll be good!'

'Well, Emma, perhaps the mere sight of my cattle whip has taught you a lesson. But you're still going to be punished. You deserve it, don't you?'

I gave a sob of assent.

'Now, Bridgit, give me the little thin cane and then start turning the wheel. Nice and slowly ...'

I screamed again as my hair brushed the floor. Slowly my head rose up again as the wheel turned, before dipping down back towards the floor. It was a horrible feeling.

But this time, as my head came up, I felt Ursula stroking my hair.

'You know, Bridgit,' I heard Ursula say, 'one day I'm to have all this removed. She'd look very slave-like with a completely smooth bald head, like some other young girls I have seen. They can kill off all the hairs these days so that the girl has a permanently shiny little head. I'd have my crest tattooed on it. That would stop her running after men!'

My God, I thought. No! No! I remembered how I had only just escaped having my head shaved in the Countess's castle. But this permanent removal of my hair would be even worse. I must never let Ursula do that to me. And did her remarks about men mean that Ursula had guessed that I was still seeing Henry from time to time?

Then just as my head was beginning to drop yet again towards the floor, as the wheel turned, I heard another whistling noise as Ursula brought the whippy little cane down across my flesh. I screamed.

'Yes, yes, scream away,' shouted Ursula, bringing the whip down again, 'and just think that this would not be happening if you had not so stupidly shown your jealousy.'

I sobbed, partly from the realisation of my own stupidity, partly from fear, and partly at the humiliation of being flogged in front of the hated Bridgit.

Slowly the wheel turned. My head began to rise up again towards the ceiling. Suddenly the cane came down across my breasts. Again I screamed but I realised that the pain was nothing like what it might have been. Ursula was clearly more interested in giving me a fright than in really hurting me.

I screamed and screamed as the whole process was repeated several times as the wheel slowly turned. But even as I screamed, again more in fear than in agony, I realised that even using the relatively innocuous thin whippy cane, my flogging could easily have been very much worse.

'Enough of this wheel, Bridgit,' Ursula suddenly called out. 'I want you! And I want her to watch. Put her back in the cage and chain her wrists to the bars so that she can't touch herself. Then get into my bed and wait for me.'

'So, Emma,' came Bridgit's foreign sounding voice from the bed, 'you're going to watch the Mistress and I having pleasure together whilst you're tied helpless in the cage . . . Just remember that you can't please her like I do – or she'd have chosen you. I'm her favourite girl. You're too old. Old! You're horrible. She hates you!'

'It's not true,' I wailed. 'She loves me, not you.'

'Bah! If she loved you, then she wouldn't have birched you, nor would she have thrashed you on the wheel. You're nothing to her – just something to use.'

I was shaking the bars of my cage with rage, as Bridgit

continued to taunt me. My wrists were chained round one of the bars, holding me kneeling up close to the front of the cage.

'You bitch . . .' I began to scream.

'If I hear another word out of you, Emma,' said the young girl very coolly, 'then I shall tell the Mistress when she comes. You know what she says about little caged dogs having to keep silent – or else!'

Overawed, I relapsed into silence behind the bars of the cage.

Desperately I wanted to turn away in my cage, but my wrists were chained to one of the bars and I was unable to. It was so humiliating seeing how Ursula was enjoying that bitch Bridgit, and having to listen to their cries of ecstasy. Again I shook the bars of the cage in fury.

I knew that I, who had been expensively trained to please women, could have given Ursula far greater pleasure than that inexperienced young whipper-snapper. What made it even worse was that Ursula was actually giving pleasure to Bridgit, something she hardly ever bothered to do for me. She was treating her almost as if she was an equal, and not just one of her slaves. It made me feel so jealous – I could have killed that smug young Bridgit.

The pain from the birch on my back and bottom had eased – as had the pain from the whip on my thighs, belly and breasts. But the mental anguish of having to watch my rival in bed with her beloved Mistress, had more than replaced the physical pain.

It was all so humiliating and frustrating. How could Ursula be so cruel?

6

The beautiful villa at Cap Ferrat

Suddenly the telephone rang.

It was Sunday morning. I ran in from the garden, panting and out of breath. Could this be Ursula? I did not want my husband, John, to answer it, lest it was her. All day I had been waiting for her call, ever since I had made my morning report to her answering machine. Jealously I had been wondering where Ursula was spending the weekend – and with whom.

'Is that you, Emma?'

It was her! The same rather dry and husky voice with the foreign intonation.

'Yes, Mistress,' I answered, thrilled.

'You remember that I told you that I was thinking of renting a villa in the South of France from some friends for a couple of weeks?'

'Yes, Mistress.' I was struggling to keep my voice calm. Cap Ferrat, the European millionaire's playground! Blue skies . . . blue seas . . . glamorous women . . . warm nights . . . handsome men . . . gorgeous villas . . . lovely gardens full of mauve and orange Bougainvillaeas and dark blue Morning Glory . . . fantastic parties . . .

'Well, I'm going ahead. Can you get away?'

'Oh, Mistress . . .' I answered, my mind racing. Could I get away from the office? Of course I could! And John would not object to me going off to stay with another woman. Indeed it was the apparent innocuousness of seeing another woman that made having an affair with a woman so much easier than having one with a man. I knew I would do anything to be with Ursula again – and for two whole weeks.

'I thought it might be rather fun if you were the maid,'

continued Ursula with a laugh. 'A cook-housekeeper comes in daily, but we shall need a maid. So why not you? You like being treated as my maid, don't you Emma?'

'Yes,' I whispered. It was indeed very exciting being treated by Ursula as her submissive maid servant.

'Good!' said Ursula, now more coldly. 'You will be paid of course – as a maid. But you'll have no time off. I shall expect you to be at my beck and call the whole time. Well?'

Gosh! Dressing up occasionally as a maid for Ursula had been rather fun. But this sounded more serious. Much more serious.

'Well, Emma, yes or no? If you won't come as my maid, I'll take one of my other girls who will.'

I felt a pang of jealousy.

'Yes, Mistress,' I quickly replied. Come what may, I knew that I could not miss this opportunity of being with my Mistress and of being her personal maid for two whole weeks! 'Yes, of course, I want to come.'

'You will also have to serve Bridgit, you understand.'

'Oh, no!' Not that nasty, stuck up, young German girl who spoke little English. I could now hear her hated girlish laughter in the background.

'Yes, Emma, if you come then you will have to obey Bridgit – or you'll be punished. You will have to call her Miss and obey her orders as if they were mine. Do you understand?'

'Yes,' I answered, contritely. I would, I knew, put up with anything just to be with Ursula. But to have to take orders from that chit of a girl, that spoilt brat with whom Ursula seemed besotted!

'Good, then I'll have your tickets sent straight to you. You will fly to Nice in a week's time, and I'll meet you at the airport.'

'But what clothes should I bring?' I wailed. 'I shall need a new hot weather party dress and a new swim suit.'

'Emma, you obviously weren't listening. I said you would be a maid – the whole time. Maids don't wear party dresses, nor do they swim in their Mistress's swimming pools, or if they do, then they swim naked – and under supervision. Do you understand?'

'Yes, Mistress,' I replied, crestfallen.

'So, bring nothing at all. As I said, you will be dressed here as a maid – the whole time. And you will be naked under your uniform – except for your chastity belt which, of course, you'll also wear the whole time.'

'Oh, no!' I exclaimed. 'No please!'

'Yes, Emma! I don't want my maid to start having ideas above her station. And I don't want you to start picking up men on the flight, either. So, you are to travel wearing that rather dowdy nursemaid's smock I've given you. And put on those rather ugly boots – they're enough to put off any man! And wear that ugly felt nursemaid's cap to hide your pretty blonde hair. And don't you dare take the cap off! I shall arrange for one of the stewardesses to keep an eye on you. So be careful, little girl!'

I could well believe it. Ursula had friends everywhere.

'And,' Ursula went on, 'if anyone asks you what you are doing, you are to say that you are joining your Mistress, for whom you work as a nursemaid. Not a nanny – just a nursemaid. Understand?'

'Yes, Mistress,' I whispered.

'So just think of being my paid maid servant for a couple of weeks! Are you excited, little girl?'

'Oh yes, Mistress! Oh yes!'

'Good! Well so am I. But remember, no laziness or sulkiness, or you'll get the cane really hard!'

The phone went dead.

I have been rushed off my feet ever since I arrived at Nice airport, to be met by Ursula and a smirking Bridgit. From the very outset, my place in society as a mere servant had been clearly established. Ursula curtly told me to get into her car alongside the elderly chauffeur and to keep quiet, whilst she and Bridgit sat in the back talking loudly, in English for my benefit, of the exciting parties they would shortly be going to – without me.

Arriving at the villa, Ursula had handed Bridgit a carrier bag.

'Put it on her straight away,' she had ordered, 'and bring

me the key. I can't stand the idea of a servant girl playing with herself behind her Mistress's back.'

Bridgit had led me into the little maid's room off the large bedroom she shared with Ursula. She had opened the plastic bag and, to my dismay, had drawn out Ursula's dreaded new chastity belt. It was, I saw, similar to the one that Isabella had used on me.

'Hold up your dress!' she had ordered in her strongly accented English. 'Step into the leg rings.'

Then, without a word, the cruelly smiling young girl had deftly fastened the belt round my waist and pulled the slotted centre piece up between my legs. As with Isabella's belt, I had felt my thighs being pulled together and my beauty lips being squeezed into the covered slot. Then seconds later I heard the click of the padlock. I would, I knew, now have to walk with little mincing steps and be quite unable to get at myself.

It was a very exciting feeling, but not one, I was sure, that would continue for very long. But I was wrong, for as the days went past, much to Bridgit's delight, Ursula showed no sign whatsoever of wanting to release me from the belt – not even when she made me pleasure her with my tongue and fingers in her bed.

I was kept busy from dawn until late at night, first cleaning up the house and kitchen, then ironing the clothes that I had had to wash the previous night, then humiliatingly having to accompany both Ursula and Bridgit to the bathroom when they awoke, and finally having to bring them breakfast in bed. This was followed by running their baths, washing and drying them and laying out their freshly washed and ironed clothes – with the ever present fear of a beating should the slightest crease or wrinkle be found.

Ursula and Bridgit would then enjoy a game of tennis on the villa's private court, with me being kept hard at it, acting as ball-girl. This would be followed by showers during which I had to wash and dry them, and then help them into their swim suits, before preparing the long reclining sun chairs and parasols by the side of the pool.

Then I had to slip away and clean the house – being only

too aware that another beating would result if Ursula's eagle eye detected the slightest speck of dust anywhere – or if Bridgit found any. I didn't mind too much being beaten by Ursula but, as an older woman, I found it highly degrading when Ursula tossed the cane to Bridgit and told her to beat 'that lazy slut of a maid'.

By this time the cook house-keeper would have arrived and prepared a delicious lunch which I had to serve round the pool. Often other women friends of Ursula's would join them, and some men as well. Some of them would recognise me and take a delight in ordering me to bring them food, towels, drinks and cushions, complementing Ursula on the obedience of her new maid.

'It's obedience that only results from fear of the cane, I'm afraid,' Ursula would laugh. Indeed the cane was always present, lying on one of the tables by the pool.

Ursula was very strict in not allowing me any of the delicious food, maliciously saying to her friends that I was putting on weight and had to be kept on a diet of yoghourt. Twice Bridgit had found me, ravenously hungry, trying to steal a delicious cold cutlet from the refrigerator. Then, grinning with delight, she had run off to report what she had seen to a furious Ursula. On both occasions, the result had been a dreadful thrashing by the side of the pool, in front of the guests.

In the heat of the afternoon, Ursula would retire to her bedroom for a siesta, taking Bridgit to bed with her. I would have to put them into frilly long nightdresses, and then remain silently standing in the corner of the now darkened room, consumed by jealously, as the two of them alternatively made love and slept.

Occasionally, my heart would leap into my mouth as Ursula beckoned me, too, into the bed. But the chastity belt always remained on, and often even the maid's costume did as well.

In the evening I had to serve drinks and food to Ursula's dinner guests, and then jealously watch them all go off to enjoy themselves at the Casino, or to a party at another villa.

Before locking the front door, Ursula would cruelly lock a short chain from a ring in the middle of the doormat to a little ring hanging from the bottom of my chastity belt, between my legs. The chain was intended to be fastened to the collar of a guard dog, but was equally effective in keeping me on guard crouching down on all fours on the mat behind the locked door until Ursula and Bridgit returned – often slightly drunk and again in an amorous mood.

I would have to undress them, hang up their expensive dresses and help them into their night dresses. Once again I would have to remain present and on duty whilst they made love, only being allowed to crawl to my own little cot when they were overcome with sleep.

I was so disappointed at being confined to the villa. It seemed such a waste to be in such a glamorous place and to see nothing of it. And how jealous I was of the way Bridgit was allowed to sunbathe and relax by the side of the pool, whilst I had to trot to and fro bringing her and Ursula fresh drinks, delicious little sandwiches and dry towels.

But at least, I told myself, I was with Ursula.

7

The terrifying wrestler

'It's about time she earned her keep,' I overheard Ursula
say nonchalantly in a low voice to Bridgit. Idly I wondered
who she was talking about. Obviously not me! 'I'm certainly not going to be out of pocket over her! And she could
give us an amusing little spectacle into the bargain.'

Lazing on a sun chair by the swimming pool of the delightful villa, Ursula helped herself to an iced drink from
the tray that was being proffered to her by a pretty and
mincing, but obviously very nervous, maid servant – me!

I was dressed in a plain knee length black maid's uniform with a white pinafore and a starched little white cap.
A puff of wind stirred the pine trees that shut the garden
and swimming pool off from the neighbouring villas. It
also made my short maid's skirt swirl, to reveal a little
silver chain linking two metal rings round my legs just
above my knees – the short chain that made me walk with
such mincing little steps. From each ring, two little chains
led upwards towards my waist.

As I served drinks to Ursula and her guests, I saw that
Bridgit kept clapping her hands with delight and nodding
eagerly. But it was only later that I realised why. How she
would have been thrilled at the idea! She would love to see
me really put in my place!

How she loathed me, her older rival for her beloved
Ursula's attentions. How disappointed she had been, I had
learnt, when she realised that Ursula was going to invite
me to the villa. It was she who had suggested, however,
that I should be treated as a maid servant – an idea that
Ursula had accepted with enthusiasm. It was a humiliating
position that Ursula had often forced Bridgit, herself, to
accept in the past.

But now she was really enjoying bossing an older woman about: making me wash her panties and complaining to Ursula that they were not properly ironed – even though I'd done the job perfectly. Not only did I then have to do them all over again, but Ursula had ordered her to give me six strokes of the cane. How Bridgit had enjoyed that!

Bridgit had made her enjoyment clear as she made love to Ursula in the hot afternoons in front of me. Ursula had made me stand in the corner of the room, facing the wall like a naughty child. There, driven mad with jealousy and frustration, and locked into my chastity belt, I had had to listen to it all and not dare to turn round to look.

And then how she had enjoyed it when, afterwards, I had to wash and clean her, as well as Ursula, in the bathroom – seeing for myself how my rival had been allowed to enjoy herself whilst I was kept frustrated.

'But she'll have to have a nasty fright, for I don't want her getting a taste for men again,' I again overheard Ursula say as I went past with my tray of empty glasses. I wondered who she was talking about.

Then, I saw Ursula turn to the large African woman who was staying in one of the bungalows in the villa's garden, and was reclining on a sunbed on her other side. 'What do you suggest?'

'Well, I know one of the wrestlers taking part in the big international competition in Cannes,' whispered the black woman. 'He's African and a huge ugly brute of a man – and he's certainly won enough money to pay handsomely to get his hands on a beautiful white girl like her, even in front of us!'

'An ugly great wrestler! That sounds ideal,' laughed Ursula. 'Tell me more! Can you really fix it all?'

'Yes, at a price!'

'Ah!' said Ursula.

'My price will be to have the girl in my bed for a whole night!'

'Oh! Well, I don't know . . .'

'Go on, agree!' cried Bridgit. 'That'll really put her in her place!'

242

'May be,' said Ursula to Bridgit. Then she again turned to the black woman. 'Tell me about this monster of a man . . .'

Still quite unaware that it was me who was being discussed, I picked up the empty glasses, gave a little curtsey, and turned to return to the kitchen.

Ursula was watching me as I made my way awkwardly down the little steps. Doubtless she was thinking what a success that new type of chastity belt was proving. I saw her smile, probably remembering how she had had me thrashed by Bridgit earlier that morning for asking to have it taken off. Ten strokes of the cane for impertinence! I certainly would not ask again! And she knew how I hated being caned by a younger girl.

Perhaps she was also remembering the previous torrid night of love-making with Bridgit on one side of her, and her maid on the other – wearing her chastity belt, of course, unlike Bridgit. Both had had to compete to give their Mistress the greatest pleasure, with the loser – the maid, of course – then being forced by the Mistress's cane to pleasure the younger woman, under her Mistress's eagle eye.

Yes, the chastity belt had definitely ensured that I had been kept pure as snow ever since my arrival in the villa several days earlier. And although I did not then know anything about it, Ursula would doubtless now have been thinking how it would ensure that I would also be kept fresh and tight for my forthcoming performance – something that could come as a horrifying surprise for me . . .

I was thrilled!

At last Ursula had taken off my chastity belt. She gave no explanation and I did not dare ask why, lest she changed her mind and told Bridgit to lock it back on me again.

It was evening. Ursula sent for me and told me to make myself look as beautiful as possible. To my delight she also told me to take off my ugly maid's uniform, and then she took off the awful chastity belt. But then she washed me out and greased me behind. But I knew that Usula often liked to take me from behind with her dildo – something I hated, but which often led to other things . . .

So despite the discomfort of these preparations, I felt madly excited at the thought of what was going to happen.

Then Ursula gave me a beautiful silk sari to wear. No underwear, no bra, no slip, no blouse – just the transparent silk sari. I looked in the long mirror. A truly ravishing creature stared back at me.

I could feel my erect nipples pressing against the tight silk. It was so thrilling! So exciting! What was going to happen? I still did not dare to ask. But obviously my Mistress, my wonderful and so exciting Mistress, was going to use me – at last! So much for Bridgit! With my belt removed I could feel my self becoming more and more moist, more and more aroused.

Not even when my hands were tied behind my back did I dare to say a word of protest. It made it all the more exciting. I'd show that little trollop Bridgit how a grown woman could really give pleasure to another woman!

I did not even mind when a metal collar was locked round my neck. Once again, all the more exciting! And it was yet more exciting when a chain lead was fastened to the collar.

Ursula put her hand down and touched me. I almost exploded.

'Yes, she's nice and ready now,' Ursula called out to Bridgit. 'Lead her through into the drawing room.'

I was dismayed to see Ursula hand her cane to Bridgit. I was even more dismayed when the young girl picked up the chain lead. She gave me a sharp tap on the buttocks, which were covered only by the sheer silk of the sari.

'Come!' the girl said, giving the chain lead a sharp tug.

Wonderingly, I followed the girl into the large brightly lit room. I looked around. Astonished, I saw that a group of Ursula's friends, mainly women, were sitting bolt upright on little chairs. Then I turned towards what they were looking at. My jaw fell. My eyes almost started from my head. I started to scream.

I tried to turn and run from the room. But Bridgit grimly held the chain fast, and with my hands tied behind my back I felt helpless.

'No! No!' I was screaming.

I could not take my eyes off the huge figure of a man, a bald headed African, a vast muscular man, a terrifying cruel looking man, a man whose little pig eyes gloated as he looked me up and down.

'Oh, yes!' he said, flinging off a short silk dressing gown; the sort that boxers wear. He now wore only a leather jock strap against which his large genitals were straining. He looked even more huge and muscular – like the pictures I had seen of professional wrestlers, but even more repulsive and brutish.

'No!' I screamed. I turned to Ursula. 'No! Don't let him touch me!'

'Nonsense, Emma. It'll be very good for you to have a nice boyfriend again. But I dare say that after this lover, you won't be so keen on other men again for some time!'

'No, please, no!' I screamed.

'Oh yes, Emma! Oh yes! And just remember that I'm being very well paid for your services! Just think of that!'

My God! I thought.

Then Ursula pointed to the cane in Bridgit's hands. 'Now keep quiet and do what you're told or you'll be thrashed!'

Ursula turned to the huge wrestler.

'Well? Do you like her?'

'Yes, Ma'am,' he grinned. He spoke with a strong African accent. 'She's worth every dollar I've paid to have her.'

'Good!' said Ursula with a smile.

'Yeah! I want her now!' he reached towards me. I was now cringing, and just looking petrified at this monster of a man.

'But first why don't you put her on your knee and have a good feel,' smiled Ursula, pointing to a large armchair.

The huge wrestler sat down. I struggled ineffectively as Bridgit dragged me up to him. She kept hold of the chain. In fact she was to keep hold of it throughout the whole performance – to accentuate my helplessness.

As the excited spectators watched in silence, the wrestler reached up to me and pulled me down onto his knee. I felt so small and helpless by comparison to this horrible giant of a man. He began to grope, feeling my breasts and squeezing my nipples. Then, he gently began to run a hand down between my legs, touching my beauty spot – the little bud that had been shut away behind the belt for so long.

With my hands bound behind me, I was powerless to resist.

Horrified, I began to feel my body reacting to the nearness of the male: a huge naked and aroused male. Ursula had ensured that I was well aroused before I came into the room and into close proximity to this naked male, and the touch of his hands on my nipples and beauty bud was devastating.

'Now kiss your lover,' ordered Ursula. 'Lick him under the chin!'

Again horrified, I found myself being driven by my own body to obey. Although one part of me was repulsed by this huge creature, another part was adoring being made to be his helpless slave. I hesitated.

'Go on, Emma!' warned Ursula. 'He's paying several hundred pounds for you and you're damn well going to give him his money's worth! So go on. Lick!'

Appalled, I found myself licking up at his chin. I felt a complete whore. I was earning my Mistress money!

'Now I think it's time you did a little work, Emma! Go on, kneel down between his legs, you little slut. Go on kneel down!'

Shamefacedly I slipped down to my knees. Shocked, I saw that this giant of a man had slipped off the jock strap. Horrified, I saw the man's huge great dusky manhood thrusting up between his outstretched legs. Like a terrified rabbit hypnotised by a stoat, I simply could not take my eyes off it.

Then, Bridgit gave me a sharp tap of the cane on my buttocks.

'Go on, you little slut, you little whore!' cried Ursula.

I lowered my head, as I knew I must . . .

* * *

Soon I was kneeling over a couch. My hands were still bound behind me, but my head was now held down by Bridgit, making me raise by buttocks – offering them to the huge wrestler, who was now standing behind me. I felt him part them with his hands. I heard him grunt with satisfaction when he felt the grease.

'Up higher!' Bridgit tapped my buttocks with her cane, making me proffer myself even more invitingly.

Suddenly I felt something huge and hard pressing against me. I screamed in protest and tried to turn my head round to see what was being done to me. But Ursula slapped my face hard.

'Don't you dare look round. You go on looking straight ahead. And head up!'

I screamed again as I felt him penetrate me and press deeply into me. Then as he slowly began to work in and out, I felt his hand on my beauty bud again. The combination was breathtaking, utterly overwhelming. I was this giant's helpless plaything – a plaything he had paid to use. Gradually I felt my buttocks moving rhythmically in response to him.

'That's better you dirty little slut,' murmured Ursula, her voice rising. 'You're just a dirty little slut aren't you? Aren't you? Say it!'

'I'm just a dirty little slut!' I heard myself scream . . .

Minutes later I felt the man surge deep within me. My own climax followed seconds later.

There was a little round of applause. Ignoring me, Ursula handed the man a congratulatory glass of champagne. Never had I felt so ashamed.

'Now, Bridgit,' said Ursula smiling at her friends, 'turn the little slut over, and let's see how she responds when it's done from the front.'

I was now pulled back over the couch and held so that whilst my feet were still on the floor, my head was right back and I was looking up at the ceiling. The huge African leant down over me.

After days locked up in the chastity belt, I was almost as tight as a virgin. The huge African was now grunting with pleasure as he slowly began to open me up.

It was awful, but several minutes later, the room again resounded alternatively to my little screams of pain and delight.

The same scene was repeated on three other occasions during my stay at the villa.

I never knew when it was going to happen. And each time, Ursula drove home my position in her household by giving the delighted Bridgit a quarter of what the giant African had paid to use my body. I got nothing, of course.

After each performance I resolved that never again would I go through with it. Ursula had no right to have me used in this way! I would refuse, I would fight against him, I would be cold and give him no pleasure.

And yet, every time, I finally found myself revelling in my violation – much to the amusement of Ursula and her friends who, stop watches in hand, would bet on how long I would hold out this time.

Even worse I found that during the day I was constantly thinking of the wrestler's huge manhood, thinking of it with a mixture of fear and excitement – just as Ursula knew I would.

And all the time was the awful knowledge that the horrible fat friend of Ursula would be coming back the day after each peformance to claim her promised reward – taking me to bed. That was something that I really hated, and only fear of the cane and the woman's sheer brute strength made me accept it.

All in all, I tell myself, as I write up this diary in the plane on my way back to dull old London, staying in Ursula's villa at Cap Ferrat had been one of the most exciting, but deeply humiliating and degrading, times of my life.

Then, as I looked down on the lights of London, a wave of realism swept over me. It was disgusting what Ursula had done to me. She was like a drug, an evil drug, and I must keep away from her. But could I?

8

Henry!

Henry always seemed so busy, always about to announce his engagement and then running into difficulties.

Twice I had tried being purely platonic with him. After returning from Cap Ferrat, I had invited him over for lunch to a large house with a lovely garden which Ursula and I had borrowed from one of my husband's grand relations. Ursula meanwhile was working on a nearby exhibition. I had learnt that Ursula was going to be away for the day.

'I'd love to see you,' I told Henry on the telephone, 'but you must promise – no touching. I've promised Ursula, and she'll beat the living daylights out of me if I break the rules.'

'Then just don't tell her,' Henry said angrily.

'It won't work, darling,' I replied. 'She'll get the truth out of me in the end. She always does. So, please, please, no touching!'

'All right!' Henry finally agreed in a temper.

I found it thrilling to meet him in this new way. It was a new game. I was longing to throw myself into his arms, as we picnicked in the sun loggia that overlooked the spacious lawns. But I was also wildly excited by the fear of the consequences of doing so. I had wondered, after all the wild excitements of being with Ursula again, whether I would now find Henry rather dull. But the mere sight of him had made my heart pound again. It was even pounding as I listened to him complaining about the waywardness of the woman he was still trying to marry.

For once Ursula had not left me locked into a chastity belt. I rather wished that Ursula had, for later, strolling hand in hand with Henry round the pretty lakes, I could feel myself becoming more and more aroused.

Indeed only the realisation that Ursula would shortly be returning, prevented me from acceding to Henry's pleas, and pulling him up into the bedroom I was sharing with Ursula.

Henry, the Brute, the Bounder, as Ursula disparagingly referred to him, in my Mistress's bedroom! My God, I thought, what would Ursula have done had she suspected the truth? She would have killed me!

Oh how exciting it had been.

Then on another occasion, Ursula and I had been staying at a hotel near Henry. Ursula had just had my breasts slightly enlarged and firmed up in a private nursing home. It had cost her a pretty penny. She had also had my nipples pulled out further. The combined effect was fairly dramatic. I had been delighted with the change and longed to show my new curves off to Henry. It was so frustrating being so near to him and yet not allowed to contact him.

Luckily, I discovered, Ursula would have to leave early the next day and then meet me again in London. Making an excuse, I had slipped away to a telephone, and quickly phoned Henry and suggested he meet me for breakfast – but once again, no touching. Once again it had been thrilling – though I scarcely knew whether it was due to the presence of Henry, his obvious admiration of my newly enhanced bosom, the excitment of being determined to be faithful to Ursula, or the fear of what Ursula would do if she ever found out that I had met Henry – no matter how innocently or briefly.

In my happiness at being Ursula's slave I longed for Henry to also find happiness with the charming woman he was already half living with. But the months passed by and there had been no announcement of an engagement. Finally, a few weeks later, angered by Henry's continual inability to bring his marital affairs to a conclusion, and genuinely besotted with Ursula and her continual strict control – a control that thanks to the telephone was just as demanding even when we were separated – I told Henry that everything was over between us.

Life had moved on, I cruelly told him on the telephone

– the same telephone that only minutes before I had used, excited almost out of my mind, to make my humiliating morning report to Ursula. I now had a more satisfying relationship, I said to Henry, one that offered far more excitement and intellectual stimulus than he had ever provided.

The next morning, scarcely had I sat down at my desk in my small private office, feeling wretched and miserable and uncertain what to do with my life, than in walked Henry. He must have driven for half the night, since long before dawn.

I was appalled. I was looking like nothing on earth with my hair screwed back any old way and wearing a dreadful old dress – the first thing I had found in my wardrobe that morning.

I had been driven half crazy by Ursula's demands and controls, by my jealousy of Bridgit, by the way Ursula just ignored the fact that I was a married woman with a home and a husband, and by the apparent finality of the break with Henry. I had just escaped to the privacy of my office to try and recover from it all – to get my breath back so to speak, and to concentrate on my business ventures.

And now here was Henry, the man I had finally cut out of my life the day before. He was, I quickly saw, looking terrific. Clothes were so important, and he was looking as self confident as always, in a well cut grey Prince of Wales check suit, a pink shirt and a contrasting blue tie. If he was distressed, and I knew he must be, then there was little sign of it.

I was so overcome, that I could only bury my head in my arms, folded on the desk. I knew that he would repeat his theory that Ursula was an evil influence on me. I half knew that it was true but how could I possibly give her up? And yet here he was, sacked by me only the day before, and yet the next day he had had the guts to drop everything, drive a couple of hundred miles, and come and confront me. Would he beat me in a rage? In my own office?

He was laughing away at his own audacity, as if my misery was the funniest thing in the world.

'You can't get rid of me as easily as that! And look at yourself – what a mess!'

I hated him. But at the same time I could not help admiring him.

Silently now, he put his hand on my bowed shoulder. He stroked my cheek. Angrily, I turned my head away and buried my cheek in my arms. I could feel the tears were about to flow. He stroked my hair. I burst into tears, sobbing my heart out into my arms as I sat at the desk.

'Why, oh why did you come back?' I wailed.

Then I was in his arms.

We walked in the park. We had sandwiches in my favourite hotel. Then I led him to his car and we drove out into the country. I knew the place. It was isolated and muddy. He dropped the back of his seat. I knelt on the passenger seat and lowered my head. I would please my Master before he set off back home again!

There would be plenty of bumpy rides with Henry after that, and several more exciting scenes with Ursula, but it was I knew, and as Henry also smilingly knew, once again the beginning of the end of my second affair with Ursula.

9

The reluctant bride

I felt exhausted by Ursula's constant demands.

She was simply over-powering. In small doses she was fine but, after three days of being constantly badgered by her on the telephone, I was left utterly limp.

So when Henry, out of the blue, suggested a weekend away at his lovely cottage, I was delighted. I longed to go away with him if only to show Ursula that I was not just her slave. Alas, however, I had already promised Ursula to spend the weekend with her. What was I to do? On the one hand, Ursula had made special arrangements to take me and some friends to a country cottage she had rented on a large estate, and on the other hand this might well be my last chance to spend a weekend with Henry before he became engaged. What a dilemma!

Ursula had also promised all sorts of fun and games there, including the presence again of Bridgit. But, of course, it was really the dreaded Bridgit, of whom I was so jealous, that used to upset me so much. I had tried to hide my jealousy, but Ursula had deliberately goaded me by paying more attention to that young chit of a girl. Indeed, I felt that I had been ignored whenever Bridgit was about.

So, I was in very bad form when I arrived at Ursula's town house. I had not slept for two nights, thinking of Bridgit and Ursula being bedded together.

Sure enough the first thing I saw was Bridgit coming out of Ursula's bedroom. Bridgit, I thought bitterly, was the perfect submissive slave. Unlike me, she didn't even have to act many of the parts that Ursula demanded. Whereas I was very strong minded in my day to day life but adored being submissive in my sex life, Bridgit was just a born slave – 'born to lick', as I used to say to her contemptuously.

I was even more put out when another very pretty girl came out of Ursula's bedroom and walked past me with her nose in the air.

My brain was now in a turmoil. On the one hand I wanted to tell Ursula that I would not be spending the weekend with her, and yet on the other I felt so jealous of the other two girls that I naturally didn't want to leave the field to them. What should I do?

But any idea of broaching the subject delicately with Ursula had to be abandoned for I learnt Ursula was giving a special dinner party for a dozen close friends that night, and for the next few hours everyone was rushing about making last minute arrangements.

It was in the middle of the dinner that Ursula suddenly announced that the dinner was to celebrate her forthcoming marriage.

There were gasps all round. Marriage? Ursula?

'Yes,' laughed Ursula, 'I'm going to take a bride and enjoy her during a honeymoon in the country.'

I was struck dumb.

'But,' added Ursula with a laugh as she pointed to the horrified me and to the two laughing younger girls, 'I shall also be taking two bridesmaids.'

'Who will be the bride?' the guests all cried. 'And who will be the bridesmaids?'

'Oh, I think it would be great fun making Emma attend on one of the younger girls,' laughed Ursula. I choked in rage. 'But in fact the bride's going to be . . . going to be . . . Emma!'

My mouth fell wide open.

'And how's she going to lose her virginity?' asked one man.

'Oh! For that I've got a special rubber manhood ready to strap on for the wedding night.' Then Ursula lowered her voice so that I could barely hear. 'And it's going to be specially loaded!'

There were gasps and laughs from the guests.

'And the bridal dress?' one woman asked. 'Let's see her in the bridal dress and the bridesmaids in their dresses.'

So it was that, highly embarrassed, I returned to the dining table a few minutes later, dressed in a long white wedding dress, carrying a bouquet of flowers and attended by Bridgit and the other girls both dressed in matching bridesmaid dresses.

'But this is only a rehearsal,' explained Ursula to her guests. The real wedding – and its consummation – will both take place in the country tomorrow. And you're all invited to attend!'

'Will the bride be taking any vows?' Ursula was asked.

'Oh yes, she'll have to vow to be utterly faithful!'

'And to obey?'

'Of course!'

Horrified, I realised Ursula was quite serious about 'marrying' me. Two months previously I might well have been thrilled at the prospect of making a commitment to Ursula. But not now. Not now.

'And tonight the bride will sleep with me, innocently like a little girl – in readiness for her deflowering by me tomorrow!'

That night I lay awake in Ursula's arms. The other two girls, her so-called bridesmaids, had been banished to another room. Ursula was sleeping deeply, dreaming no doubt of the events that were planned for the following day.

Finally I could not keep silent any longer.

'I can't be your bride tomorrow, Madam. I've arranged to spend the weekend with someone else!'

Ursula awoke with a start.

'What! What did you say, you silly little girl?'

I repeated what I had said.

Ursula sat up in bed, switched on the light and smacked me hard across the face.

'Don't you dare to speak to me like that, you ungrateful little wretch!' she shouted.

'But it's true' I moaned. 'I'm sorry, but I've arranged to go away with . . . you know . . . him.'

'Him!' screamed Ursula. 'You mean the Brute ... the Bounder. You mean you're not going to go through a marriage with me because of that wretched man? You must be mad!'

'It's just to say goodbye!' I cried. 'It's my last chance. He's getting married.'

'Ha! You've said that before, you slut. I'm not going to share you with any man! And just to teach you a lesson, you're now going to get the thrashing of your life, my girl,' said Ursula menacingly as she got out of bed and opened a cupboard door.

'Look!' she cried. 'It's a new birch I've had made – specially in case I had any trouble from you. See! The thorns are still on the rods. Now bend over and pull up your night dress – we'll then soon see just how serious you are about that man of yours!'

The next half hour was just about the most painful of my life. But steadfastly I refused to call off my weekend with Henry.

Finally, the furious Ursula threw away the birch.

'All right, get out of my room and go and sleep on the corridor floor. But I warn you, Emma, you'll rue this! And I shall enjoy making Bridgit my bride instead of you. We shall have such fun together – all the weekend. Much more fun that I would have had with sour old you. She's young and exciting. So just think of that whilst you're with that ghastly man of yours!'

Ursula's words were still ringing in my ears when early the next morning I stumbled painfully out of the house. They were still ringing in my ears as I drove to meet Henry. Nor could I get out of my mind the memory of Bridgit's smug face when Ursula told her with a kiss that it would be she, and not me, who was going to be her bride. It was a memory made all the more painful by my sore little bottom.

'My God!' I murmured, as the feeling of acute jealousy built up, 'What have I done?'

Fun and then ... disaster

Henry arrived at our agreed meeting place in his usual exuberant form – all fun and raring to go.

As we drove down to his home, I longed to talk to him about my feelings and how distressed I was after the scene with Ursula. But as always when I wanted to talk to Henry, he was not in the mood to listen. He was too tied up with his own problems. When, plucking up my courage, I told him that I had been thrashed with a birch with the thorns still on as a punishment for going away with him, he merely laughed.

'Serves you right for going about with that bitch!'

I was so on edge that I began to feel irritated by Henry, and by the things that usually amused me about him. This time I felt he was just tiresome, and I was relieved when next morning he went out hunting. I could then have time to myself.

I knew I was being a masochist as I lost myself in thoughts of what Ursula and that bitch Bridgit were getting up to. Finally I couldn't bear it another minute. I picked up the phone and rang up Ursula.

'Oh, so it's you,' came Ursula's cold voice. 'What do you want?'

Nervously, I replied, 'I was just ringing to say that I hope you are having fun.'

'Oh, fun! Yes, you are missing out, Emma. You're obviously not having much fun with the Bastard – you poor thing! Bridgit says you must be desperate to go with him.'

Then I could hear lots of giggles down the phone. Smouldering with suppressed rage, I rang off. How dare Bridgit think that I was desperate because I was with Henry? What did she know about all the fun I have had with Henry? She knew nothing – the silly little creep!

I could feel myself getting all worked up, as I paced up and down Henry's house. I was in such a state that I did not notice the passing of time and was surprised when suddenly Henry rang on his mobile phone to say that he was on his way home. I decided that I would concentrate on Henry and put all thoughts of Bridgit out of my mind. And, to my surprise, when I found Henry in his hunting boots and spurs, I really did forget Ursula and that wretched Bridgit. I could even feel myself getting aroused as I pulled them off.

'Kiss the soles of my boots!' Henry roared. I loved it. I was now getting into the real role of a submissive slave, kneeling before her demanding Master . . . I undid his zip, and found his manhood throbbing.

'Suck!' he yelled raising his hand as if to smack my face. 'Work you little bitch, work!'

Poor me! I sucked as if my life depended on it, and indeed I knew that I would get ten strokes if I didn't.

'Now wash me!'

I gave him a bath and made him some tea and eggs.

'Crawl!' he then cried. 'Crawl on all fours to the bed!'

I love being treated like a dog. To lick my cruel Master all over like a bitch on heat . . . He was very aroused now. His nipples were hard and the pupils in his eyes were dilated. I crawled between his legs, licking him deep down.

'Drink it all!' he suddenly yelled. 'Drink it – and hold me whilst you do it.'

Soon he was pulling me up by my hair. 'Crawl up, little dog!'

I was now so choking with excitement that I thought I would surely burst. But, like a clever violinist playing the final sonata of a Mozart concert, he kept playing on my little bud – until I screamed out, 'Woof! . . . Woof! . . . Woof!' and then collapsed in a heap.

We both slept soundly, and we even continued to sleep the following morning. But Henry had to go out for drinks, leaving me curled up satisifed, but eager for a little more domination.

This longing to be dominated always came on strongest

after I had climaxed. I almost wanted to be beaten to bring on another climax. I thought about how good Ursula was at this, and how disappointing men usually were. They had all the right ideas, but so often it was just a fantasy. They liked to think about it, but when it came to actually doing it they were not so good as women.

Pondering this, I found that I simply couldn't resist telephoning Ursula. I was in such a good mood, that I thought I would tell Ursula how much I missed her domination . . .

The telephone was not answered for ages. I was about to give up, when a foreign sounding woman answered.

'Is Ursula there?' I asked.

'Miss Ursula is not available,' said a harsh voice.

'What do you mean?' I shouted. 'She always speaks to me. Please say it's Emma.'

A few minutes later, the same harsh voice came back. 'Miss Ursula says she is having fun with Bridgit. She will ring you back. What is your telephone number?'

I was livid with rage. I banged down the phone and screamed out aloud, 'The filthy bitch!' I screamed even harder. 'That wretched little Bridgit! Oh, how I hate her!'

Tears started to run down my cheeks. I just couldn't stand it another minute. I rang back.

'I insist on speaking to Ursula!'

The next minute, I heard a very husky voice.

'So what are you disturbing me for, Emma? My little darling Bridgit is being the most divine little slave . . . Just listen.'

I listened.

'Crawl, Bridgit! Now kneel!'

I could hear the swish of the cane on Bridgit's bottom and little Bridgit's cries for mercy.

'Under my dress you go, Bridgit. Now lick, little bitch! Lick your Mistress the way you were taught!'

I felt like slamming down the telephone, but then a mixture of horror and disgust made me glue my ear to it. All the things that I had thought were unique to me and Ursula, all the reasons why I had thought we had such a special relationship, were all being betrayed. Ursula had always led me to believe that I was the only one who could bring her to a special climax – and now I could hear Ursula crying out to Bridgit as she had never done with me. I could even hear Bridgit's little licks.

I heard Ursula's breathing quickening. She was moaning and crying out. Then I heard Ursula beating Bridgit – giving her at least twenty strokes, because she wasn't licking fast enough.

'On all fours, little slut!' I heard Ursula scream. Then there was a humming noise followed by Bridgit's little whimpers of joy.

I was breaking out in a sweat. This was unreal. I felt mad – insane with jealousy. I had myself enjoyed little threesomes with Ursula and one of her girls, and these had excited me considerably. But that was because I had always felt the other girl was no threat to me.

Only a few weeks before, Ursula, me and another girl had spent almost all one weekend in bed together. How exciting it had been when I was kissing and licking Ursula between her legs and the other little girl had been licking me from behind.

But this was different, quite different. Could Ursula be faking it all?

Still transfixed to the telephone, I could hear them both simultaneously climaxing, screaming, laughing, and yelling. Bridgit was crying 'Woof! Woof!' for all her worth, and Ursula was crying out in ecstasy, sounding like an opera singer stuck in a high contralto note.

Again, I longed to slam the phone down. Of course, I realised afterwards, I should not have tormented myself. But the damage was done. I felt sick. Huge tears were falling on the floor. I was desperate, quite inconsolable. I had loved Ursula and what, I asked myself, do other people know about love, real love?

Suddenly I looked at the clock. It was nearly one o'clock. My God, I thought, the Bounder will be back in a minute. Oh, God, I can't bear to look at him! Perhaps I should tell him the truth straight out? But he wouldn't understand the depth of my feelings and despair.

I had promised him some wonderful love making on his return. And here I was, feeling sick, anti-sex and utterly depleted. In a way I also felt a huge anger against Henry. I knew I had to lash out at somebody.

I felt like getting in my car and driving straight off to confront Ursula and that slimy little bitch Bridgit – and hitting them hard, especially that horrible little smug wretch. But then I remembered that I had left my car at the hotel where I had met Henry. I was without a car and stuck. Oh God!

Henry arrived back. I can't, I thought, I simply can't. I couldn't bear him to even touch me. I hated everybody. He'd probably do an Ursula on me next.

I festered under the bed clothes. I heard his manly foot-steps. I smelt his arousal in the bed. God, I thought, I'll make him, or her, pay for this. I was now so confused that I could see no difference between Henry and Ursula. Everything was betrayal, I felt. I meant nothing to any-body. They all just regarded me as a convenient tongue to use between their legs.

The Bounder was getting agitated in the bed. I was not satisfying him. His whip touched my buttocks.

'Please your Master, you little bitch!'

Four strokes followed.

But I remained motionless.

Ten strokes and I kept thinking, 'The bastard, he's no different from her.'

All the venom I should have poured on Ursula I was now pouring on him. 'Look at him,' I told myself, 'the swine, with his masterly indifference to her and to her wor-ries, and his anger because he was not being satisfied. Ugh! do him good! Let him sweat!'

Finally I could stand it no longer.

'Go away. Get out of this house!'

'Certainly not!' came his angry reply. 'This is my house!'

'Bah!' I thought . . . his house . . . his bed . . . his bloody car. What did I care? I was now quickly losing myself in an abyss of despair – a mad place where people took on horns. Henry was no longer Henry. He was a huge dinosaur. Ursula was a grotesque lizard. Everything was topsy-turvy. I must get away fast.

But Henry just smirked at me. 'Feeling a little upset, little girl?'

This made me even more angry. A little upset indeed! What did that smug bastard know? All he ever thought about was himself.

'Dress yourself and clean yourself up,' he ordered. 'You look so ugly squatting on the bed like that.'

That was the last straw. I leaped out of bed. I looked for something to hurl at him.

'Go away, you creep, go away. Take me home!'

I was now quite out of control. The pent-up anger and terrible frustration, I had suffered with Ursula, mixed with the memories of the unbelievable good times I had also had with her, all came flooding back. And here was Henry goading me on, goading me on with his supercilious smile and his studied indifference. And then to finally add insult to injury, he started to have an intimate telephone conversation with another of his girlfriends. He's just like Ursula, thought I.

The fuse blew. The lights went out for me and it was a she-devil that took over. I became another person. My whole face changed, and so did my voice. All sense was now gone. I hurled abuse at Henry. I hated him. I broke everything I could see.

He acted oblivious. He looked bored, which made me wilder than ever.

Then he started to get the wrong end of the stick.

'Oh, so you're jealous of my other girlfriend, are you?' he laughed. 'Oh, well I must confess that I do love women.'

On and on he went, showing off.

If outwardly Henry was keeping cool, inwardly he was appalled. All the anticipation with which he had felt for this much longed for weekend together had turned into ashes in his mouth. And yet it had been so wonderful at first. He had seen me taken over by this devil before. On the other occasions it had always been caused by jealousy – jealously of his other girlfriends. Unaware of my telephone calls to Ursula, he was mystified this time. He knew that I would not change back to my normal bubbly self for another day and that meanwhile I would be impossible.

He read the Sunday papers whilst I sat huddled in the corner, silent and consumed with rage, my face still twisted with hate. Finally he got bored with my tantrums.

'All right,' he said sadly, 'get in the car. You might just as well go home for all the use you are to me.'

I grabbed all my things, stuffed them into a bag and got into the car. Shaking with hate I snarled at Henry every time he tried to make conversation during the long two hour drive. Yes, he had grown horns.

EPILOGUE

Whilst the cat's away . . .

I was again beginning to feel destroyed by Ursula.

At first it had been thrilling to return to her and to describe to her the utter failure of my weekend with Henry. I felt exhausted and in a turmoil ever since I had returned shamefacedly to Ursula; she had been so ghastly to me on the phone when I was staying with Henry, and had been delighted to hear of the utter failure of that visit.

I realised that I had made an utter fool of myself with Henry, but felt that I simply could not explain to him why I was so upset. In fact I had felt relief when Henry had assumed that I was just jealous of another girlfriend of his with whom he had been hunting.

But I was now far too taken up with Ursula and her incredibly demanding routine to worry about all that. It was indeed a twenty four hour commitment – total submission to my Mistress. Ursula was certainly having her revenge for when I had broken away for one weekend – a weekend that I had already promised Ursula that I would spend with her.

Cruel Ursula! I thought, as I picked up the phone in my office to ask permission to relieve myself. Gosh, how cruel she could be! Supposing Ursula was out? I looked at the page in the loose leaf book in which Ursula made me record all the times, each day, I received permission to perform my natural functions and then record the result. I would have to fax the page to Ursula before going home in the evening.

The telephone just rang and rang. Ursula must be out shopping. Desperately I wondered if I dared go to the loo without permission. Before sending the fax that evening, I would have to sign that it was a complete record. Ursula seemed to have a sixth sense for noticing when it was not quite right – and then, as I knew to my cost, Ursula would be on the phone! There would be no argument, no excuses – just the announcement that I had earned myself another ten strokes of the cane for lying and deception. One word of protest, and it was twenty!

Two days previously, before sending me back to my home in the country, Ursula had locked a chastity belt onto me. I could spend a penny through the little grille, and awkwardly holding the rod slightly to one side of my rear entrance, I could with difficulty relieve myself there too. That morning I had to do just that, telephoning Ursula for permission beforehand, recording it all on a mini-cassette, and then telephoning her again and playing her the cassette, after I had washed myself clean. It was all too shame-making, but fear of the cane was uppermost in my mind – and anyway, I had to admit, it was also very exciting being under such incredibly strict control.

Not daring to go to the loo without permission, I began to think of my astonishing life, and I waited with increasing urgency for Ursula to return to her house and answer the telephone ...

My thoughts turned to Mark. He, of course, was blissfully unaware of the depth of my relationship with Ursula. He just wanted an understanding wife! I had been stunned when he popped the question. I knew it would suit him well to have a wife in name only – a cover for his other little fancies. I had been adept at turning a blind eye to such activities. I wasn't really being very clever or forbearing – it was just that I had so many exciting things going on in my own life, that I just hadn't time to care about what he got up to, or about anyone else, now that Ursula had so taken over my life.

Or so I was thinking to myself when sudenly the telephone went. It was Henry! Telephoning out of the blue to suggest a meeting: 'a business meeting,' he had said.

I had sent him one of my short stories for fun and he, of course, had recognised my writing immediately. We both laughed together over it on the phone and I found myself softening up as I talked to him about the fun I had had with the other 'maids' in the story. I spoke of the thrill as one of them, Scarlette I had called her, had taken off her panties and spread her legs. It had been even more thrilling when Scarlette had opened me up whilst I was standing stock still as Big Judy was beating me on my buttocks – making me moist for Scarlette's mouth.

Whilst I talked to Henry on the telephone I could feel my nipples almost stretching through my silk blouse and, despite Ursula's damn chastity belt, I could feel my panties were already wet – just from his voice.

Oh dear, I thought, Ursula would have me bent over the table when she smelt that! But I was so excited at talking again to meet Henry that I almost didn't care, and in an unguarded moment I agreed to meet Henry at my office. Then fear of Ursula almost made me cancel it – but surely a 'business meeting' could be no harm.

However, a few days later, I learnt that Ursula was going to New York for the opening of a friend's exhibition. She had begged me to go with her, but I couldn't and anyway, I thought, 'whilst the cat's away, the mice can play!' – especially as Ursula had agreed that her visit would be too long to leave me locked up in her awful chastity belt!

I decided that I certainly did not want to play cat and mouse with Mark – he was so exhausting! He was the sort of man who always wanted to be entertained, whilst Henry, on the contrary, entertained me. So it was that I started to think of Henry again and, as I did so, I could feel that tingle again inside my little panties. In fact, as I was no longer wearing a chastity belt, I could not resist putting my fingers inside my panties and playing with myself. I was getting so steamed up that I rang Henry and suggested booking a room!

Henry seemed a bit surprised. 'A room?' he queried.

I thought to myself how slow off the mark he was – but I was now almost climaxing and didn't care. 'Yes,' I said, 'a room!'

'Right! Go ahead!' said the now delighted Henry, and so

I went ahead and booked a lovely room over-looking a nearby large lake. It reminded me of Switzerland and so, of course, of Henry.

I now could not wait to see him again. Oh, if only I could put Mark off, and meet Henry earlier! But I simply could not do so. Mark was offering me the moon – and he was after all a very rich man with a fabulous lifestyle. Did I really want to give all that up? It was too tempting. I decided that I would go on with the charade of pretending that I loved Mark for a little while longer and see how things developed at home. My husband John was so dependent on me, that I just couldn't bear to leave him. Anyway neither his relations nor mine would ever speak to me again if I did so.

'Why, why does everyone at home depend on me?' I would scream. Henry didn't! He did as he pleased – and secretly I could not help admiring the 'devil may care' Henry. He laid down the rules – and if you didn't abide by them, well tough!

'Wednesday at last!' cried I, jumping for joy as, with a light-headed feeling, I woke up. I kissed the sleeping Mark on the forehead, and gently eased my way out of bed and headed home. Stupidly I had left my car there and had been brought down to Mark's estate by his chauffeur. So now I had to go back with him – which was a bore.

Arriving home I had a late breakfast with John who was just rushing off to his office.

'Lovely to see you, darling. I've been so busy at my office these last few days that I just had to stay over at a hotel,' I happily lied. Then I left an order at the village shop for groceries, and headed for the lake.

My heart was beating fast. I was also driving fast, but fortunately there was little traffic on the road that day as I scorched round corners and shot over cross roads in my frenzy to reach Henry – the old Foxhound. He's always hunting someone new – it's in his blood laughed I. But I didn't care.

The seat of my car was now wet; I had removed my

panties and was fantasising about my cruel Master. I knew he could be cruel – like my Mistress. I could almost feel his cane coming down across my naked bottom, and I wondered what he would think of my new 'Open Canal' as Mark called it. He had arranged for me to go to a nursing home and be operated on by an Indian doctor so that he could enjoy taking me like he took his young men. It was rather exciting.

Suddenly I almost crashed the car.

He was there!

Henry, the old Hound, was looking like a forty year old – all fit, new clothes and cock a hoop! And what a cock! I was simply longing to get my mouth onto it. I wanted to start immediately, but the Hound suggested a romantic walk. Secretly I longed to lie down on the wet grass – and maybe the odd nettle – with Henry perhaps letting himself go all over me.

But, still, it was heavenly walking alongside Henry, listening to his stories and to his plans for new chapters for his book. Later I read some in the bath. They were terribly exciting . . .

Suddenly I heard my Master call out: 'One . . . Two . . . Three . . .'

I crawled into the bedroom and up under the bedclothes. I was hungry for his manhood. But it seemed so big that I almost choked on it. But the sheer excitement of licking him down there, and of knowing that if I did not please him I would get fifteen strokes, made me work all the harder. I longed for his hands to touch my beauty bud, to make me scream, to make me burst out with pleasure . . . But as usual he kept me waiting.

Now that my rear entrance had been widened, I longed for him to take me there. Previously he had been too big, but now I was ready for his rocket. In he went!

Then he turned me round and took me straight on, making sure to play with me afterwards until I collapsed almost sobbing with sheer joy.

It was tremendous! I felt wildly elated. My eyes still glittered feverishly and I could feel my breath coming in great gasps, my nipples still sticking out like thimbles.

I longed for it all to happen again! I wriggled and Henry parted my sodden thighs again. I heard myself begging him for a pause, but I knew it would not be long before we would be at it again . . .

I rang home and made excuses to stay out that night. I simply could not leave Henry. I was back again as his little slave.

Mark was always saying he liked a Duchess in the drawing room but a whore in the bedroom, and I loved playing the slut. I knew that most men adored sluts because, with them, they could really relax and amuse themselves. Some wives learn the art, but how sad that so many never do.

As I fell asleep, I thought how I longed to spend all the next day with Henry . . .

Then suddenly, it seemed, it was time to be up and gone!

A Brief Encounter indeed! I thought, as I drove away.

This was real life – fun without any entanglements. I went cold thinking of how pinned down I would be married to Mark. I would never have any freedom again – I would have to report all my movements to him. In other words, I would just be a bought slave – sold by myself for a huge sum.

I recoiled and decided that I would have to make an excuse to Mark. It wasn't money I wanted, it was freedom – just like Henry. Because of that his plans to get married seemed to have been put on ice. It was nice to be on a lead at times, but freedom to break away was everything: freedom to break away from Isabella, from Mark, from the Countess, from Ursula and even from Henry. Oh, the excitement of breaking away, and then the even greater excitement of going back – or of being dragged back and punished.

Who would I be going back to next?

NEXUS NEW BOOKS

To be published in June 2004

PRIZE OF PAIN
Wendy Swanscombe

Britain is to host the most bizarre TV game show ever, as hopeful submissive males enter a lottery to appear on 'Prize of Pain'. One day soon discreetly perfumed black envelopes will slip through the letterboxes of five lucky men and they will receive their instructions from the Domina de Fouette. Public humiliation awaits, and attempts to cheat will be detected and cruelly punished. Four men are unworthy and will fail the ordeals She sets them: one only will win through to the ultimate prize. The prize of pleasure . . . and of pain. Who wants to enter Mistress's Lair? And no coughing!

£6.99   ISBN 0 352 33890 3

DOMINATION DOLLS
Lindsay Gordon

Is it a beauty treatment? A fashion statement? Or the costume of a sinister cult? How do these masks of transparent latex transform ordinary women into beautiful vamps, dominant mistresses, and ruthless femme fatales? A timid socialite and her shy maid suddenly become merciless exploiters of male weakness; a suburban mother changes into a cruel mistress who takes an assertive interest in a prospective son in law; a mysterious female traveller leaves a trail of bound, disciplined and thoroughly used men behind. These are some of the stories of the Domination Dolls and the men they walk upon. Confessions collected by the librarian chosen to work in London's secret fetish archive, a woman who turns detective but soon succumbs to the temptations of female domination.

£6.99   ISBN 0 352 33891 1

LESSONS IN OBEDIENCE
Lucy Golden

What would you do if a young woman arrived unannounced on your doorstep one day to make amends for someone else's sins? And what if you detected, beneath her innocent exterior, a talent and a willingness to submit you'd be a fool not to nurture? Faced with that challenge, Alex Mortensen starts carefully to introduce his pupil to the increasingly perverse pleasures that have always featured in his own life. But what should he do when she learns so fast, catches up with him and threatens to overtake? A Nexus Classic.

£6.99   ISBN 0 352 33892 X

To be published in July 2004

THE PLAYER
Cat Scarlett

Carter, manager of an exclusive all-female pool tour, discovers Roz in a backstreet pool hall. When he sees her bending to take her shot, he can't resist putting his marker down to play her. But when he signs Roz up to his tour, she discovers that the dominant Carter has a taste for the perverse, enforces a strict training regime, and that an exhibition match is just that.

£6.99   ISBN 0 352 33894 6

THE ART OF CORRECTION
Tara Black

The fourth instalment of Tara's series of novels chronicling the kinky activities of Judith Wilson and the Nemesis Archive, a global network of Sapphic corporal punishment lovers dedicated to chronicling the history of perverse female desire.

£6.99   ISBN 0 352 33895 4

SERVING TIME
Sarah Veitch

The House of Compulsion is the unofficial name of an experimental reformatory. Fern Terris, a twenty-four year old temptress, find herself facing ten years in prison – unless she agrees to submit to Compulsion's disciplinary regime. Fern agrees to the apparently easy option, but soon discovers that the chastisements at Compulsion involve a wide variety of belts, canes and tawses, her pert bottom, and unexpected sexual pleasure.

£6.99   ISBN 0 352 33509 2

If you would like more information about Nexus titles, please visit our website at www.nexus-books.co.uk, or send a stamped addressed envelope to:

   Nexus, Thames Wharf Studios,
   Rainville Road, London W6 9HA

NEXUS BACKLIST

This information is correct at time of printing. For up-to-date information, please visit our website at www.nexus-books.co.uk

All books are priced at £6.99 unless another price is given.

------ ✂ --------------------------

Please send me the books I have ticked above.

Name ....

Address ....

....

....

.... Post code....................

Send to: **Virgin Books Cash Sales, Thames Wharf Studios, Rainville Road, London W6 9HA**

US customers: for prices and details of how to order books for delivery by mail, call 1-800-343-4499.

Please enclose a cheque or postal order, made payable to **Nexus Books Ltd**, to the value of the books you have ordered plus postage and packing costs as follows:

UK and BFPO – £1.00 for the first book, 50p for each subsequent book.

Overseas (including Republic of Ireland) – £2.00 for the first book, £1.00 for each subsequent book.

If you would prefer to pay by VISA, ACCESS/MASTERCARD, AMEX, DINERS CLUB or SWITCH, please write your card number and expiry date here:

....

Please allow up to 28 days for delivery.

Signature ....

Our privacy policy

We will not disclose information you supply us to any other parties. We will not disclose any information which identifies you personally to any person without your express consent.

From time to time we may send out information about Nexus books and special offers. Please tick here if you do *not* wish to receive Nexus information.   ☐

------ ✂ --------------------------